The Precious Pachyderm
An Evangeline Adams Mystery

Karen Christino

ISBN: 978-0-9725117-3-5
Stella Mira Books
StellaMiraBooks@cs.com

• Acknowledgements •

Adam Kraar's unflagging enthusiasm, as well as his critical eye, gave me the confidence to see this project through. Sue Christino, Joan Aldrich and Ebba King each provided much-needed feedback, with Ebba's party idea adding immeasurably to the result.

Frederick A. Margolin has given me the rare opportunity of meeting so many unusual people who have enriched my life. The wonderful folks at the Bogliasco Foundation were generous enough to welcome me to their study center, where I was able to draft a good part of this book. Lina Accurso, Nick Dagan Best, David Hernandez, Enid Newberg, Vivian Soren-Myers, Norm Winski and Donna Woodwell also supported me with their own enthusiasm for Evangeline Adams and her work.

I've been reading about the 1920s for many years and a number of books added significantly to my research. Carl Sferrazza Anthony's biography of Florence Harding briefly mentioned Evangeline Adams and sparked my imagination; Evalyn Walsh McLean's delightful autobiography helped me create her fictional counterpart. Louise Brooks' memoir provided inside information on the Manhattan show business scene in 1926. E.M. Forster's *The Hill of Devi* brought princely India to life for me, and histories by Ian Copland, Angma Dey Jhala, Ann Morrow and Coralie Younger all helped me better understand life at an Indian court. Harish Johari's *The Healing Power of Gemstones* introduced me to this metaphysical topic.

I'm forever indebted to: Bruce Scofield, who had the fortitude to publish my biography of Evangeline Adams; Ed Dearborn, who nurtured my love of the history of astrology; and Bob Zoller and Al H. Morrison, who unstintingly shared their astrological expertise.

I've also been very fortunate to continue to uncover additional biographical information on Evangeline Adams and I hope this story brings her to life in a new way.

• Chapter 1 •

Mary sat poised with her pencil and pad, pretending to take dictation. Miss Adams had repeatedly told her not to waste anyone's time relaying back to the clients their own unconsidered thoughts and obsessions. *It would probably make them more aware of how they'd actually spent their time and money*, Mary thought. But then again, she certainly didn't feel like typing up Mrs. Fiske's self-absorbed spiel. So it was better this way.

Evangeline Adams seemed to have infinite patience and Mary did not. It was clear that Mrs. Fiske was in an emotional loop. But it also seemed obvious that much of it was of her own making. If her husband continually kicked her under the covers and shouted obscenities in his sleep, it was time for one of them to sleep on the couch. Or a divorce. But Mrs. Fiske's husband appeared to have some money and she seemed to want to keep him. Mary paused to study Mrs. Fiske. She definitely did not have the sylph-like figure currently in vogue. She was over-dressed for the occasion, and if she didn't calm herself, that fox fur around her shoulders was likely to spring back to life and jump for her jugular. Her makeup, Mary's daughter Jeannie would have said, looked like it was applied with Crayola crayons. That was an exaggeration, but it had some merit. It made Mary smile. She appreciated the challenges of women aging. She felt bad for Mrs. Fiske. But not that bad.

"But what am I do to, Miss Adams?" Fiske asked impatiently as she leapt from her chair, fingered her wrap and began to pace the floor. "I simply cannot tolerate him anymore. What do you think I should do?" She turned to face the astrologer.

Mary looked again at Mrs. Fiske. *Typical Gemini*, she thought. *She could spend the whole half hour talking*. Mary was already identifying people by their zodiac signs. Whether or not it worked, it made for a convenient way to think about things. And Miss Adams often had something very practical and realistic to say. Mary didn't know if it was wisdom from her astrological expertise or a canny understanding of human nature. The clients didn't always hear her; they didn't always listen. But Adams was right to the point.

"Well it seems to me that you need to analyze your options. Which appears less evil: staying or going? Once you make a decision, the rest is easier. You then adapt yourself to that reality."

Evangeline Adams' gray bob, frilly dress, chunky build and petite stature made her look like a dotty older aunt. But her eyes, a clear, intense blue, could be riveting in their intensity.

"I would wait until Saturn has passed your Mars. You may feel frustrated and angry, but that will pass. If you have faith that things will return to normal again, you'll get through this time. I know it seems very troublesome now. But things will right themselves quickly enough. You experienced this aspect from Saturn before, about twenty-nine years ago. What happened then? Around 1897."

"I was married," replied the client, sitting down again in the chair in front of Adams' desk. "It was quite a difficult adjustment for me."

"So you see, as the cycle repeats itself, you may again need to make some adjustments in your relationship. In another week, things will begin to turn around. You'll feel a weight lifting, you'll see. Saturn is very reliable and well-timed. For now, take things as they come, do what you can on a day-to-day basis, and try to adapt to the demands of the moment. In the meantime, why don't you slip out of bed once he falls asleep?"

"He would never stand for that!" Mrs. Fiske scoffed. "He can't tolerate being alone at night."

"But he'll be asleep, dear, and never to know." Evangeline could be almost hypnotizing with her compassionate insight. Her voice was soft and clear, and her patrician Boston accent gave her a certain upscale authority. "In the morning, you simply pretend you got up early," she said soothingly. "Do that and I think you'll feel better and get through this difficult time."

The alarm bell on the desk rang softly, signaling the end of the session. Mary and Evangeline Adams both stood up as the astrologer continued speaking exactly as before. "Believe me, I've taken the sleeping draughts myself, on occasion. But if you do it every night, you're avoiding the issue. If you address things now, compromise, and make constructive changes, you've not only solved your immediate problem, but you've learned a valuable lesson, which will put you in good stead when Saturn challenges you again in seven years. So good to see you again, Mrs. Fiske. Mary will type up your session and get it out to you soon."

Mrs. Fiske blinked for a moment. The time had shot by and she hadn't even gotten to the part about her houseguest going through her jewelry case. A half hour was a short appointment. Next time she'd have to organize it more carefully. She got up and followed Mary out of the room.

Mary returned to her desk and made the expected gracious noises as the client left the office. It was no problem putting together something suitable for this lady. As she'd been instructed when she first started working for Miss Adams, she'd simply type out Evangeline's side of the conversation, which was not that long. Then she'd add some of the mimeographed boilerplate forecast interpretations that had already been prepared. Saturn opposite Mars was not a fun astrological transit, to say the least. But Mrs. Fiske would be delighted. Well, maybe not delighted. But people rarely complained. They seemed, as Miss Adams had so often said, to need to talk. And they always came back.

Mary looked out at the Manhattan skyline from her tenth-floor window and remembered her own first interview with Evangeline Adams. That was over three years ago: it was 1923, she was then thirty-three years old and had been employed by a large law firm for nearly ten years, having worked her way up to a partner's assistant. There was a lot of correspondence and she also typed and re-typed wills. That was the most annoying part of the job, having to re-type an entire will because her boss had changed his mind about some detail, then changed it back again. He never understood that it was not that simple. The whole document often had to be redone, since it had to be perfect.

Mr. Williams was a bland and boring guy, but his wife, who stopped by the office regularly, often at the wrong time, was a real pain in the neck. Williams would inevitably be in conference with an important client when Mrs. Williams dropped in. And then Mary was in a quandary. Did she appease the wife and face the boss's anger at being interrupted? Or should she advise the wife to wait and have to listen to her tirade of abuse? It was never an easy decision but that was the worst part of the job. Until Mr. Williams became interested in her.

It started casually enough. "Oh, I've spilled some coffee on my collar, could you go out and buy me some more?" Or, "I don't like these cufflinks my wife bought me. Maybe I should have you pick them out for me next time."

Mary was able to keep the relationship cooperative and professional for a while, until what she'd come to think of as "The Episode." She was in the narrow filing room the Friday afternoon before Labor Day, putting away some folders. It was quiet and many of the attorneys had taken the day off. But not Mr. Williams. And while he'd always stayed in his own designated office space before, suddenly he was with her in an area few entered, and seemed to be in an expansive mood. He began with, "Thank you Mary for not interrupting my meeting yesterday. I know Helen can be a little difficult, and I appreciate your having her wait."

Then he quickly pulled a file drawer all the way out, barely pretended to look for something, and stood on the other side to block Mary's exit. He smiled broadly and Mary could see a foamy spittle at the corners of his mouth.

"You know, my wife doesn't understand me. We work so well together and I think I prefer you."

Mary didn't quite know how to react to his sudden change in attitude. As he leaned in, she could also smell an aura of what she took to be cheap grain alcohol surrounding her boss. "I'd like to give you a big raise," he purred as he reached for her left breast.

Mary screamed. She rammed the file drawer back, shoved him aside, and dashed out of the room, grabbing her hat and bag from her desk and practically running out of the office. She was stunned. There was really nothing to predict such behavior. She went down the block to an empty automat for a sandwich, but couldn't eat. The corners of the yellow processed cheese slice were dried out, the bread was stale and the lettuce leaves wilted. She did not want to deal with Mr. Williams again. But she didn't want to lose her job, either. So she returned to the building and spoke in general terms with the office manager. He took her seriously and listened attentively. But finally, he put his hand on her arm in a kind, avuncular way.

"Look, I'm not going to tell you it hasn't happened before. But he's a partner and we can't complain. So you have two choices: you can stay or you can go. I can advise you on how to deal with it but I can't get involved. If you leave, I'll make sure you get all your vacation and sick pay. And I believe you have some coming. Take some time and think about it."

Mary didn't want to. The spittle on Williams' lips had totally disgusted her. She wasn't afraid of him, she knew she could work things out if she wanted to. But that foamy spittle was the last straw. It was as if it represented all the creepy things that were bubbling and oozing out of Williams and the whole office. She felt trapped. She wanted to put it all behind her. And she suddenly realized that she had felt like that for a long time. And so she escaped.

Back home in their apartment, her daughter Jeannie was ecstatic. "Thank God, Mom! You finally got out of that dead-end boring job. You work too hard anyway. Take some time off for a change."

"How can I take time off? Who'll pay the bills?"

"You know you have savings. You never spend any money. Now we can find you a fun job. My friend Brenda's mother is an employment agent. She has lots of interesting positions. Why don't you go see her?"

So Mary Adler dutifully dressed in her best business suit and went down to the Sixth Avenue offices of Myrna

Bernstein, Employment Agent. Myrna was a lively, energetic woman with dark hair and a sharp eye. She appraised Mary's experience quickly and seemed to like it. But then she turned and looked at Mary critically. "I do have a really nice position that you are very well suited for. Are you religious?"

"I don't understand. Is this job for a church?"

"No, but it's very unusual. It's for a lady astrologist. She's very successful at reading horoscopes for high society. It's steady work, but I can't tell you it's not odd. Some people wouldn't approve."

Horoscopes? Mary wasn't sure what that meant but didn't care. It was working for a woman that she was thinking about. Gone with the foamy spittle. "Is she nice?"

"She's very nice. I've met her personally myself. She actually gave me a reading and it wasn't half bad." Myrna laughed, remembering. "She's around sixty years old. Just a little eccentric is all. And you'll probably be used to the work: steno, typing, billing, correspondence, some figures, dealing with clients. It's a small company in the Carnegie Hall building. She's the boss and you'd be her manager and personal assistant. The pay is $160 a month. Are you interested?"

"I would like to meet her." Mary could hardly believe it. $160 was noticeably more than her current salary after working her way up for so many years.

"OK. There's just one thing. I want you to get this job. But you'll have to look a little more modern."

Mary shook her head and frowned, not understanding. Myrna continued.

"You've been in a very conservative environment for years. Times have changed and Evangeline Adams is a modern woman; she keeps up with the times. You've got to cut your hair. There's nothing that makes a woman look as old-fashioned as long hair. I'll take you down to the salon myself, right now. I'll even pay for it if you'd like, because you're the most qualified applicant I've seen and I think you can get this job. But you have to trust me." She paused. "Do you have any other appointments?"

Mary admitted that she had already stopped at another agency and had two appointments scheduled for the following day.

"And for what?" Myrna queried. "Nothing as good as this, I don't think."

"Another law firm and an accountant who specializes in estates."

"Are you interested in those positions?"

"Not really. But I need a job and that's what I know how to do."

"No one knows how to work for an astrologer. She needs someone reliable and discreet; that's you. If this doesn't work out, and I have a feeling that it will, I'll find you something just as good. Is it a deal?"

Mary nodded.

"Who set you up for tomorrow?" Myrna asked.

Mary opened her purse and gave her the man's business card. Without a word, Myrna picked up her telephone and got him on the line. "Mr. Howard, this is Mary Adler, I was at your office yesterday . . ."

She's pretending to be me! Mary was surprised. She couldn't imagine she'd get away with it. Myrna was nothing like Mary. Wouldn't he know it wasn't her? But then she realized: it's just a phone call. Mr. Howard probably saw a dozen people yesterday. But she was amazed that anyone could imagine such a ruse.

Ten minutes later, they were at the beauty parlor. Mary's long, auburn hair lay on the floor, and a fluffy bob soon curled around her face. Back at the office, Myrna made the appointment with Evangeline Adams, then took her into the ladies' room to make her up. Mary felt a little overdone with powder, rouge and lipstick, but she decided that Myrna Bernstein knew what she was doing. And she was right: Mary had gone to the interview and was hired on the spot.

• Chapter 2 •

Now, as she gazed out the big windows overlooking West 56th Street from their tenth floor offices, Mary thought about how strange it had been, ending up here. The job was far from perfect, but it was much more engaging and she had a lot more responsibility. Mary started as the adjoining door burst open, interrupting her reverie.

Clara Cosentino rushed excitedly into the room. "Mary, Jesse just said, while I was walking past, 'How much do you think she weighs? Add twenty pounds for that butt alone.' He's getting completely carried away; he'll say anything. I *know* it was about me! Not that my butt is that big, that's just his style. He likes to make these comments when people are right there. It's a perverse thing, as if he wants them to hear him and wonder if it's about them. Or like a kid, to slip one over on you. He even did it with Miss Adams last week! And his lewd comments all the time make me sick. About women *and* men. Richard laughs at them. I guess he has to, since Jesse's his supervisor. Jesse just wants to attract attention any way he can. Always talking about what hot stuff he is! Mary, I can't take it anymore!"

Mary took her friend by the arm. "Calm down. Sit here, next to me. Let me get you some water." As Mary went to the water cooler and brought her back a drink, Mr. Jordan purposefully strode into the room.

"Clara, I'm here to speak with Miss Adams, but I really wanted to talk to you. I don't like to bring up this delicate subject, but now I have no alternative. Perhaps Mary should excuse us."

"No, I prefer it if she stayed." Clara sat down in the chair next to Mary's desk; her olive skin was flushed.

"Very well, have it your way."

Mr. Jordan was forty-ish, tall, slim, and bespectacled, with dark hair slicked back from a center part and a sallow complexion. And try as he might, Mary knew he was no authority figure. He was in fact a real pill, but he was still in charge of the outer office where Clara worked. Jordan continued.

"Jesse Bauer is very upset. He says you've been making loud comments about him in front of him and Richard. They're both very uncomfortable. Now he tells me that you've made a lewd comment about his, ah, physique . . ." Jordan searched for a word that would be accurate but inoffensive. "His 'backside' to be precise. He is your manager and I don't need to tell you how inappropriate this is."

Clara was stupefied. She could almost not speak. Mary had never seen her flushed so red before.

"I? Made comments about *him*? Mr. Jordan, he's making it all up! *He's* the one that made comments about *me*!"

"You know he's very popular with the entire staff, and I've heard nothing like this from anyone else."

"Have you heard anything like this about *me* from anyone else?"

"No, but it's not hard to see why you'd be attracted to him," Jordan chuckled.

Mary put in, "Mr. Jordan, Clara has a boyfriend. She's not interested in Jesse Bauer."

"I promise you that I'll look into this further. But I don't need to remind you that I've known the Bauer family a good long time. And Jesse is a veteran of the Great War; he's made no secret of that. He's due your respect, if nothing else."

"Mr. Jordan, I've done nothing wrong!" retorted Clara hotly. "Jesse is very disruptive. He talks about himself all the time."

"Now that simply can't be true since his billing is done conscientiously every week. I review it myself. He runs a very tight ship, I can tell you."

"Mr. Jordan, Richard does all the billing!"

Jordan didn't listen or hear her, Mary noticed. He continued on, "And I want to point out that some of your co-workers have stated that *you* talk too much."

"Who said that?" Clara demanded.

Jordan became smug: "I'm not at liberty to divulge particulars. But if you don't change your attitude, there will be a reckoning, I can tell you that!"

Miss Adams, overhearing the commotion, stepped into the inner office. "What's all the fuss about, Mr. Jordan? Clara, you look distressed."

"I'm handling it, Evangeline. There've been complaints regarding Clara's conduct, that's all I can say right now. And I have no place for her to sit since she's upset Jesse Bauer and he refuses to work alongside of her any longer."

"Mr. Jordan," Evangeline replied, "I will see to it," she said breezily. "Clara, you can stay here at the extra typing desk. There's plenty of room. You don't mind, do you, Mary?"

Adams didn't wait for a reply, Mary noticed. She went on: "Clara can continue to do her work from here. Mary and I rely on her quite a bit already."

Jordan was now annoyed. "I shouldn't be bothered by such nonsense when I'm so busy," he defensively replied. "I don't have time for this. That's what I hired an office manager for!"

"I know," Evangeline soothed him. "It's all settled now. You may return to your office."

Jordan glared at Clara with his murky gray eyes; he had to have the last word. "All I'll say is that this is a business office. We try to do some good here. But we need people to cooperate. And I need to have some peace." With a curt nod to Evangeline, he turned quickly and left the room.

For a few years, George E. Jordan, Jr. had maintained offices right below them on the ninth floor where he'd set about building Evangeline's business. He and Miss Adams had been married a little before Mary started working there, but Jordan hadn't become actively involved until he'd expanded the astrology studio. Before Mr. Jordan arrived, it had been a much nicer place to work. Mary drew up horoscopes and managed Evangeline's affairs, along with a few assistants, who typed and calculated the horoscopes for the mail order work. Now, after Jordan's expansion into much more mail order work, there were usually at least ten secretaries working next door in the outer office, Clara among them. Jesse Bauer was their reputed "office manager," and along with his assistant Richard, worked with numerous part-timers and floaters who came when available or needed. The larger office suite where they worked, adjacent to Mary and Evangeline's offices, had been added for the business managed by Mr. Jordan. Mary and Evangeline were separate from the larger suite, but now shared a common reception area. And somehow they were never really able to keep themselves apart from the increased activity on the other side. Mr. Jordan was definitely not a "hands on" manager and something always seemed to come up that needed attention.

Evangeline turned to her office and called inside. "D'Artagnon! Come here." A young orange Pekingese, barely more than a puppy, eagerly trotted out at her command, sat down, wagged his tail and looked about him brightly. "Come and sit with Clara for a while," the astrologer said as she picked him up and put him in Clara's lap. "I know you love the dogs."

"I do," Clara tearfully replied as she hugged the little dog.

"I'm very mindful of the fact that it was your aunt who brought me my beloved Sonny fourteen years ago. Of course Sonny's getting to be an old man now. But he was always such a beautiful, courageous animal. Have no fear that you shall always have a place here with us, if you would still like it." Evangeline paused. "Clara, you know that a lot of these men came back from the war shell-shocked."

"I know, Miss Adams, but Jesse was never even near the front lines! He ran telegraph and telephone wires for the officers in Paris."

"Nevertheless," Adams said kindly, "it's an extremely frightening experience and if you don't come from a stable home like you do, you cope as best you can. Now we're left with all of these wounded men and we're afraid to live with them, and they with us. I don't believe in war, but I did forecast it astrologically, so I think on some level the general population has little control over it. Jesse Bauer was swept along with those difficult planetary tides, as so many were," she said with a sweeping motion of her hand. "His father did Mr. Jordan a large kindness some years ago, so he's committed to keeping him. It's not my way of doing things, but I don't like to interfere."

Mary had never gotten used to Adams' Victorian formality of referring to her husband as "Mr. Jordan" in the office. It seemed very old-fashioned.

"Now, relax for a few moments," Evangeline instructed Clara. "Then collect your work and carry on as if nothing has happened. I'm afraid we're all turned upside-down a bit by Mercury retrograde this week. We can expect misunderstandings. We must try to re-examine things, to look at them with fresh eyes. Perhaps we'll learn something. It will straighten itself out, you'll see. And where is Miss Coleman?" Evangeline asked Mary a little impatiently, looking at her wristwatch. "She's late for her appointment and I was looking forward to meeting this Aquarian flyer." She sighed, returned to her office, and closed the door.

"She's right Clara," said Mary. "She's always talking about this Mercury retrograde. And we have it for another week or so." Mary had typed revisions to the Mercury retrograde report page many times. It was a time when errors were more likely to happen and communications could be misunderstood. Mercury retrograde could also reveal mistakes in thinking. It lasted for about three weeks, three times a year. Mary didn't like it, and she grudgingly admitted that she often found herself making typing errors and getting the wrong idea during the Mercury retrograde phase. And they were in the middle of it now.

Clara stroked the sweet little dog, who cuddled into her lap and seemed to soothe her. "Mary . . . Do you think I talk too much?"

Mary admitted, "Well, sometimes, when . . ."

"I'm sorry!" Clara choked. She clutched D'Artagnon so tightly to her that he let out a yelp. "I don't want to be the loud, obnoxious one."

"No, no, no, don't be silly. You could never be obnoxious. You don't talk too much. You know Mr. Jordan just made that up to have something to say."

"Or Jesse Bauer did. He's a real heel. He can't stand to hear anyone else talk but himself. I do feel bad for him. He's been through the war. At first I thought he was a very unusual person. Most people don't want to talk about the war. But after a while, the same story about burning down the latrine, just to get attention. I think I've heard him tell it a hundred times. Mr. Jordan doesn't understand. He would if *he* had to sit next to him for just one day. Jesse flirts with all the girls and they put up with it. They know he could get them fired. And they don't have to sit next to him, either!" She paused a moment, then added, "Of course, he has to live with himself *all the time*. Which must be excruciating."

"Mary," Clara asked a little sheepishly as she petted the dog, "how would you feel about going to my desk and getting my stuff? I don't even want to look at him right now."

"Clara, it's no big deal. Just ignore him and go get your things."

"Please?" Clara wailed. "I'll never ask you for another favor as long as I live. I promise."

"Well, all right," Mary agreed, not really wanting to indulge her. "But just this once. He works here and we all have to get along with him."

"Thank you, Mary! You're a real sport."

Mary opened the adjoining door to the larger suite, and went to Clara's desk to collect her things. "Clara's moving to the other room," she said to Richard. "Good luck with Jesse."

Richard quietly said, "Thanks." No one knew what to make of Richard. He was polite enough and hardworking, but Mary had never gotten to know him very well in the months that he'd been working there. Clara and the other secretaries felt the same way. The only thing one could say was that he was nice enough and was attentive to his manager, Jesse.

Jesse, himself, looked pretty good at first glance. Mary appraised him: about thirty years old, he was six feet tall and slim; he had fair skin, nice features, and light brown hair. He seemed to have good taste. But there was something a little off about him if you looked for more than a few seconds. His ties were too loud, his pants were too baggy, their colors a bit too bright for office wear, and his hair always seemed to have too much Brilliantine in it; she wanted to give him a towel.

Now, as Mary collected Clara's pencils, charts and purse, Jesse was at it again. Leaning back in his chair, he relaxed with his legs crossed on his desk as he held the phone mouthpiece against his chest and the earpiece with the other hand. Mary couldn't tell who he was talking to or what it was all about. It surely didn't sound as if it had anything to do with his work for Mr. Jordan. He was speaking loudly as usual.

"What can I do when I'm just one person? I got complained to when I asked for help. I'm doing like twenty things right now and next I'm doing fifty things. I've got a hundred people calling me. I don't know why they're asking me; I'm the manager, I don't do this. It's not gonna happen magically, do it yourself. You didn't listen to me and now you want me to fix it for you? Sorry. I've got to be nice to them and they really don't know what they're doing. I can't fix stupid," he finally said dismissively, then paused a moment to listen. "When I don't have time to wipe my own ass? Forget it."

Mary quietly finished gathering up Clara's belongings, shook her head to herself, and returned to the other room to join Clara.

• Chapter 3 •

It was nearly 2:30 in the afternoon and time for the last appointment. Superficially, the day had been routine, and four clients had already arrived for their half-hour slots for astrological readings. But something felt wrong. Maybe it was the distraction of Clara sharing the room or Mr. Jordan's annoying personality. Maybe it was the Mercury retrograde that Miss Adams had talked about. But Mary felt ill at ease. She couldn't focus. She liked Clara, but the chaos of the outer office was now spilling over into her space. She didn't need to see more of Mr. Jordan and she didn't need any more of Jesse's drama. Mary enjoyed working for Miss Adams because she had a relaxed personality and rarely got excited. She knew exactly what to expect from the job, she liked their routine, and she was afraid that it might be changing.

Miss Adams was still in consultation with the aviatrix, who had indeed been late but who very much wanted advice on her career, when the inside door opened and four slender men in orange robes entered the office. They all wore yellow turbans on their heads. Their leader, a man in his sixties, stepped forward to address Mary. He had weather-beaten brown skin that fell in deep wrinkles on his face, and a long white beard. His eyes, though, were vibrant and smiling and seemed to twinkle as he spoke.

"I am Swami Yogananda Puri and we are holy monks from the most ancient Vedic order of the Sannyasins in India."

At that the four bowed in unison. They seemed to each represent a different decade in life, as they appeared to be from old age to youth. Mary already had Swami Puri's name on her list for the 2:30 slot. The monk continued speaking in his mellifluous and cadenced Indian accent.

"We have recently left from the port of Dwarka and are now come to see Miss Evangeline Adams in New York. We are very happy to be here in your country as guests of the Vedanta Society." They all bowed again, as if on cue.

"Miss Adams will be with you in a few minutes," Mary said routinely, although intrigued by these unusual guests. "Would you like to sit down?"

"Oh, thank you very much my lady, but we are all very comfortable standing as we are and looking out onto your most impressive city through these beautiful windows." The three other monks joined in agreeing excitedly in their own language.

"You are lucky indeed to work for such an honorable and talented lady astrologer. In our country, lady astrologers are rare." Puri gazed out of the large windows. "See what monuments of stone your people have built, a great accomplishment! Swamiji told that you have prosperity here in America, but not inner peace. Remember that no matter how grand the skyscraper, it is a trivial thing indeed compared to the limitless life of the spirit."

As Mary listened to the monk, she felt herself somehow lifted out of the room and into the sky. Sri Puri said she would be going on a journey, not on the earth but of the mind; that she must have courage but that she shouldn't worry as he would be there to support her. At least that's what he communicated. It was less like speaking and more like an infinitely gentle embrace. And then in a twinkling, Mary was back at her desk and the monk was continuing to talk just as before.

"The forces of the world are very strong here and they will always throw you off your balance. But astrology may help to develop your reasoning ability and thus attain some knowledge. Mental discipline is one of the paths to freedom, lady. Remember that, and you will discover the truth, the most precious of jewels."

Miss Adams opened her office door and said goodbye to Miss Coleman, who observed the Indians with a little surprise and hurried out. The swami looked at Adams and greeted her warmly.

"Ah! It is you. I have seen you in my dreams lady." He bowed again and the other monks followed, regarding Miss

Adams with great excitement and anticipation as she smiled and ushered them into her office.

"Wasn't that odd?" Mary asked.

"I like them," Clara said. "The old guy seemed to know what he was talking about when he was looking at the sky. He made me feel better."

Mary had to agree. She and Clara looked out of the big windows together for a while. Mary wondered if she might have actually imagined leaving her desk. Something about their brief encounter made her shiver with excitement, anticipation and even anxiety. *What had the monk said? A journey of the mind? What could that possibly mean?* She gazed out over the Manhattan skyline for a few more minutes, then once again returned to her work.

At the smaller typing desk by the wall, Clara continued what she had been doing in the other room earlier in the day. As part of the office's mail-order work, she would calculate the full horoscope charts for the customers who had provided their exact times of birth. Then she'd pass the charts along to the other secretaries in the outer office, who would then pull Evangeline's mimeographed sheets pertaining to each planet and zodiac sign in their birth chart, and bind them into a nice report. The customers would then receive a somewhat personalized report without the expense of a personal interview.

Mary was putting together the report for Mrs. Fiske. She had already typed up Evangeline's descriptions and advice from her interview earlier that day. She now turned to the same mimeographed pages, which would describe the salient astrological aspects in more detail than Miss Adams had time for. She pulled the page for "Saturn afflicting Mars," the transit for which Adams had advised patience, Mary recalled. She could almost hear Evangeline's voice as she read, "This transit can make one feel abused and ill-treated, as it sometimes brings treachery and stirs up jealousy and enmity. One should avoid feeling bitter or vengeful and also avoid cruelty, unfeeling acts, and unkindness, and work toward a forgiving spirit. It is apt to bring very trying experiences and often brings accidents, especially if Mars is afflicted. The accidental condition is very important, and must not be overlooked."

Mary sighed. Life, too often, was not always the happy scenario we hoped for. And, as she had unfortunately learned, the challenging astrological aspects seemed to have a way of making themselves felt, while promised good luck didn't always materialize the way one would like. She wasn't convinced that all of it worked all of the time, but astrology did appear to be an influence. She looked up as a young smiling face came through the door.

"Hi, Mary. How's it going?" asked a slim young man; he waved to Clara with a large envelope. It was Joseph Mankiewicz, the newest of the writers that Evangeline had hired to work on her autobiography. He had a round face and an energetic, open personality. Joe had gotten the assignment to do the finishing touches on the book.

"It looks like you have the manuscript ready?" Mary asked.

"You bet." He sat down on one of the client's waiting chairs in front of Mary's desk and leaned forward. He was excited and eager to talk.

"The draft Mr. Collins gave me was very good already. Very good. I just thought it could be funnier. And I wanted to communicate Evangeline's warmth. So for instance, in the scene where she first comes to New York and gets kicked out of the hotel for practicing astrology? I have it all happen in one day. It's more dramatic and makes for a more involving story. And then—listen to this gag—" he paged through the manuscript quickly and read aloud. "She says, 'I must have made a neat picture of youthful determination as I staggered along under the weight of my carefully over-packed portmanteau. Of course, I didn't know that I was committing a social error by carrying my own bag in so fashionable a neighborhood; but I should have experienced a certain wicked pleasure if I had known it.' What do ya think? Good, huh? Huh?"

Mary tried to collect her thoughts. She thought it sounded dreadful. "But I'm sure that's not how it was. She always had an assistant and I know she's actually very good at packing for a trip. Very organized."

"It doesn't matter. Who cares?" Joe dismissed the idea with a wave of his hand. "All those details are fine but they're not very compelling. What's the real story, the event? We get the meat of the story across this way. It's better writing."

"If you say so . . ."

"Look, let Miss Adams read it, you'll see. She told me that with all my planets in Aquarius like hers, I would know exactly what she wants. She felt I'd be able to put her over and I think I have."

"But to make her funny? You know, she's not very funny. Maybe unintentionally so at times. But she's a very serious person."

"Everyone likes a good laugh. She'll love it. Trust me."

Mary was skeptical, but she took the manuscript. They had been working for months on the drafts. First they'd collected Evangeline's press clippings from her entire career, and then typed up Mr. Jordan's first draft. It was a big project and many of the secretaries in the outer office had spent time on it, but for Mary and Clara especially, it had been a big commitment. Next a professional writer, Frederick Collins, had turned it into something that sounded like a real book, and it was back in typing again. And finally Collins had recommended Joe for the polishing. He couldn't have much experience, Mary thought. He was only a teenager, although already at Columbia University. But he was definitely sure of himself.

"Miss Adams is in an interview right now," Mary advised him. "But I know she wants to look at this right away because we have a deadline with the publisher soon. How do you feel about coming back tomorrow morning and seeing her then? By that time she'll have had a chance to go through it. Give me a call before 5:30 tonight and we'll set up a time."

"Sounds good. I'll see you later!"

Mary looked after him as he closed the door. "He's only a year older than Jeannie—can you believe it?" she said to Clara. "He's already a sophomore in college and getting himself freelance writing jobs. I don't know how mature he is, but he's a lot more motivated than my daughter."

"She's a good kid, Mary. And you know, when it's your own kids, you never see them like the outside world does. Don't worry about her so much. She's Sagittarius—things are easier for them."

"What do you mean?"

"Miss Adams once said that when you're Sagittarius, if you drop by someone's house, they're usually there. You're Capricorn. If you drop by, no one's gonna be home. You have to make an appointment."

Mary considered this. "You know, that may be true," she said.

"And don't compare her with Joe. Probably his mom wants to throttle him because he gets his hair in the soap all the time. You never know."

"I guess you're right."

They each returned to their secretarial chores. When the half hour had passed, Miss Adams appeared in her doorway once again as the monks took their leave. "I've asked Mr. Jordan to give you a donation," she said. "If you go down to him, just below us on the next floor, he'll give you a check. Thank you for stopping in; it's been lovely to see you," she said, charmed. They all gave a final bow and left the office.

Evangeline looked after them wistfully. "You know, they don't require much, but that's how they survive, by donations alone."

"They said they were from India?" Mary asked.

"Yes, they are Hindu monks and devotees of my old guru, Swami Vivekananda. They were retracing his path through India to the United States. But as they landed in New York, Sri Puri had a dream, or a vision of some kind, so here they are. He feels certain that a sacred relic of some sort will be put into my care. It disappeared from the temple centuries ago and they expect to rescue it and return it to India. Very curious."

Mary was immediately curious, too. *These monks had come halfway around the world and Evangeline Adams was their first stop?* It didn't make any sense. She wanted to ask about the sacred relic, but Adams gushed ahead with happy memories. When she wasn't listening to her clients rattle on, Evangeline herself could be a little long-winded.

"How they take me back," she reminisced. "Swami Vivekananda came to attend the Columbian Exposition – the Chicago World's Fair – in 1893. I was just twenty-five at the time and I believe he was under thirty. He was an unforgettable personality, quite handsome, you know, and young. He stood up on the platform, very striking in his yellow turban and orange-colored robe, the same costume these gentlemen wear. And as he began to speak, the whole audience – and it was quite a large lecture hall, mind you, perhaps over five thousand people – the audience reverberated with an electricity that I have never experienced before or since. He had hardly said anything, 'Brothers and sisters of America,' but they all stood up at once and gave him a standing ovation. Quite extraordinary. That magnificent bronze bell voice, his dignity, his authenticity. He was Capricorn with the Sun rising in his horoscope, and I must say he was quite the embodiment of the Sun, very dynamic and shining. And he was an exceptional authority, you see. His family had been rather well off, and he'd had an excellent education. But he'd thrown all of that aside to follow Sri Ramakrishna. He had an encyclopedic knowledge of all of the Sanskrit holy texts, but also the Bible and the Koran as well. Science, psychology, multilingual. He was astounding, a brilliant mind. And he did it all with such humor and tolerance.

"He had a vitality, an essence, that was connected to something larger. Everyone in that audience felt it. You couldn't describe exactly what it was. It doesn't come across in his writings and you don't see it in his photographs, I'm afraid. It wasn't what he said, although he was always insightful. But he made you realize that you were in *Eternity.*"

It was odd, but Mary did understand. She had felt it for a moment, too, when Swami Puri was with them in the room. That feeling of being present but at the same time detached and seeing things from a more objective, peaceful view, where we were all somehow connected and part of one another.

Adams continued talking about Vivekananda. "He made us all understand the triviality of the material view compared to the limitless life beyond. We were lifted up, for that brief time that we heard him speak. And you must understand, this was over thirty years ago, and he was a colored man. Things were very different then, not as progressive as they are now. Yet none of it mattered. I attended all of his lectures at the fair. And my mother, who was in declining health, she no longer always had her own mind about her, she came with me. And it was such a blessing for her to connect with God in that way, before she passed to the other side.

"A year or more later, Vivekananda was lecturing in New York; so of course I arranged to come. By this time he had devotees. There was a lady who gave him the use of her townhouse, and he spoke in her sitting room several times a week. And there was an English gentleman who copied down everything he said. But it wasn't the words *per se*, it was that charisma, you see. It wasn't sexuality; it was nothing like your Rudolph Valentino or Ramon Navarro. It was something beyond that. A majestic calmness, I'd say.

"He could be rather casual at times and one morning I arrived a little early. I have a very clear memory of him sitting cross-legged on an armchair in the Indian manner, joking, smoking and speaking quite informally. And he told us a story about a jewel that made a great impression on me . . ."

Oh, we're finally coming to the point of the story, Mary hoped. *What about the jewel?* She wanted to know. Adams continued.

"Over here, stories about jewels are always associated with their value—how much a wealthy couple will pay for them, and so forth. But India is quite different. To Vivekananda, India was a country of great spirituality; they had it in spades. But there was immense poverty there, too. Here in America, we had our material success, along with the technology and medicine and what have you, and that was why he came here, you see, that was why he made this tremendous pilgrimage halfway around the world. We had material prosperity but no inner peace. They had a connection to the divine but were so poor, almost no one could read. He saw that we needed each other, and he was right.

"And the story of this jewel comes from some of the scriptures of India going back over a thousand years. And it's a myth, of course, it's a legend, told in visual terms that would be memorable to the listener. There was a devout man who worshipped the Sun, and the Sun god appeared to him one day as he was praying at the beach. But he couldn't see him for all his brilliance. So the god took a jewel off of his neck, which was the source of his outward splendor, and placed it on the man in honor of his devotion. No one recognized the man as he walked home, as the magnificence of the enormous ruby gave him an aura of vibrancy and blinded everyone around him. It was said that the jewel would bring protection to the land and prosperity to its people. And it was soon magically producing eight bags of gold a day. Lord Krishna suggested that the man share it with his fellows, and give the jewel to their ruler. But he would have none of it. The man's brother wore it one day and was killed in a freak accident. I think he fell from a tree and was strangled by the necklace, just like that!" Evangeline snapped her fingers. "What a disturbing image. And, as you might suspect, the bad luck didn't end there, and the man was eventually murdered and the jewel stolen. And after the thief made off with the ruby, and Krishna left the earth, the city no longer had protection, and was submerged into the sea. Quite a tale!"

Was this the same item the monks were after? Mary wondered. But it couldn't be. Miss Adams had said this story was a myth going back a thousand years. And it didn't sound like it could be true.

"So what are the lessons of the story?" Miss Adams asked. "They relate to the Sun, of course, which we know about from astrology. We should shine. We should be open. We should be generous. We should not be too attached to material things, should we? Because they do not last, and we can become entangled in them, to our detriment and loss. And we should not place ourselves above the gods; we should realize that we are human, and know our place in the scheme of things. Man is not the Sun. Divinity comes from within, not from without. Which was what Vivekananda was always telling us. And of course he would understand everything about this story, with the Sun rising in his own horoscope. He was lit from within. Jesus Christ had such divinity that a touch of the hem of his tunic healed a woman of the female problems she had suffered for twelve years, an entire Jupiter cycle. He was totally connected to God, and that energy flowed into everything about Him. Not the other way around. It doesn't come from a jewel or gold coins or a new motor-car or anything outside of us. I was told of a particular incident, that as Swami Vivekananda talked about Jesus, his entire body radiated with a golden glow, like the halos you see in religious artworks."

"Really?" asked Clara. "That's like a miracle."

"I didn't see it myself. But all the people in the group he was addressing observed it. And I believe it. If you had known the man, it was in keeping with who he was. But it's hardly a miracle. More marvelous things happen all the time. We are all part of the divine. Even Jesse. But we're all part of the earth, too, and that gets in the way and confuses people. We must learn to discover that eternal part of us, to get in touch with it, to uncover it. And to recognize it in everyone and everything around us, for it is truly there.

"That's what these monks are all about. They're keepers of the flame, so to speak. Vivekananda died almost twenty-five years ago now, still quite a young man, but he was not of this world, you see. They remember him and are following his path in the U.S. I haven't thought about him in a long while. I didn't realize how much freedom I had when I was young and how lucky I was to be able to study with him." Evangeline turned back to her office, then suddenly stopped and snapped her fingers. "Syamantaka, that's the name of the stone in the story, I remember it now." She repeated it aloud, slowly and distinctly enunciating each syllable as if the word itself had a magical effect. "*Sy-a-man-ta-ka.*"

• Chapter 4 •

The next day, Clara sat at her new desk in the inner office with Mary, relaxing with her coffee and the daily paper. Evangeline Adams hadn't come down yet from her apartment upstairs, and it was quiet. "Mary, listen to this story in the *Daily Eagle*," Clara shared with her friend.

"*While her father Iacio Lettiliano of 225 Avenue B spent the entire night searching subway stations for her, seven-year-old Marie Lettiliano was sleeping peacefully at the home of a friend of the family.*

"*The father, who had boarded a BMT subway train at Queens Plaza with his daughter on Saturday evening, reported to the police that he had fallen asleep and when he awoke at DeKalb Avenue, found his daughter missing. He then rode back over the entire route he had travelled, questioning agents at every station, but was unable to find her.*

"*A friend who lived on 15th Street said he found the child crying in the subway station at seven o'clock in the morning on Easter Sunday. He took her home and notified the father that his daughter was safe.*

"*Meanwhile, many of Marie's friends believe the safety of the girl the direct result of thousands of prayers for the child in the wee hours of Easter. Marie's father called it a 'miracle' when he spoke about the unexpected appearance of the girl yesterday morning. 'My sister is a nun, Sister Laurentia. I telephoned her right away and she and 1,500 members of her order prayed unceasingly for Marie.' The 67th Police Precinct declined to comment.*"

Clara looked up. "Mary, do you think it could be true? That the nuns saved her?"

Mary thought about it. "It's very hard to know. At one time I would've scoffed at astrology. But after working here, I think there's more to it. Things happen; we don't always know why. It might just be a coincidence. But then again . . ."

"Yeah," Clara agreed. They thought about it for a moment and then returned to what they'd been doing.

Every morning, Mary would prepare the horoscope charts that Evangeline would read for the day's appointments.

Regular clients had already had their birth charts drawn up. These were filed in the rows of oak filing cabinets next to Mary's desk, and she would pull them and place them in order. The rest she'd calculate.

For each new chart, she would consult a large book called an Ephemeris that gave the positions of the planets, Sun and Moon for each day. Mary had soon learned to understand the symbols for the planets and their placement in the sky. Evangeline said the horoscope wheel was simply a two dimensional map of the sky, drawn for the moment a person was born. Mary liked the idea of it; it was relatively simple, though Miss Adams certainly seemed to be able to extract a tremendous amount of information from it.

They also had atlases for the longitude and latitude of many places in the U.S. and around the globe. A Table of Houses provided the Ascendant or rising sign for the horoscope and the divisions of the twelve houses, the pie-like slices of the horoscope wheel. "I'm highly skilled and well paid," Mary thought glumly, "but if I ever need another job, all of this experience will be worthless."

She straightened the charts for the day; all were returning clients. Miss Adams almost always gave clients half-hour appointments, but today was unusual. Anita Stewart, an actress, was coming at 12:30. A Mr. Holkar was given an entire hour from one o'clock to two, and then the wealthy Wendel twins. Mary inwardly groaned. The twins always took a full hour. And they always wanted dictation. But Mary only typed one report since they were born so closely in time. Adams was fascinated by the twins as astrological oddities and gladly gave them the extra time. Mary found their bickering annoying. She reviewed the charts to be sure all were in order, then stopped as she noticed something odd.

"Clara, come over here. What do you see?"

Clara put her white china coffee cup down in its saucer and came to look over Mary's shoulder. "A horoscope. Tom Holkar. Sagittarius. What should I see?"

"Don't you notice anything strange?"

"No. Why, what's wrong?"

"I drew up most of the recent charts in these filing cabinets. If they're for older clients, then Betty or Hazel already did them. Sometimes Miss Adams does them herself if I've been out or it's a friend of hers. Whose handwriting does that look like?"

"Oh! All capital letters. I can't tell. It's not Miss Adams', that's for sure. And it's not your style, either. Hazel, then?"

"No, she had a very fine script. This is nothing like it, or Betty's. The planet symbols aren't drawn very well, not that smooth. And I know it's not yours."

"Or Alexa, either, or Dorothy. Wait a minute—give me that! Clara sniffed the paper. I knew it! Smell it, *smell it!*"

Mary put the paper to her nose and inhaled. "Tobacco?"

"Pipe tobacco. *Jesse's* pipe tobacco. The paper still stinks of Jesse's intolerably stinky pipe tobacco!"

"Clara, Jesse isn't responsible for everything wrong in the office."

"Mary, I'm telling you: it's him. And look, it has a coffee splotch on it, too. You know how he's always slurping away at his desk!"

"But why?"

"I don't know. Who is this Holkar guy, anyway?" Clara asked.

"I don't remember. It says he was born in India. She's giving him the whole hour. Let me look in the card file." She turned to her big box of index cards that noted the names, birth data and contact information of each of their clients, along with the dates of their visits. "He was here last year and then another time before that. Huh. I guess you can't remember everyone. But why in the world would Jesse be going into our chart file?"

"Mary, this guy could be rich. Jesse sees the times when Miss Adams tells him to be careful of a loss, and then he goes after his dough."

"Clara, I know he's a nut, but is he really a thief?"

"Well, then he wants to get to know this poor slob so he can infiltrate his way into a high-paying job with him. He could be a big businessman or broker and Jesse wants a job in the stock market. He seems to spend a lot of money."

"But why would he get rid of the old chart?"

Clara thought a moment. "Maybe he changed the horoscope! He doesn't want Miss Adams to have this Tom Holkar's true time of birth. Then her forecast won't be as good and Jesse will step in and offer his services as the replacement astrologer."

"No, it can't be that, because the card file has his correct time. See? It's the same."

"I don't know what he's doing. But I know it's Jesse," Clara said firmly.

"You know what it might be," Mary suggested. "Miss Adams could have made notes on the chart during the reading. Now they're gone. Maybe he removed some information. Something was on the original chart, and now only he knows what it is."

"That's it!" Clara cried. "It's a trade secret or something, and he has to stoop to underhanded methods because after all, who would hire him?"

"No, Clara. He could get another job. He makes a good impression. He's not unattractive and he dresses pretty well. He has a position and title. Mr. Jordan would recommend him. "

"True. But eventually he'd be expected to do some work. And he's not capable of it." Clara turned and went back to her desk.

Mary opened the narrow desk drawer in front of her and placed the charts in it, closing the drawer and locking it for safe-keeping. She had never done that before. The key was on her keychain with all of her other keys to the office and her apartment. She placed it in her purse and put it away in her bottom desk drawer.

"Hey, Mary. Hi Clara." Mary looked up. Young Joe Mankiewicz had opened the door and greeted them enthusiastically. How's it going today?"

"We're just getting started," Mary said with a smile. She liked Joe. He was a likeable kid. "I think I heard Miss Adams in her office but she hasn't opened the door yet. Let me buzz her."

Mary leaned to the intercom box on her desk and pressed a lever. "Miss Adams? Joe Mankiewicz is here about the manuscript. Do you want to see him?" There was no reply, but almost immediately, the door to Evangeline's office opened and the astrologer appeared in a flurry of congeniality.

"Ah, Mr. Mankiewicz. Congratulations! A wonderful job. I predicted it, didn't I?" she said delightedly.

Joe stood up, beaming, and shook Adams' hand. "You sure did, Miss Adams. I guess I captured that Aquarius spirit of yours?"

"Oh, you did, indeed. You're a very talented young man and I also predict you'll be going a long way. And that's not an astrological prediction, mind you, that's based upon the quality of your work. Top of the line. Mr. Collins, I don't mind telling you, is a first-rate writer, a thorough-going professional. He did an excellent job on his draft. But your work takes it to a far superior level." She chuckled to herself. "Carefully over-packed portmanteau, indeed."

Mankiewicz laughed. "And how about the story of your meeting Mr. Jordan? That was my favorite. What'd you think?"

"Just lovely. Wonderful story. Now, I've just been looking at your horoscope and I was curious about the man behind it. I must tell you that when Mr. Collins suggested you, I was a bit skeptical. You are young."

"So I'm told."

"Mr. Collins says you're attending Columbia University, is that right?" The boy nodded. "That's very commendable. What are you studying?"

"I usually do well in school, and I had an idea that I wanted to become a psychiatrist. But that requires science classes, and when it came time to dissect the frogs—well, that kind of thing was just not for me."

"Yes, yes. I see. You have a feeling for the other creatures."

"There are lots of requirements for the pre-med program, and my first year I got an F-minus in Physics. I had never heard of an F-minus before; I thought F was the lowest grade. So I went in to see the professor and asked him, 'What gives?' And you know what he said? He said, 'I feel I must distinguish between mere failure and total failure such as yours.'" Joe laughed. Mary and Clara joined in.

"That's not right, not right at all. From an educator, no less." Evangeline shook her head, frowning. "Disgraceful."

"But now I'm an English major, it seems to be working out much better all around."

"Most assuredly so. I would stick to the writing. Your horoscope is very strong in that regard and you could go a long way with it. Mr. Collins also said that your brother is the man who writes the theater reviews I enjoy so much in *The New Yorker?*"

"Sure, that's my older brother. He writes for the *New York Times* every week, too."

"Some of the things he says just tickle my fancy. I always read his column. I recall he once said, 'If they took the plot and about three-quarters of the dialogue out, it wouldn't be such a bad play.' Delightful irony."

"Oh, well, that's Hermie for you. I feel I have a lighter touch."

"You do indeed. And I hope you may be able to help us again. I have other books planned. It's hard to find a good writer who also has a feel for astrology, but I think you may be our man."

"I'd be keen to give it a try." They shook hands once more.

"Thank you again. You paint beautiful pictures, my dear. It's lovely to meet you. Now, if you go downstairs, Mr. Jordan will give you your check." The astrologer once more disappeared into her office and closed the door.

Mankiewicz turned to Mary. "I was right, wasn't I? Miss Adams really seemed to like what I did!"

"OK, I was wrong. I'm not a writer," Mary grudgingly acknowledged.

"And let's not forget it," the teen said teasingly, then added more sincerely, "Thanks, Mary. You're a good sport. I guess I'll return to the halls of academia. I've got to be at Victorian Poetry by 9:30," he said as he looked at the clock on the wall, "and I think I'll just about make it."

"We'll call if we need anything else," Mary advised him as he opened the door. As he left, she turned to Clara. "I haven't heard her gush like that since she adopted "D'Artagnon," she observed.

"She's his new number one fan," Clara agreed.

The phone rang and Mary absent-mindedly picked up the earpiece and leaned toward the receiver with her usual, 'Miss Adams' office.' She listened attentively for a moment. "Thank you," Mary said and hung up, shocked.

"What is it?" Clara asked. Mary said nothing; she rushed to Evangeline's door and knocked as she went inside. Her boss was sitting at her desk quietly reviewing some correspondence. Mary announced breathlessly,

"Henderson Fiske is dead!"

Chapter 5

Evangeline Adams looked at Mary with her penetrating gaze. She leaned her elbows on her desk, sighed heavily, and took off her spectacles. "One likes to solve problems," she paused thoughtfully. "But I'm sure that's not what Mrs. Fiske had in mind. What happened? Heart attack? Accident?"

"I'm afraid he was killed. Bludgeoned to death; hit on the head in his parlor early this morning."

Miss Adams brooded on the news for a few moments. "Poor Mrs. Fiske. Saturn to Mars acts like clockwork; always very well timed." She paused. "All right, Mary. Type up the semi-personal sympathy letter and I'll sign it whenever you're ready."

Mary was often perturbed at the way Evangeline Adams could detach herself from personal involvement with her clients. She was extremely compassionate, yet somehow didn't get emotionally involved.

Evangeline changed the subject as she lifted the stack of pages from Mankiewicz. "About this manuscript. I'd like to get the new changes in typing this morning. I don't like to give you such a rush assignment, but I'd prefer to have it all done for Mr. Jordan's review before he leaves this afternoon. It's not a tremendous amount of work," the astrologer said as she handed the book pages to Mary. "You can ask Clara to help you and even Alexa if need be, whoever is available."

"Oh, and Mary," Evangeline called her back, "Is your daughter coming today to walk the dogs? Mr. Jordan will probably be leaving while I'm in with clients and I'd like to be sure it's all set."

"She'll be here this morning. She says she can come before school and in the afternoons during the week. After June, her schedule is more flexible."

"That sounds just fine. I'd like to get someone to take care of them regularly. They appreciate the emotional support. Mr. Jordan and I like to walk them ourselves, but we're so pressed for time lately. And we don't want to neglect them.

If she likes them and they warm up to her, I hope you'll consider letting it be a more steady engagement."

"Oh, I think she'd like that."

"Very well, then. Thank you, Mary. I hope the typing won't take too long."

Mary returned to her desk and flipped through the pages of the manuscript. Mankiewicz had handwritten numerous anecdotes to be inserted and had changed others, but there were a lot of good typists on staff, so she wasn't daunted by the work. She split the stack in half and gave one part to Clara.

"It's only nine o'clock. Let's start it ourselves and see how we do. We don't have to retype the whole thing. I think we can just add these additional pages as inserts, and re-do the pages where he's made edits or deletions." They started work.

Mary loved her new typewriting machine. Its shiny black casing still glowed, and its face and paper support were brightly embossed in gold with "Underwood," the manufacturer's name. The keys also shone with bright golden letters. The touch was more responsive; she didn't have to use as much force as before. It was somewhat noisy, but she didn't mind since there were only two machines in this office. And she liked the friendly little bell that signaled the end of a line when it was time for her to return the carriage to its starting position. Mary's long fingers commanded the keyboard as she deliberately worked. She favored accuracy over speed and generally succeeded.

Clara, on the other hand, typed fast. Her smaller, plump fingers quickly travelled all over the keyboard. But Clara had become an expert at using the round pink rubber eraser to correct her work.

"Mary, listen to this." Clara read a section she was about to type. "*Sometimes the gratitude of my clients takes a very embarrassing form. On my desk in Carnegie Hall is a small ivory elephant, one of many which represent one of my pet hobbies. The young woman who gave me this particular elephant had the horoscope of a kleptomaniac. I told her so as delicately as I could.*

And she firmly denied it. But the next time she came to see me, she brought this exquisite little figure. I hesitate to accept presents from strangers, and protested against this one on the ground that it was too expensive. 'That's all right,' she called back, as she disappeared through the door; 'it didn't cost me anything. I lifted it!'" Clara smiled as she finished reading. "Who was that?" she asked.

"I never heard that story before. Joe probably made it up."

"But I think I've seen that ivory elephant. It's in the case, isn't it?"

Mary raised her eyebrows. "She always says that one was from Charles Schwab."

They returned to their work. Mary liked the project as it focused her mind and kept her thoughts from straying back to the disconcerting events in the office. She still had a vague sense of unease but tried to shake it off. After a little while, Clara got up and turned the bolt on the unused door in front of Mary's desk, the one marked "Private" on the outside, with a drawing of a hand pointing towards the reception area further down the hall. All the clients now had to be screened by Dorothy in reception at the other entrance. Clara peered into the hall outside, then quickly closed the door.

"Mary," she said, speaking *sotto voce* as she sat down in one of the client chairs. "I hadn't gone to the bathroom in a couple of days so my mother gave me some prune juice this morning."

"So?"

"Normally I could wait, but now it's coming through."

"OK, I understand." Mary didn't like discussing such things, especially at the office. "I don't need to hear all the details."

"And Jesse's in the hall smoking his pipe. He always does that around this time. I used to be so glad when he stepped away from his desk for a few minutes so I could relax. But now I wish he'd go back in. I guess I'll see if I can wait him out," Clara concluded somewhat skeptically and sat down.

"Just go."

"I can't go!" Clara quickly replied. "He'll know what I'm doing."

Mary was impatient. "Do you realize you're letting that man take control of your life? Just go to the furthest stall in the back and forget about him. He won't even notice you. And we're not supposed to use that door. Miss Adams doesn't want anyone coming in or going out that way. We have to go around through reception."

"OK, you're right. I'll go. It'll echo through the room though."

Mary said nothing; she did not want to encourage further conversation on the topic. After a few minutes, Clara got up and walked around through the adjoining door to the outer office. Mary turned back to her typing. Some of the stories she was adding were very entertaining. She was having fun typing what Evangeline supposedly said about the Morgan twins' horoscopes and had forgotten all about Clara, when she returned, looking somewhat uncomfortable. She sat down next to Mary's desk and lowered her voice.

"He was still in the hall so I just nodded to him, but no one was in the bathroom. I went to the furthest stall. Everything was going OK. But the movement was pretty big and there was a lot of gas trapped in there, and there were some loud explosions as it went down. So I don't know whether he heard it or not. I think he must have heard it."

"Clara, listen to yourself! We all have to go to the bathroom. Do you think he doesn't go?"

"But now he has something else to torture me with. I'm so embarrassed."

"Saturn is in Scorpio. These things happen. You're ignoring him anyway, right?"

Mary liked Clara, but having someone share her space took getting used to. She still felt a little off-balance and keyed-up. But soon, Mary found herself in her usual seat on the sofa by the window in Evangeline's office. Her sixteen-year-old daughter, Jeannie, was sitting in the client's chair, not for an astrology reading, though Miss Adams had insisted upon reviewing her horoscope before considering her for the job.

If astrology worked, Jeannie proved it, Mary thought. With her Sun and Mercury in Sagittarius, she seemed the quintessential blunt and direct idealist described in Evangeline's mimeographed pages. Friendly and open, Jeannie was a good mixer with a spontaneity and charm that Mary knew she herself lacked. Her daughter was a quick study, and to Mary's relief, she would soon finish high school. But she tended to lack focus, Mary thought, scattering her energies with friends and activities. Despite Mary's promptings, she had no clear picture of what she'd like to do when she completed her classes. But at least she would be walking Adams' three dogs while Mr. Jordan was away. That was something. And she was being very professional today, Mary thought, noting how Jeannie sat quietly with her hands clasped in her lap. Her hair, a little redder and curlier than Mary's, was nicely combed, and she wore her new dress of pale green voile with ruffles on the white collar, cuffs and button placket. Jeannie had smoothed the flounced skirt neatly to the side of her legs.

"Before you take them out this afternoon," Evangeline said, "I'd like to talk to you about the dogs." D'Artagnon trotted over to Jeannie, who leaned over to pet him. She then picked him up and put the little dog on her lap. The oldest dog, Sonny, was snoozing under the couch by Mary, and Lover lay upright next to Mary at the end of the sofa with his forepaws outstretched and his hind legs tucked under him like a little sphinx, relaxed but alert.

Evangeline sat back in her chair, straightened her spectacles on her nose as if to collect her thoughts, took a breath and continued. "Now, Jeannie. I know you have a good feeling for the dogs, which is why I wanted to offer you this position. But you must always remember that you are their guardian. It is your duty to be sure they're kept from harm. And they do have minds of their own. They are royal beings, you see, these Pekingese. They guarded the Emperor of China for over four centuries and their spiritual side was so developed that the Panchen Lamas kept them as well. They've been bred to be special for so long that they consider themselves entitled, and I spoil them dreadfully, too, I'm afraid." Evangeline paused as she looked around and smiled at her beloved pets. "In a way, they are my children." Jeannie smiled too, and nodded in understanding. Lover looked like a little gargoyle, passively bearing witness to every word. Like their mistress, they seemed relaxed and complacent during most of the visits to Evangeline's office. If anything, they were generally unaffected by the range of emotions often displayed there, and enjoyed the company.

"But look here: you must show them who's boss, that's the cardinal rule," Evangeline said. "Because they can be willful. Lover, especially. He's a Leo and their leader, and is used to getting his way. He does have that male Leo flaw: he has an ego."

Lover had a beautiful golden coat, but was a little haughty and stuck-up, lording it over the other two. Mary had to laugh at his miniature ego; he never deigned to pay her much mind except to gaze at her with a certain disdain. Miss Adams had said that all Mary needed to do to make friends with Lover was to flatter and praise him, but she somehow couldn't bring herself to do it. Now the little dog sat there next to her, puffing himself up. He had gotten the idea that he was being talked about, and, added to Jeannie's awe and attention, this made him take himself even more seriously than usual. He threw out his chest and looked back and forth at the women with great pride. For someone whose main occupation was lying around and keeping Evangeline company, Mary thought, this was a momentous day.

"Sonny there," Evangeline gestured to the inert form under the couch, "is the eldest and he's mellowed somewhat, but he can be stubborn, too. He's Scorpio. D'Artagnon is still a boy, really, and he's not as strong-minded with the Sun in Gemini. But he will follow the others as they're his superiors; that's his nature."

Old Sonny had white and brown hair and it often hung, long and lank, by his face. His eyes could be runny, but even so, when awake, he never stopped staring about him with vigilance. Little D'Artagnon, a funny name, Mary thought, for a small orange fluff-ball, was still young and not yet completely indoctrinated into the little canine cult. He would come to Mary to be petted and would sometimes lick her hand. Yet the way that he so religiously followed the actions of the two senior members of the team was a little unnerving. And he had the same watchful black eyes. With their snub noses and sharp little rows of teeth, the three at times looked to Mary like little monkeys, and were even sometimes disturbingly human. Mary had heard many of Evangeline's stories about their heritage before.

Miss Adams went on, "In China, these dogs were bred to be companions to the royal household and guarded the royal family as well. In turn they had their own bodyguards — eunuchs — to care for them. As puppies, they were suckled by the ladies of the court and were treated like one of the family. They were fed from the finest porcelain bowls and their personal servants slept at the foot of the dogs' beds so that their every need would be instantly met. Citizens were required to bow before them."

Jeannie was obviously impressed by the story. Mary could tell, though, that she probably had no idea whatsoever what a eunuch was, and the reference to suckling by the ladies probably also shot right past her without recognition. Mary sighed. She couldn't help thinking of the more sophisticated and ambitious Joe Mankiewicz. Had she done something wrong in raising her, or was it just the girl's horoscope? But Jeannie had always been attracted to animals and was enraptured by the ancient history. And this seemed like a good way for her to start a real job with some responsibility, Mary thought.

"It's only in recent years that they've come to the west," Evangeline said. "They were sacred to the Emperor and represented his health and power. Those who removed them from the palace would suffer the death of a thousand screams. So of course, very few took the chance."

"Wow!" Jeannie exclaimed.

"The Pekingese were bred for their resemblance to the lion. The imperial lion of China is a symbol of strength, pride and prestige, just as it is in the zodiac, and this is why I'm so attracted to these animals, you see, since my Moon is in Leo in the sixth house of pets. The Foo dogs, as they're called, represent the animal passions subdued and channeled. And don't underestimate their small size, either. They are very strong and can be fearless fighters when the occasion demands it. Sonny here once wrestled with a man's shoe that came too close to my path."

Mary imagined the sleeping, paunchy Sonny drooling on someone's shoelace and being ignored. She bit the corners of her mouth to keep herself from laughing. Sonny was now napping, flat on his back with his legs thrown out. He was the largest. Even so, Mary reckoned that he couldn't weigh more than ten or twelve pounds, if that. Here in Manhattan in the twentieth century, with their owner feeding them off of her own plate, it seemed that this was Evangeline's fantasy of herself as a royal pooh-bah, with these mini doggies her magical subjects. But suddenly, the steam pipe behind Mary's sofa began clanging, signaling that the heat was rising. This disturbed the sleeping Sonny, who growled grumpily, snorted a bit, and rolled over. D'Artagnon leapt out of Jeannie's lap and ran to scratch and yap at the exposed pipe against the wall, hoping to catch the noisemaker.

"Jeannie, bring him back," Evangeline asked. "It's all right," she added soothingly to the dog as Jeannie immediately jumped up, lifting him back to her seat. She stroked him calmly until he settled down.

"You see?" Evangeline observed. "You've just demonstrated an instinctive care and concern, along with the ability to take action. Well done," she said, very pleased.

Jeannie and D'Artagnon were both pleased, too, and the little dog soon relaxed again and forgot all about the noisy pipe. Sonny yawned and went back to sleep.

The three Pekingese were in fact Evangeline Adams' darlings, her dears, her surrogate children. They were the real partners in her life, notwithstanding the role that Mr. Jordan played, Mary suddenly realized. She admired Jeannie's bright hazel eyes and cute sloping nose; she was clearly right at home with D'Artagnon in her lap. Mary was proud of her daughter and Evangeline was proud of her little brood, too. And they were about to entrust them to each other.

Evangeline continued: "They are good dogs and they are devoted to me. But you must be firm with them. They can be very joyful and mischief-making, but don't let them take advantage of you."

"Oh, I won't, believe me," Jeannie instantly replied. "I can be strict."

Mary wanted to roll her eyes at her daughter's comment, but controlled herself.

"Now," Evangeline continued, "You'll meet with Mr. Jordan at lunchtime and then come back this afternoon after you finish class?"

"Yes."

"Good. Mr. Jordan will show you how to brush and feed them. He usually feeds them before their walks. I feel it would be best if they had their own permanent guardian, don't you? It will make for much more harmony among them and for us all. Let's see how it works out."

"Miss Adams," Mary asked, "I'd like her to stay out of the park, don't you think? It's not safe."

"Oh, it's perfectly fine, nothing to worry about," Evangeline replied offhandedly. "Thank you, Jeannie. We'll see you later."

Mary stood up with her and said to Jeannie, "I'll talk to you when you come back at lunch, OK?"

"All right, Mom. Bye, Miss Adams." Jeannie put D'Artagnon down and waved as she dashed out the door.

"Miss Adams," Mary began, "they say there are a lot of fast automobiles in Central Park. And it seems very crowded — I've heard there's crime there."

"I often take the dogs to Central Park myself and I've taken particular note of the crime figures in the papers: they're very low, especially in the daytime. The park is not maintained as well as it once was, and some of the dying trees simply give it a spooky appearance. And Jeannie has

Jupiter in her seventh house. There will always be someone to help her. Don't worry." Evangeline concluded. "And of course, the dogs will protect her in any case."

The dogs? Mary thought to herself incredulously. The three little puffballs she thought of as coddled canines? But she realized that Adams did go to the park often and that she was probably right.

"Oh, and Mary," Adams added as she was leaving. "Call Marco and see if he'll take a look at that radiator. It's getting disruptive again."

• Chapter 6 •

Mary returned to her desk and the typing project. Clara had already made some headway, but they decided to enlist Alexa Chenko, a secretary from the outer office, to help them finish.

"Mary," Clara began confidentially. "When I was coming back from the ladies' room, Jesse was talking to Alexa in the hall. He was taking her arm and she looked annoyed and wrenched away. I didn't want to interfere, but I think something was going on."

Mary turned to her inquiringly. "Do you think he was making a pass at her?"

"I'm not sure. It just seemed weird."

"Well," Mary thought out loud, "I don't know her as well as you do, but I think Alexa can probably take care of herself."

"She did seem to be," Clara agreed. "She talks about these stage-door men who come after her. They see her onstage, and she leaves a show with all that powder, rouge and eyelash tint. They think she's really swell, but it sounds like she holds her own with them. I guess you're right," she said, not convinced.

Mary's phone rang three long times: it was the signal from the receptionist, Dorothy, at the switchboard to "watch out," that something urgent was happening. Mary was immediately on her guard; Dorothy rarely used that signal. She instantly picked up the earpiece, leaned toward the phone and said expectantly, "What is it?"

Dorothy came over the line, speaking low but with some urgency: "Mary, there's a police detective coming back to see Miss Adams! He wouldn't take no for an answer!"

"*Oh, no!*" Mary cried as she rushed to her boss' room. This was not good. Evangeline Adams always handled all of her clients' problems in a professional, detached manner. And she did so with most of her own affairs as well. But the police were another matter. She'd already been arrested three times for fortune-telling, and had gone through a lengthy court proceeding in 1914. Mary remembered the arrest in 1923, when she first started working there. A female undercover detective had come in with an appointment for a horoscope reading, talked and listened for the half hour, and returned later with other officers to drag Miss Adams down to the courthouse. Adams' lawyer had gotten the case dismissed, but it was not a pleasant memory. Evangeline had a tendency to cavalierly flout conventional authorities, but at the same time, an absolute fear of them. She was at her worst when dealing with officials like the police who questioned her motives and sincerity. Her Martian, combative side came out, as well as her emotionalism, making her both argumentative and defensive.

"Miss Adams!" Mary called as she knocked sharply on her door and opened it. Evangeline was at her desk, quietly reading a new astrology book. "Dorothy says there's a detective on his way back here—"

"A detective? Again? I thought we had done with those dreadful people!"

She had barely finished the sentence when a large middle-aged man strode into the office with a younger sidekick. Jesse, always with a nose for news, followed closely behind. Mary quickly shut the office door to shield Miss Adams, and turned to face the interrogators.

"I'm Detective Sergeant Thomas Brophy and I'm here to speak with Evangeline Adams," the man said roughly.

"Do you have an appointment, detective? Miss Adams only sees people by appointment." Mary could smell the stale scent of cheap cigars clinging to the policeman.

"I don't need an appointment. I'm the *law*. I take it this is Miss Adams' office that you're blocking?"

Evangeline came to the door from the inside and opened it; Mary tottered backwards unsteadily for a moment.

"Miss Adams? I'm Detective Sergeant Brophy, ma'am, and I'm here to ask you a few questions," he said, taking off his hat. Lover and D'Artagnon roused themselves from their napping places on the sofa and came up to stand by Adams inquiringly.

"I remember you, detective," Evangeline said coolly, regally holding herself up to her full four feet, eleven inches. "You were the officer who came to arrest me three years ago. As you may recall, the case was dismissed. I'm still doing nothing wrong or illegal. Continuing to give horoscopes as I've done for thirty years. Remaining a positive force in society as you can see if you read this month's issue of *Collier's*. So good day to you. If you have any further questions, Mary will give you the name of my lawyer."

"This is not about astrology. It's about another matter entirely. I'd like to sit down so we can talk."

"Well . . ." Evangeline considered. "Very well, then, if you must. I hope it won't take long. I have clients arriving soon," she said, resigned. "Mary please stay with me and take notes." Mary grabbed her steno pad and sat on the couch by the window as she did in client interviews. D'Artagnon and Lover trotted back and sat with her as they often did. Sonny, from his position under the sofa, regarded the policeman warily.

Brophy's assistant stood in the doorway with a notepad and made a show of licking the tip of his pencil. He raised an eyebrow and eyed Mary challengingly as if to say, *"I'm the real note-taker here."* Mary ignored him. Sergeant Brophy moved his heavy frame into the office and plumped himself down in the client's chair opposite Miss Adams, uninvited. "Ah, I see you have a lot of elephants here in your office, Miss Adams," he said, gesturing toward the figurines. Little D'Artagnon came over to investigate and sniffed Brophy's shoe. He let out a small yelp as the detective nudged him aside. Lowering his feather-like tail, D'Artagnon scurried back to join his two friends and sat beneath the sofa with the older dog, unnoticed by Evangeline.

"I've collected them since I first began practicing in Boston, over thirty years ago. They represent strength and stability and remind us to respect our peers." Evangeline's tone had the slightest tinge of sarcasm to it. "They also signify luck and fortune in both the Indian and Chinese traditions."

"It looks like some of these are quite valuable." Brophy looked about him with an attempt at geniality.

It was a beautiful collection, thought Mary. There were too many of them, of course, but individually, many were absolutely exquisite. Evangeline could never turn down an elephant. Mary had listened to Miss Adams talk about them often, and she enjoyed hearing the stories and examining the fine handiwork in gold, bronze, jade and hardwoods. Almost all were gifts. The first had come from Evangeline's teacher, Dr. Smith, who had presented it to her not long before he died. They were meaningful philosophically and by now were a valuable collection, but Adams clearly had a sentimental attachment to her parade of small pachyderms.

Mary followed Brophy's gaze as he inspected a tribe of diminutive ivory figurines on Evangeline's desk, and the large elephant lamp closer to him. Some elephants were scattered on the top of a bookcase behind the astrologer. But the more valuable ones were in a locked glass case to the detective's left. It was these that he now seemed most interested in. The dogs watched his movements intently.

"Are these gold? Gemstones?" He got up to take a closer look. Evangeline followed him, warming somewhat to one of her favorite topics. Perhaps, Mary thought, this will be a routine matter and he'll leave soon enough.

"The one in the corner was from Mr. Morgan, the elder. He found it on an Egyptian dig. It's teak, I believe, with gold plating. That ivory one is from a royal collection in India. It was a gift from a wealthy British industrialist. Many of my clients give me these little treasures as tokens of their appreciation. They often feel that the help I offer them cannot be repaid with my usual fee alone. The gold one balancing the jewel on his trunk is one of my favorites; it came from a terminally ill businessman. He spent most of his life accruing a large fortune, but all he wanted to do was paint. His horoscope agreed with him and I told him so, although his wife did not see it that way. It was a most difficult decision, but he was happy in the end because of the assistance from astrology. And so he gave me that lovely creature. It was designed by Mauboussin in Paris."

Brophy sat down again heavily, smelling as if a cloud of cigar smoke had wafted out of him. "Now Miss Adams," he opened. "I take it you know Mr. Henderson Fiske, the prominent broker?"

"I read the papers. I know who he is. I've never met the man."

"Oh, no? But his wife is a client of yours, isn't that right?"

Here we go, thought Mary.

"I'm sorry, Detective, I most certainly do *not* discuss my clients with anyone. People know when they come to see me that the consultation is absolutely confidential."

"Miss Adams, we know that Mrs. Fiske is a client," put in Brophy's young assistant from the sidelines, smugly. "You saw her for a consultation yesterday afternoon. Her family and friends have told us so."

"Well if that's what they said, then why do you question me?" Adams asked somewhat testily. "I'm not going to dispute them."

"Mr. Fiske was found dead this morning in his sitting room at his home on Fifth Avenue and 9th Street," Brophy stated with an attempt at dramatic effect.

"I'm afraid I already heard that news earlier this morning. A horrible business."

"We believe he was hit with a blunt object—a club or a bottle or something of the kind. Killed instantly."

"I am very sorry to hear it. There is unfortunately a lot of violence in the world."

"Quite right, quite right," the detective agreed, then paused for effect. "Now Miss Adams, when Mrs. Fiske would come to see you, would she speak of her husband?"

"Most women in consultation will speak of their husbands. That's the commonest thing in the world, nothing wrong in that. They need an outlet and they often don't have the freedom to share their feelings with friends in their social set, or their family for that matter."

"And what would she talk about?"

"I'm afraid, Detective, as I've already told you, that I cannot speak of such things as they are confidential in nature. I will tell you that Mrs. Fiske's concerns were purely domestic. And that she was determined to have a healthy and successful relationship with her husband."

"I see. Well, what can you tell me about Mr. Fiske?"

"Why, I've already told you. I know next to nothing about him. I know from his wife that he didn't approve of or respect astrology, I can tell you that. He was an enemy of the science. So you see, Detective, he had nothing whatsoever to do with *me*."

"Well if that's the case, Miss Adams, perhaps you can help me understand this." Brophy casually produced a small leather-bound booklet from inside a large jacket pocket. "This is Mr. Fiske's personal appointment book. It says at the top of this page for the week of April 4th, *E. Adams: Elephant.* That's this week."

Evangeline took the book from Sergeant Brophy and stared at it, mute. It seemed to shake her. "Detective, as I've said, I know nothing whatsoever about the man. Adams is a common enough name. It could refer to anyone." She handed him back the book.

"Doesn't that strike you as too much of a coincidence?" Brophy countered. "How many Adamses have such a connection with elephants?" he asked as he raised his hands to encompass the room. He repeated, "*E. Adams: Elephant.* What do you think it means?"

Mary could see Evangeline blanch. "If you think that this in any way relates to me, I would ask Mrs. Fiske for her opinion. She loved the elephants—*and* astrology. He did not, insofar as I know. Perhaps he wanted to purchase her a gift and was planning on making an appointment to see what type of thing his wife might have liked." Mary could see the anxiety creep in. Evangeline was blinking and had now begun what sounded like a monologue; she was no longer making the most sense.

"It may be that I surround myself with too many of them; my friends have told me that. Then again, perhaps it's a comment upon me. With my large ankles and nose, sometimes I think I'm becoming one of them myself. Or, it could be symbolic. Maybe he had a change of heart and wanted to learn about the bounty that astrology and elephants might hold for him . . ."

"Or perhaps you were buying a valuable figurine from Mr. Fiske, eh?" Brophy interrupted.

"Nonsense! That is ungrounded speculation of the worst kind." Evangeline had regained her forcefulness once again.

"Mr. Fiske was representing some high-priced gems for the Maharaja of Indore. He had a valuable jeweled elephant statuette at his home, which has now disappeared. His employees and we, too, I'm bound to admit, feel it may be connected with his death. So I ask you again: did Mr. or Mrs. Fiske contact you in connection with this elephant?"

"Sergeant Brophy: you are inventing stories. I do *not* pursue the elephants. The elephants *come to me*. That's the way it has always been, as is indicated by my horoscope." She folded her arms and sat back in her chair defiantly. "Mary, show these gentlemen out."

The dogs again woke to attention on hearing their mistress raise her voice. Mary stood up and as if on cue, Mr. Jordan, followed by Jesse, now dashed into the room. Jesse had run for help. Sonny and Lover came forward and began to bark at the commotion. D'Artagnon, perhaps not yet recovered from his recent insult, sat up on his haunches and let out a long series of piercing yowls.

"Now see here, Detective!" Mr. Jordan snarled. "That's just about enough! My wife knows nothing about this affair and I'll thank you to leave. I've telephoned our lawyer and he'll be with us directly." Mary was pleasantly surprised: Jordan looked a slender tower of strength as he stood over Detective Brophy. But as the detective unfolded his six-plus feet of tobacco-ey bulk from the chair, it was clear that physically at least, he could crush the bookkeeperish Jordan if it came to it. However, he seemed to cave under threat of litigation and coolly picked up his hat.

"That's all right. We're finished. For the moment. Thank you, Miss Adams, for your cooperation. I'll see myself out." He turned to go, and with a glance the supercilious assistant accompanied him. Jordan followed to be sure they left the office.

Jesse called after them, "Ya big bullies!" But the detectives were already out of earshot.

Evangeline fanned herself with a file folder as Sonny climbed up on her lap and the other dogs sat by her feet. "Mary: *brandy!*" She petted Sonny who was panting from his recent exertions. A long thread of his saliva dribbled onto Adams' dress. She didn't notice.

• Chapter 7 •

By the time Mary came down the small staircase from Evangeline's private apartments with a snifter of brandy, she and Mr. Jordan were deep in conversation. Mary placed the glass on Evangeline's desk, quietly closed the door, and returned to the inner office and Clara.

"I tried to listen, but I didn't want to put my ear right to the door . . ." Clara started.

Mary sat down and turned to Clara. She spoke quickly and quietly. "Mr. Fiske had an expensive elephant statuette and someone's stolen it; they think that's why he was killed. And they also think that Miss Adams had something to do with it."

"*What?!*" Clara was incredulous.

"That's right. And there's something else." Mary lowered her voice even more. "Mr. Fiske actually called the office last week, before his wife came in. I thought it had something to do with her appointment. He was kind of rude. Well, he was definitely not gracious. He asked for Miss Adams and when I told him she was in an interview, he was annoyed. I didn't even take a message at the time; he said he'd call back."

"Well, what did he say? What was he calling about?"

"I have no idea. Sergeant Brophy also said that Mr. Fiske was selling a bunch of jewelry for some guy called—" she stopped to look at her notes. "—the Maharaja of Indore. Does that name sound familiar to you?"

Clara thought. "It does sound vaguely familiar. But I don't know why."

"I felt the same way. I don't know where Indore is, but she meets some of these royals sometimes when she goes to Europe."

"Maharaja of Indore," Clara repeated to herself. "Maharaja of Indore. Wait a minute! It's right here; did you see the morning paper?

Clara leaned over and picked up her newspaper from the windowsill. "I read it this morning on the subway." She put the paper on her desk and excitedly leafed through it. "What did I tell you? Listen." She began to read.

"*Former Indian Ruler to Peddle Fabulous Gems. Maharaja Who Lost Throne Over Dancing Girl Visits New York.*

"*Jewel collectors are excited over the prospect of seeing, and obtaining if their purses are long enough, some of the most famous of the many priceless collections of gems in India. His Highness, Tukoji Rao III* — funny name! — " Clara interrupted herself, "*former Maharaja of Indore (who lost his throne over the beautiful dancing girl Mumtaz Begum) is in New York and ready to sell precious stones in order to make up for the revenue he has had to surrender.*

"*When the ex-Maharaja left India, virtually at the bidding of the British government, he brought with him practically the whole of the Indore state jewels. He abdicated in order to avoid an official inquiry into his share of the murder of the Bombay merchant Bawla, and the attempted abduction of Mumtaz Begum. The former Maharaja has decided to make his headquarters in Lucerne, Switzerland, where he has purchased a magnificent estate and castle-like chateau.*

"*The value of the jewel collection which the ex-ruler must dispose of, at least in part, in order to maintain himself in magnificent exile, is understood to be almost fabulous, for he inherited jewels and treasures worth far beyond the traditional 'king's ransom' — the accumulation of centuries of warfare, looting, tributes and legitimate collection. Indore is one of the richest states in India and the jewelry worn by its ruler on state occasions has long been famous, even in a land of lavish display and regal magnificence.*

"*Just what the Indore jewels are nobody knows, with the exception of a few confidential agents whom the deposed ruler has called in to advise him. Naturally the ex-Maharaja is not going to stand in the marketplace and offer his jewels for sale personally. The utmost secrecy surrounds the negotiations, and anxious will be the consultation between the former ruler and his advisors as to the stones that are to be sold.*"

"And Mr. Fiske was a broker for the jewels!" Mary concluded.

"That must be it." Clara agreed.

"So Mr. Fiske takes an expensive elephant figurine home to show to his wife. Or maybe just for safe-keeping. And someone finds out about it and comes in the night to steal it. There's a scuffle and Mr. Fiske is killed. They get away."

"And just because Miss Adams collects elephants they think she was involved?" asked Clara.

"Well, Mr. Fiske also had her name in his appointment book with the word 'elephant' next to it. She was completely surprised when he showed it to her."

"She obviously had nothing to do with the murder," Clara said. "But if she also knew this Maharaja, maybe she knows something about what's going on."

They both sat still, pensively.

What did Evangeline know? Mary wondered. *And why did Mr. Fiske call? What had he said?* She searched her mind. She could recall his unusual basso voice over the wire. She remembered the name and she remembered his distinctive manner. "Evangeline Adams, please," he had said bluntly. "Henderson Fiske speaking."

"She's in an interview" Mary had replied, as she so often did. "May I take a message and have her return the call?"

"*Damn!*" she thought she had heard him say under his breath. And then he just sat there. She thought he'd hung up, but there was no click on the line.

"Hello? Hello? Mr. Fiske?"

"I'll call back," was all he said, gruffly, as he abruptly got off the wire. Mary had forgotten about it. People called, sometimes they left messages, and sometimes they didn't.

"Mary," Clara said thoughtfully, "you know what I think? Mr. Fiske had the jewel from the Maharaja. The Maharaja is from India. And that Mr. Holkar is from India, too," she said significantly. "How many people do we get from India? And Jesse took this Holkar's chart."

"It is a weird coincidence. And what about the monks? They're from India, too," Mary added.

"It's very suspicious. Jesse's involved in this somehow, I just know it—" She stopped abruptly and cried with surprise.

Mary jumped with a start, too, as the hall door opened from the outside, the door that no one entered anymore, that was always to be kept locked.

"Oh, Mr. Simon! You startled me!" exclaimed Clara. "People are supposed to go through reception down the hall. Didn't you see the sign? Didn't we lock the door?"

It was Robert Simon, the recent new owner of Carnegie Hall and its adjoining apartments. He was a nice-looking middle-aged man with a full head of brown hair feathered with gray. He looked fit and trim in a business suit. Simon was interested in astrology and had been to see Miss Adams for a number of readings in the past. He laughed as he jingled his keys.

"You forget who owns the joint," he joked. "I have a pass key. The receptionist wouldn't let me in the regular way. She's pretty tough. I wonder that anyone gets through."

"She has Saturn in the seventh house in her horoscope," Mary informed him. "That's why she was hired: to keep people out who don't have appointments." She smiled. "I have Mars in the seventh and I was hired to fight off the people who *do* get through."

"You can't be serious?"

"Of course I'm serious. Miss Adams screens all of us before we're hired to be sure we have the right astrological credentials. Kind of like the dogs."

"The dogs?"

"She won't adopt one unless their horoscope is compatible with hers."

Simon sat down next to Mary and brought out his billfold. "I have some tickets today. What are you girls interested in?" *Sunny*? That's got dancing. *Craig's Wife* at the Morosco. And at the Hall, there's the Boston Symphony this week. I'll leave them here and you can choose what you like." He placed the pile of tickets on Mary's desk.

"Who's out there with you, Mary?" Miss Adams called from inside her office. She opened the door and stepped out. "Ah, Mr. Simon. Are you answering our calls to fix the radiator pipes that are waking us up every day at five o'clock in the morning and disrupting our work?"

"Don't worry about that," the landlord replied as he got up. "The maintenance crew is handling it. I wanted to talk to you about Mr. Fiske; you heard the news I suppose?"

"Yes. Sad. Very sad."

"Mr. Fiske gave me a call last week to suggest I buy a unique stone," began Simon. "You know I'm an erstwhile collector and I make the odd investment here and there. Fiske had brokered a deal for some jewelry for my wife several years ago. Got us quite a nice price, too, I'll admit." He paused a moment. "You know I like the elephants; how many times have I asked to buy yours? But this one was special. He had it from some Arab Sheik or something. He described it to me: it had once been on the head of a cane. An elephant, on a base, rearing up on its hind legs with its trunk upraised. But here's the kicker: it had been carved out of a single ruby stone. It sounded fabulous. And it was flawless; or so he said. Well, I thought it over and I mentioned it to my wife, and you know, it's a one-of-a-kind item. That type of thing only comes along once in a lifetime. I called him back, but by that time he had left for the day. And then of course he left this world. Now that it's out of my reach, I find I want it all the more!" He laughed. "I know my wife certainly does. But being that it was an elephant, I thought of you."

"I believe you're right. People will be asking me about this matter," Adams said thoughtfully, then looked him in the eyes with that peculiarly intense gaze of hers and carefully changed the topic. "Well, Mr. Simon, what theater tickets do you have for me today?"

Simon picked up the pile from Mary's desk. "*Ghosts* by Ibsen. *The Coconuts* with the Marx Brothers. Will Rogers will give a show at the Hall on Thursday evening: *All I Know is What I Read in the Papers.*"

"Oh, Will Rogers, please. Just one; Mr. Jordan will be out of town, and I can use the diversion. I have enough ghosts and nuts in my own life to want to see them after hours," she noted drily as he handed her a ticket. "Thank you. Now what about the radiators? Every year they send Marco. Marco is kind and polite and eager to help. But he doesn't see the big picture. I ask that *you* see the big picture, Mr. Simon. We are still in the heating season. I have banging in my pipes whenever the heat comes up. It is very distracting and some of my clients have complained. My husband hears the identical banging downstairs, too. This suggests to me that it is a *system-wide issue,* not a local issue, which is why no matter what vent or pipe Marco installs, the banging always begins anew after a few days.

"So I ask you to give me your word, in good faith, that you will hire an engineer or whomever is best qualified to repair the boiler. This is the twentieth century! The Age of Aquarius is dawning. The technology is over a hundred years old. It's an elegant system, but it's not working properly. If you will promise to do that, I will speak to you about this 'fabulous' gem as you put it."

"Yes—yes, of course," Simon quickly agreed. "Whatever you say."

"Now I know you're a busy man, but if you have time for this ruby, you have time to fix the pipes. And it will be a benefit to everyone in the building. You're a businessman; it will save you money in the long run. Mr. Carnegie's people didn't care about that. They didn't have to make a go of it. We were left to the benign neglect of Marco. But now that you're here, things should be different."

"I promise you, Miss Adams, that I will take care of it."

"Very well then. Come in and I will tell you what I know."

Mary and Clara watched as Adams' door closed. They looked at each other. They both wanted to listen at the door but neither of them would be the first to admit it. They reluctantly returned to their typing.

Chapter 8

Ten minutes later, Miss Adams was leading Simon out of her office. He paused to ask, "Whatever happened to Mrs. Harding's elephant collection? Do you know?"

Adams had become more expansive. "I haven't the slightest idea. Of course, her collection didn't exist until she saw mine. She immediately associated it with the Republican Party. She tried to offer me large sums of money to buy me out, but I turned her offers down. It took her some time and effort to amass what she had. Now it's probably been distributed to a distant relative. Or in storage. Who knows? But no one's ever come to me with any of them. Thank goodness. I don't like to turn an elephant down, but I don't care for the association. Tainted by corruption and aggressive behavior."

Simon changed the subject: "You know, the colored girl in reception did a terrific job of keeping me out. If you ask me, though, I'm not sure that's the best idea for growing your business. People will—"

Evangeline interrupted him briskly: "And I don't ask you. But if you must know, the young lady in reception is named Dorothy. She's a concert pianist and has taken master classes with Paderewski."

Simon interrupted her in turn: "Excuse me, I didn't mean to—"

"—Her father is a brilliant radio technician and I recommend you to his shop. In fact, Dorothy herself understands more about the switchboard than anyone who's ever sat at that desk. And she keeps the wrong people out. My business is larger than I can handle, thank you, and I do not appreciate your insensitive comments!"

"But I only meant—"

"Good day, Mr. Simon. Please remember the pipes."

Simon bowed and left through the outer office door. Adams watched him leave disdainfully. She turned to her assistants.

"You see, everyone's looking for an elephant now."

Clara asked, "Did he mean Florence Harding, the First Lady?"

"The very same. She was obsessed with astrology, absolutely addicted to it. She'd go to every single reader in town until she found someone who'd tell her exactly what she wanted to hear. And she could afford it, too. Why, if Mrs. Harding were alive today, you could bet your bottom dollar that *she* would be in possession of that ruby elephant. A Leo woman, and a negative example of it in my view. Much energy and ability but unfortunately only used in a self-serving manner. She bought me an express ticket and had me run down to Washington, D.C. when they were in office, before your time here, Mary."

Mary nodded; she'd already heard this story. Evangeline still smarted at Mrs. Harding's treatment of her several years before.

"'A matter of national importance,'" Evangeline quoted her scornfully. "And what did it turn out to be? Please confirm Madame Marcia's prediction that her husband will die in office! Asking me to substantiate the idle pandering of some two-bit so-called 'psychic medium.' I do not do such things and I did *not* support her husband's administration. And to not pay me after that disagreeable episode, well, the audacity of it. Simple audacity."

"But," Clara asked, "her husband did die in office, didn't he? So the psychic was right."

"That is irrelevant to the discussion," Adams said, becoming more agitated with the memory. "Mrs. Harding sat here, in this very office, many years ago, while her husband's political career was only a glimmer — or should I say mote? — in her eye. She looked about her, she saw the elephants, and she was overtaken by them. And it was a revelation to her, that someone could collect such lovely objects that would also identify her politically. She offered to buy me out, all of them, on the spot. Extremely aggressive — Mars out-of-bounds in her horoscope. Make a note of it: Mars out-of-bounds, lacking evidence in the horoscope to the contrary, can make for an aggressive individual. Her husband would never have gotten out of Marion, Ohio without her constant pressure, much less made it to the presidency. When I wouldn't cooperate and sell her my collection, she had to amass her own. But I can assure you, her elephants were not gifts of gratitude or friendship, no. And she never paid me for the so-called 'emergency' session! Simply outrageous. Her friend, Mrs. McLean, later told me that I hadn't been accurate enough." She snorted in dissent. "I obviously didn't play into the little games of obsequious pandering that she demanded.

"And that Mrs. McLean—Evalyn Walsh McLean—was Mrs. Harding's great friend, and another strong-minded Leo. She *had* to have that jewel, the Hope Diamond, it's called; you've read about it in the papers, I'm sure. Big as a hen's egg, it was. A blue stone of that size can be quite dangerous. It would take an adept with the horoscope of the Dalai Lama to handle that energy properly and I told her so quite plainly. So what did she do? She went downtown to my competitor, Mrs. Pontin, whose only policy is to tell them what they want to hear. Well! I believe in advising my clients appropriately, not just making money. And it can be hard with these women who are accustomed to having their own way. Very disturbing. If I had a horoscope like Mrs. McLean's, you wouldn't find me meddling with a stone like that. I told her in the strongest manner possible. Many years ago now, she was a newlywed then. But they go their own way, you know, you can't control them." Adams paused for a moment and began to turn toward her office, but couldn't let go of the story.

"Mrs. McLean told me all about the diamond's legends and in a bit of a frenzy about it, too. It dazzled her; some romantic notion about the stone being connected to the royal court of France. And you know what happened to them, don't you? Lost their heads." She gestured across her throat. "Guillotine." She pronounced it in the French manner, "*ghee ya teen*," making it sound frightful. "Leos are attracted to the romance. And she thought she could outwit it, play games with the Universe. But a diamond that size is just like another planet, albeit a very small one. Wear it close to the body and you invite its power, whatever that may be. Well. Not for me to say, is it? They go their own way."

"Was there really a curse on the diamond?" Clara asked. "Did anything happen after she bought it?"

"Yes. Tragedy. Her young son was killed in a motor-car accident. And of course her husband is a philanderer — although you don't need a cursed diamond for that, I suppose. And blue stones, in particular, are not the best" she said pointedly. "Beautiful, yes. But a blue stone accentuates Saturn. One might argue that it's strengthening Saturn, but it will therefore also accentuate your obstacles in life. Unless you have a wonderful Saturn in your horoscope." Evangeline was becoming more centered as she always did when she talked about astrology.

"A red stone, like the ruby, accentuates the Sun, a much brighter prospect all around. Quite a different matter altogether. All stones are marvelous and animate. The Hindus call it 'Sattva,' Sanskrit for 'joyful harmony.' They are not like us but they are alive."

Mary was thinking about Mrs. Fiske; she was an old client who came often, but Mary couldn't recall her ever talking about a jewel. *What was so valuable about the ruby statuette that would get her husband killed? What had the detective said about it?* She tried to recall. Mr. Fiske was selling some jewels for the Maharaja, and the ruby elephant was one of them. But Mary didn't know much about the gem itself. She was distracted from her thoughts as Adams continued speaking.

"What's also important is not the monetary value of a jewel, but what it conjures up in its owner. Some people become captivated by a piece; it excites them and makes them feel connected to something of beauty, something larger than themselves. Some stones are larger than life. They're somehow divine. It's like the sense of recognition we get when we meet someone we really like. Doesn't mean they're good for you. And some of these jewels do have gruesome histories, especially the large ones. That becomes part of the stone's energy, too, you see.

"Sometimes it's the sentimental value that's important," she said as she put a hand to the strand around her neck. "I treasure my pearls because they belonged to my grand-mother, and my grandmother was always good to me. They live on while she could not, and so they *become* my grandmother to me. They evoke her. They take me back to a time when I could run to her with my youthful fears and sorrows. And so they are time-travelling machines as well. A little piece of 1840 or 1850 that still remains with me, that I can grasp and hold onto when I miss my grandmother's loving embrace. Oh, yes. Time travelers.

"So you see how misguided this focus on large jewels is, paying immense sums of money for something you can't begin to understand or appreciate. Remember Swami Vivekananda's story and the man choked by the necklace." She paused a moment as she thought. "My pearls have whipped cream and Nanny's blueberry slump in them. What does the Hope Diamond have? Generations of greed. Lust for power. Theft. Grappling for control over others. Any divinity it once had has become corrupted. Nice to look at, maybe, but don't bring it home. That's my view at least.

"It's become very popular with these society ladies. They come to me and want my approval of the gemstone before they buy it. I don't even need to see the stone, a description will suffice, and I can do it through the mail. And what do I charge them for this important service, Mary?"

"$10. The same as for the yearly indications."

"That's right; quite reasonable under the circumstances. But we aim to be of service."

"But Miss Adams," Clara asked, "if this lady had an unfortunate horoscope, how can you blame the diamond?"

"It's my belief. We can't escape destiny, but we should do whatever we can to uplift ourselves as described by the horoscope. You're given a roadmap. Do you purposely drive off the avenue and into a bottomless pit? No, you do not, and that's the end of it."

Evangeline returned to her office, sat down at her desk, opened the bottom drawer and brought out a large old file folder. She drew out the papers in it and laid them on her desk, leafing through them. She called out, "Clara, get us Mrs. McLean's horoscope, will you? Here are Dr. Smith's notes from the old Indian texts." Her long-dead astrology teacher's note pages were covered with small, neat, old-fashioned writing. "He studied Sanskrit, you know. This is his translation."

Mary stepped into the office. She had seen Miss Adams studying those papers before, but they had always remained a mystery.

"Sanskrit?" asked Clara, quickly returning with the horoscope.

"A Hindu language, thousands of years old. The astrological texts were written in Sanskrit. Dr. Smith was a student of the Transcendentalists, you know. Emerson, Thoreau. They studied the sacred works. And Dr. Smith, well, he was naturally attracted to the astrological part. He must have learned it at Harvard. At that time there were very few in America who knew anything about Sanskrit, Thoreau included." Evangeline turned a page.

"In this column you have the rising signs," she showed them on the page. "Then for each type of stone, what is beneficial or to be avoided. Let's look at Mrs. McLean. She has Sagittarius rising. Her stone is a diamond, ruled by Venus. Turn to the Venus page. Sagittarius rising, see? Go across the row: '*Unsuitable*.' However, Mrs. McLean's diamond is a deep blue, so we could really say that it's also ruled by Saturn. Go to the Saturn page for blue stones. Once again, go down to Sagittarius rising. '*Not suitable. Wear only if Saturn is in the first house.*' Well, Saturn is in the *seventh* house in her horoscope, see? It's the *opposite* of the first. So the blue stone would increase the malevolence of her enemies. Not good.

"In her chart, she has Venus, the planet ruling diamonds, conjoining Saturn, the planet ruling blue stones, right in her partnership sector, the seventh house. She acquired that jewel at a very young age; she'd just been married. But what actually transpired is that the blue diamond has become her partner. As plain as day! Astrology never ceases to amaze me.

"That's the basics. Very definite rules for it, too. And there are so many variables that judgment must come into play as well. You could spend your entire career studying the astrology of gems. We don't have time for that. But these notes come in very handy for these society ladies who want to know which gemstones to buy. My self-styled rival, Juliet Pontin, doesn't have notes like these. No one does, not here in America, at any rate. What a gift from Dr. Smith! A considerable intellect, indicated by my Saturn in the ninth house, of course." She neatly placed the papers back in their folder and returned them to her desk.

"Mark my words. We'll be hearing from Mrs. Pontin next. She'll want to get hold of that jewel for her own self-aggrandizement. Mars in Scorpio rising, another potentially aggressive signature. She becomes desperate for anything that's been in the papers, and she could probably afford it, too. And Mrs. McLean, the lady with the Hope Diamond, she'll no doubt be looking in as well."

"She already has an appointment," Mary announced. "Tomorrow afternoon."

"Exactly as I said. You can see the logic of it. She's an absolute bloodhound when it comes to unique gems. You don't need astrology to predict the future, just a rational and objective mind. Mrs. Harding is dead: she's been released from this plane. But Sergeant Brophy is a shrewd man and he'll see the connection as well. He'll be back here, too, I'll wager. To no avail, I'm afraid, but he'll be back."

Chapter 9

Later that day, Mr. Jordan strode into the inner office with his lanky walk. He was dressed casually, in a checked blazer and beige slacks. "You've got it for me?" he asked Mary.

"Yes," she answered.

"Miss Adams is already in consultation?"

"Uh huh," Mary replied. "Actress."

"Ah," Jordan said knowingly.

Mary was glad she hadn't been called in to transcribe Anita Stewart's session. She'd been coming in for years and had a complicated life. "Now here's Joe's original. And this—" Mary placed the new manuscript on her desk, neatly bound with a large red rubber band, "—is the typed revision. Miss Adams liked everything he did."

"Oh, I know. She couldn't stop talking about it last night. Still, I do want to review it for myself. If all looks good, I'll have Jesse take it down to Mr. Dodd in plenty of time for the deadline. You've kept a carbon I suppose?"

"As usual. And Mr. Dodd left a message for Miss Adams a little while ago. "

"Why is he calling her?" Jordan asked, put out. "Miss Adams doesn't need to be bothered by this. I'm handling it." He paused a moment. "I don't want her talking to him, it'll only complicate things. And she doesn't have time for that."

Mary mollified him. "Whatever you say."

"Good. After I see your daughter and finish checking this draft, I'm taking the train to Boston and I'll be out of the office for the rest of the week. You're sure your girl can handle the little beasts? They need a firm hand."

"Oh, sure. She's good with animals. But you'll show her how much to feed them and all?"

"I'll take her up to the apartment and give her some pointers," he paused. "There's nothing urgent that needs doing while I'm away. Miss Adams has the keys to my office, of course, in case a need arises. Jesse will be in charge on the other side. I'll give him my keys in the event he needs some information or paperwork from my studio, but things generally take care of themselves without me."

Mary nodded. Jordan relaxed somewhat and smiled to himself, hooking his thumbs into his vest pockets.

"I'm quite looking forward to this trip," he said in his best pseudo upper-class Boston accent. "It's been years since my initial training with Émile Coué. He doesn't come to the U.S. very often and I'm sure I'll gain a lot of reinforcement at this clinic. I wouldn't be the man I am today without Coué." He smiled as he smoothed the corners of his waxed moustache. "He changed my life. Oh, I could make money before. I could get a job, I could make a business deal. But was I happy?" He gestured with his hand in the air like an actor on the stage. "No. I was depressed, I hated my parents, and I couldn't find a committed path. And all it took was a positive attitude," he said, self-satisfied with his success. "*Tous les jours á tous points du vue, je vais de mieux en mieux.* How true, how true." He chuckled. "After Coué, I found astrology, I met Miss Adams and started this successful enterprise," he said, spreading out his arms to indicate the breadth of his supposed accomplishments. "I was able to attract all of these things not because I willed them to happen," he said, pointing in the air with an index finger, "but because I *believed they could!* Now I wake up every morning eager to face the day. And everyone around me benefits."

He caught sight of Clara finishing a meatball hero at her desk and frowned. "You would do well to take the training, Clara. I tell you this for your own benefit. Attitude is everything," he admonished her. "*Je vais de mieux en mieux* — that's the way!" He took his watch from his vest pocket and glanced at it. "Must be off! Send your girl to me when she arrives, Mary." He picked up the manuscript and left, as enthused as he had entered.

Clara watched him leave as she wiped some tomato sauce from her lips with her napkin and swallowed the last bite. "If he doesn't stop that mewing, the dogs'll be coming out here after him," she said matter-of-factly. She balled up her waxed paper and threw it in the trash can. "Why does he single me out? Here I am, minding my own business and he acts like I'm some kind of louse."

"He's not a very good advertisement for the method, is he?" Mary agreed. "Miss Adams thinks he's mistaken about Coué. She's read his books. She says that Mr. Jordan is too idealistic about it. It's fine that he feels successful, but she expects that when a hard astrological transit hits him, his old problems will resurface."

"His old problems have never gone away—he just wants to imagine they have," Clara replied a little testily.

There was a soft knock on the adjoining door and Alexa Chenko, one of the secretaries from the outer office, walked in. "Sorry to disturb," she began in her Russian accented English, "but Clara, can you help with chart?"

"Sure. What is it?"

Alexa closed the door and stepped inside. She was a pretty young woman in her twenties. "How we do for South America? This one is for Brazil—I think is right—we reverse, yes?"

"It's actually the same as for the U.S.," Clara said as she checked Alexa's calculations. "It's not logical, but you don't reverse the signs."

"OK, good." Alexa sat down in the chair next to Mary and exhaled. "How many times we retype book? Each time is different. Better? I don't know. Is good, is good, but . . ."

"You're right," Mary answered. "They just keep changing it. But I really think it's done now." Alexa had excellent taste and was always in style. She had bleached blonde hair, pencil-thin eyebrows and wore a lot of makeup, but Mary always marveled that she managed to look great, nevertheless.

"How's the baby, Alexa?" Clara asked.

"Oh!" Alexa exclaimed as she brightened and clapped her hands. "5:30 in morning, baby wakes up and sounds like she is singing. Just lying quiet, 'La, la. La, la.' So cute!" She laughed. "Usually she screams. Leo say, 'Oh, she is chorus girl, wait and see, or opera star,' rolls over and boom! Right away, back to sleep. Eventually I fall asleep too."

"That's cute," Clara said. "Your mother's still taking care of her?"

"Oh, yes. Mother loves baby. She never so good to *me*," Alexa said a bit tartly. "I wish I could stay home with baby, but we need money. We work it out. Leo got job for next month in Boston. Choreography and set design."

"That's great, Alexa," Clara said. "Are you all right when he goes away?"

"Is much more peaceful, I tell you that." She looked out the window, then turned to Mary. "So what's all this with detectives? Jesse says client is dead."

"It's actually the husband of our client — Henderson Fiske. He was killed last night."

Alexa shrank back, visibly shaken. "Oh my God. Henderson Fiske. I know him, you know. Killed? Horrible thing."

"You knew Henderson Fiske?" Mary asked, surprised. "The broker?"

Alexa nodded. "Remember I had part in Ziegfeld Follies last summer? Fiske one of the men who follows girls."

"What do you mean?" asked Mary.

"Lots of men — big, rich men, married men — they come to shows and they like girls," Alexa explained. "Want to buy dinner, invite to party, take out. Makes them feel like big man with young woman again. Sometimes producer — is good to know. Or talent scout. Maybe for flickers: is good pay for few days' work."

"You go out with them?" Mary asked, astonished.

"No big deal. Why not?" Alexa said nonchalantly.

"Does Leo know?" asked Clara.

"Leo knows everything. Leo wants me to go. One gave fox fur for dinner with him."

"Just dinner?" Mary asked. "It seems like an awfully big gift just for dinner."

"Is gift. They give, I make no promise. Is nothing to them. Friends see in restaurant with beautiful girl, see him buy gift, think he is big cheese. Leo takes fox fur and sells it to pay rent."

"But don't they expect more from you?" Mary asked.

"Sometimes at party, Park Avenue penthouse, they want you sit in lap. Try to touch me, I slap him. Some like slap, too, I think. Crazy world. I go to party; Leo comes later, talks to men. He thinks they hire him." She laughed mockingly. "They only think to hire *me*, not husband."

Alexa continued, "I wear little elephant, see? We see in pawn shop when we take fox fur. Is pretty, no?" She showed them a little jade and gold elephant charm she wore around her neck. "Leo buys for me—is good luck, Miss Adams says. No one hurts me. They try something, I elbow in belly. Not enough, knee in crotch."

Mary was appalled. It sounded sad and more than a little unsavory.

"We do in Russia, Paris, men same everywhere. Leo follows Serge Diaghilev to Paris after war, dances in *Ballets Russes*. Brings me. I train with company, too."

"Then what happened?" Clara asked.

"Diaghilev is bad boss. Too hard. Leo gets job in America and we come here. Whole story."

No one said anything. Alexa added, "No one wants to be in Russia any more. Except communists in New York who don't know any better. Sister moved out to farm near Bryansk with husband and family. At least they eat."

"And Mr. Fiske?" Mary asked.

"Well, Fiske one of men who come backstage, stage door men. He liked my Iberian dance," she demonstrated with a few graceful strokes of her arms. "Invites to dinner, wine. Old man, but knows a good time. I go out with him . . ." she looked up, thinking, "maybe two, three times. Beautiful restaurants, Ambassador Hotel, Ritz, wonderful food, wine."

"Nothing else?" Mary asked.

"No, Fiske, no. Leo say, 'No gift, no fox fur from this one. Why waste time?' Fiske find other dancer for dinner."

"Do you know why he might be killed?" Mary asked.

"No! Big surprise. But I only know Fiske from dinner. Maybe business is different. Maybe he's crook. I don't know."

"Alexa," Clara said, "When I saw you with Jesse in the hall this morning, he looked like he was getting a little rough. Did he hurt you?"

"Jesse?" Alexa laughed derisively. "Jesse thinks he is big timer, tries to blackmail. You know my photographs in *Artists and Models* magazine I showed you?" she asked Clara.

"Sure."

"Jesse thinks I do something wrong." She turned to Mary. "Is beautiful picture. Nude, but nothing showing, is very artistic, very beautiful picture. Jesse sees, he wants money or will tell Leo."

"What?" Mary asked, shocked.

"Oh, yes. Will show Leo, tell Miss Adams. He thinks he is big man, big operator. Ha! I tell him, 'Leo arrange for picture, Leo agent, book as model, Leo in photo studio. Leo know all about.' And Miss Adams? I don't think she cares, do you?"

"No, I don't think so," agreed Clara.

"Jesse just stupid man. Stupid, crazy man." Alexa got up. "OK. I finish chart, go to lunch. We miss you on other side, Clara, and Jesse is not there right now," Alexa said as she turned to go back to the outer office.

"I'll come sit with you later," Clara told her.

Mary turned back to her desk and got out the egg salad sandwich she'd made that morning. She walked over to the water cooler to fill a paper cup for herself. "Tom Holkar is coming at one o'clock," she said aloud. She sat down and chewed on a bite of sandwich as she considered the mystery of his horoscope chart. Jesse may have switched it, but why? Maybe they'd discover something when the client arrived.

Mary's phone was ringing. "Clara, listen: two short rings, repeated a few times. That's a signal from Dorothy."

"What do you mean?" Clara asked.

"Dorothy signals me with the telephone. When the detective came, she gave me three long rings—meaning 'urgent.' 'Interesting' is two short rings repeated. It's more light-hearted."

"But is it interesting good or interesting bad?"

Mary laughed. "We don't know—that's part of the game. But it seems interesting that Dorothy found Mr. Holkar interesting."

"You're right."

They both sat and watched the door expectantly. Mary felt somehow excited about meeting him, but a little anxious at the same time. "Maybe Holkar will want a transcript and we'll learn more about him," she said.

"Or should we try to engage him?" Clara asked.

"Ssh!" Mary warned as the door opened and a tall and attractive man appeared. He seemed relaxed and confident as he calmly walked up to Mary's desk.

"Mr. Holkar? Miss Adams is still in consultation. Why don't you have a seat? She'll be with you shortly."

"Then-kya," Holkar replied in a clipped British accent as he sat down with his overcoat over his arm and crossed his legs casually.

The two women studied him with all of their attention, uncertain of their next move and trying to glean any information possible from the client's appearance. Mary noticed that he seemed completely self-possessed, without any consciousness or concern about the two of them, while they, almost vulture-like, sat poised and waiting to feed on any opportunity to engage him.

Tom Holkar was slim and nearly six feet tall, with even, delicate features and beautiful dark eyes. Mary recalled that he'd been born the same year as she was—1890—so he was 36 and looked about that age. But something about him was distinguished, too, and that made him seem a little older. His jet-black hair and dark complexion confirmed that he'd been born in India, as they knew from his horoscope. He had a somewhat aquiline nose, a dimpled chin and a neat moustache. His ears stood out a bit from his head and the earlobes were detached, a sign that Evangeline had often said indicated a generous nature. He wore a rich-looking business suit.

Holkar removed a gold cigarette case from his jacket pocket and opened it, but then looked up at Mary and inquired, "Mind if I smoke?"

"We don't mind," Mary quickly responded. "But Miss Adams doesn't like it — she has a little asthma."

"I'll wait, then," he said genially as he snapped the case shut and put it away. "Must have her at her best!" He smiled quickly and it was a warm smile that belied any gravity in his appearance.

Clara practically leapt from her chair and asked, "May I take your coat?"

"Then-kya." Holkar stood up to hand Clara his coat and she went to hang it on the coat-stand by the door. "Hold on a moment . . ." he interrupted her, reaching again for the coat, which was a stunning rich blue in a fine fabric. Clara handed it to him. "I've forgotten something." He checked the coat's pockets, inside and out.

Mary noticed that Holkar appeared to have no distress or inhibition whatsoever about whatever he'd forgotten. He could have been in his own living room talking to a family member. He wore a large jeweled ring on his right hand and others on his left.

The client then checked the pockets of his suit jacket, slowly and calmly. "No," he stated definitively and looked back to Clara. "Be a dear and get the birth information from my secretary — the yellow Rolls Phantom at the curb." Clara immediately turned and left to follow his instructions. Mary observed the client as he watched Clara leave, and an alarm bell went off in her head.

Ugh, she thought. *He has charming manners, but he's a womanizer, and not ashamed of it, either.* He had that in common with Jesse. She didn't especially like being left alone with him. And there was something she also didn't like about the way he asked Clara to go on the errand. There was an annoying placidness in his request, a presumption of her willingness to drop everything and jump to his needs. Mary was overreacting a bit, she knew. A lot of the wealthy clients had servants and it was second nature for them to enlist Evangeline's assistants in their own needs, at times almost as if they weren't real people. Mary never liked it. But at least they could now be sure of one thing: this Mr. Holkar was filthy rich.

• Chapter 10 •

Jeannie Adler stood in front of the elevator with Mr. Jordan, waiting for it to arrive. She was dressed a little sportier today, in a navy blue button-down dress with a Peter Pan collar. The white light above the elevator lit up to indicate the car's arrival and the heavy doors opened. A young elevator operator about Jeannie's age, smartly dressed in a blue cap and jacket, asked, "Your apartment, sir?"

"Yes." Mr. Jordan stepped in and gestured for Jeannie to follow. "Todd, this is Jeannie, Mary's daughter. She'll be handling the dogs while I'm away for a few days."

"Nice to meet you, Miss," the operator said brightly, tipping his hat.

"Thanks," Jeannie answered. She had never been upstairs before and was looking forward to seeing the dogs again.

Todd leaned over and grasped the long handle controlling the heavy outer doors with his left hand, pulling them closed. He quickly pulled the handle on the inside metal gates with an efficient and practiced motion and closed them, too. Then he turned to the control box to his right and moved the large wooden lever that started the elevator on its slow ascent. They could see the big white floor numbers painted on the wall outside the elevator grill: 9, 10, and then as the number 10½ passed, indicating the mezzanine level, Todd slowly moved the control lever to its resting place. "Here we are Sir, Miss." He quickly opened the inner gates and then the heavy outside doors as the elevator bounced to a stop. Mr. Jordan and Jeannie stepped into the hallway and walked down the hall to Jordan and Adams' apartment.

"Here's our humble abode," Jordan said in his plummy accent as he unlocked the apartment door and turned on the lights. The dogs were just inside, already sitting in the kitchen waiting for them, looking like three little statues or even teddy bears. D'Artagnon was the first to break rank, as he let out a little bark and came to greet his new friend Jeannie.

"It's relatively straightforward," Jordan began. "You see their bowls right over there next to the ice box. There's plenty of food — Miss Adams tends to order too much. They eat the same things we do, and you can also give them a dog biscuit or some kibble — here in the cabinet." He stepped over to the all-in-one, opened a door, took out and shook a box.

Jeannie smiled and nodded as she looked around her at the bright yellow kitchen. The dogs sat by her feet and listened attentively to Mr. Jordan as well.

"Help yourself to something, too. There's coffee if you'd like it. There are usually plenty of leftovers. We have a new electric icebox that keeps everything fresh for days," he bragged. "They eat meat, vegetables, whatever we have. Cut it up in pieces for them. Give them some fresh water, clean up and wash the dishes when you're done. Their leashes are here by the door. You can brush them all when you get back. Clear?" he asked.

"Yes, sir," said Jeannie.

"I'll leave you to it, then," Jordan said dismissively. "Here's the key to the door — don't lose it, please." He turned to go out and left them alone.

Jeannie knelt down on the floor by the dogs and they looked up at her expectantly. She smiled at them for a few moments, then greeted them broadly with a big, "Hello! Are you ready to have some fun?" The dogs looked back at her with bright eyes and D'Artagnon yelped in agreement.

"Now D'Artagnon. That name is a little too long for me," she teased. "Shall I call you Tanny? Darty?" The little dog barked his assent. "Darty it is. And Lover — how did you get a name like that?" she asked coyly. "Whose lover *are* you?" Jeannie laughed as he observed her intently. "You're the Leo, right? I guess you're just the most loveable, aren't you?" Lover wagged his tail and snuggled his head into her hand affectionately as she petted him.

"And Sonny, my boy . . ." Jeannie began as she addressed the older dog. "Tell me something about yourself." Sonny was paying attention but made no reply. "I'll bet you're the finicky one, am I right? What do you like to eat?"

Jeannie got up and walked over to the cabinets, opening a few doors until she found some tinned food. She took down a can and read it to them. "Libby's corned beef in its own rich jelly. *Blech!*" she complained. "That does not sound good. Beech-Nut peanut butter?" There were cereals: Post Toasties, Kellogg's Corn Flakes and Quaker Puffed Rice; and canned fruits: Del Monte pineapple, peaches, pears and maraschino cherries. "Oh, do you want a cherry?" Jeannie asked. "I do." She opened a jar, took out an overly red cherry and placed it in her mouth. "Ummm" she said approvingly.

The dogs looked on attentively, waiting patiently for their meal. They had never been consulted about the menu before.

"Let's see what's in the icebox." Jeannie opened the door to the small built-in refrigerator and peered inside. It had a smooth white porcelain interior and was very cool. "Armour's Star Ham," she read. "Just the thing for an astrologer's assistants!" The dogs wagged their tails. Jeannie spotted a bowl of eggs. "I know how to make scrambled eggs – would you boys like that?" she asked enthusiastically. "I certainly would." She took out the eggs, a slab of butter and a bottle of milk, quickly found a bowl and began cracking at the built-in counter. She grabbed a fork from the drawer, shook in some salt and pepper and beat the eggs in time as she sang a popular song. "Ev'ry morning, ev'ry evening, ain't we got fun? . . ."

Jeannie turned to the gas stove, found a frying pan below it and melted some butter, cooking the eggs while singing her song. The Pekingese were enormously patient and stayed close by.

When she was done, Jeannie set the pan on another burner. "We'll just let it cool down a little, I don't want to burn your mouths." She gathered up their dishes, got a plate for herself from the cabinet and turned on the gas to reheat the morning coffee for herself, still singing. "Not much money, oh, but *Sonny,*" she said, turning to the older dog, "ain't we got fun?"

Jeannie sat down at the kitchen table and began clearing it of newspapers and mail. Then she served the four of them:

the dogs with smaller portions on the floor and she at the table. They all tucked in. "You like it?" she asked as she refilled their water bowl. "We're all going to get along just fine, aren't we? You're good dogs." The dogs had already finished and were now politely washing themselves. Jeannie poured herself some coffee, added sugar and milk, sat down again at the table and glanced at the morning paper.

Her eye caught sight of a gilt-edged invitation in Evangeline's mail. "Ah, what have we here?" she asked the pets, comedically. She read the invitation aloud with dramatic flair: "*Mrs. John Miller of Seattle requests the honor of your presence at a reception to be held for His Royal Highness Tukoji Rao, Maharaja of Indore, Thursday, the eighth of April, nineteen hundred and twenty six at half after six o'clock in the evening at the Plaza Hotel, Fifth Avenue and Central Park South.* Ooh! And there's even a handwritten note from the lady: 'I hope you can make it.' Well . . ." she said with enthusiasm as she looked at all the dogs and then particularly at little D'Artagnon. "Would you accompany me, sir, to the ball?" she asked as she stood up and play-acted a big bow, then took his front paws in her hands. "Shall we dance, my dear Darty?" D'Artagnon stood up on his hind legs as Jeannie swayed back and forth with him. Her red curls bounced as she sang, "Night or daytime, it's all playtime, ain't we got fun?"

As Evangeline's client Tom Holkar waited for Clara to return with the birth information, he stood with his hands behind his back and glanced at Mary. "Having lunch, are we?" he asked with a disarming smile, again with genuine and even charismatic warmth.

Mary looked down at her sandwich and water, a little embarrassed. "Yes. Would you like some?" The thought of offering this wealthy client the remains of her egg salad made her even more embarrassed, but she didn't know what else to say.

"Oh, no, no, no, I wouldn't dream of it," he chuckled, declining the offer. "Awfully nice of you, though. My friends are in the car and we'll be going out after Miss Adams finishes with me," he explained. "Hope to have some good news to share, eh?" He smoothed his tie and Mary noticed more jewels on his tie bar, as well as an expensive-looking wristwatch.

"I hope so," Mary answered. She generally tried not to engage with the clients, as many could be talkers. But now she wanted to learn more and couldn't think of anything else to say. Holkar gazed out the window as many clients did, sat down, and then glanced at Adams' brochure from reception. Clara returned, a little out of breath, and handed Holkar a slip of paper.

"Then-kya." He stood up, reached into his pants pocket and handed her something. "There you are," he said crisply.

Clara glanced at it in surprise, curtsied, and went back to her desk.

Miss Adams appeared at her door, ushering Miss Stewart out. She quickly greeted Holkar and showed him into her office. Mary instantly turned to her assistant. "What did he give you?"

Clara looked down. "Wow! A silver dollar."

"He gave you *a tip*? You know you actually curtsied? Why'd you do that?"

"I don't know. It just felt like the right thing to do. My mother taught me when I was a kid."

"Do you have a case on him?"

"What?"

"You have a case on him, don't you?"

"Me? Mary, he's handsome and all that. But I really just wanted to feel his coat!"

Mary smirked ironically. "If you say so . . ."

"It's the truth."

"You can go ahead and touch anyone's coat. What makes his so special?"

"See?" Clara dragged out her response a little. "You can't tell the difference, can you?"

"Of course I can tell the difference," Mary responded defensively. "It's a very nice coat. A lot of rich people come in here and many of them have beautiful things. It's nothing to get excited about."

"I thought it was cashmere. But that's not your ordinary, run-of-the-mill cashmere. It's some kind of top-of-the-line, world-class cashmere. I've never seen anything like it." Clara went over to the coat stand and held the coat out, stroking it.

"What makes you such an expert?"

Clara sat down with the coat in her lap and looked at Mary wistfully. "When I was growing up, my mother was a coat finisher. She used to bring home piece work, and in the evenings I would help her out. So you get to know the materials. A lot of the time it was just wool, or gabardine or linen, depending on the season. But sometimes it would be cashmere, and then we were in for a treat, because we loved that soft, warm feeling in our hands. My mother would collect the little bits of it left over. And they weren't very big at all because they cut it pretty close to what they need; they don't like to waste it. But she sewed them together to make a rag doll out of the scraps. I used to take it to bed with me or put it in my skirt pocket when I was nervous or upset. It was so nice and soft, like a security blanket. It never really had one color, and then after a while it was so beat up and all, it just looked like something the cat threw up. But I loved that crappy rag!" She caressed Holkar's coat as she remembered her family story.

"Anyway, sometimes it was high summer when we were doing it, because that's when they're making them to get ready for the winter. And we'd be sitting there, it might be ninety degrees, horrible, humid summer weather; we couldn't sleep anyway it was so hot. And you're dripping sweat and you have this warm coat in your lap making it even worse. But it didn't matter." Clara thought about it a little.

"It was nothing you could hold onto, it literally slipped through our fingers. But just knowing that something so soft and lovely was out there in the world kept us going. And we would talk about it; it became kind of a game while we were working. Who were the people that could buy such a thing, and how long did they have to save up to have it? Did they take care of it, or did they have some kind of accident and rip a hole in it the first time they wore it? Maybe they had so much money—and this was something we could never quite comprehend—if they had so much money, like some of these picture stars, that they'd buy a coat like that every season. Or even buy another one right away if it turned out they didn't like it." She paused a moment to reflect. "And this is one helluva coat. Mary, just feel the coat. Please?"

Mary came over and felt the expensive fabric. It was indeed unimaginably soft and light.

"And the buttons! Look at the buttons, Mary. Some kind of carved horn I think." Clara stroked the coat some more, almost as if she were petting D'Artagnon.

"I think it's vicuña," Mary stated. "One of the clients talked about it. It's supposed to be the most expensive kind of wool."

"Really, Mary, I just wanted to feel the coat. And aren't we interested in him anyway?"

"We are interested in him; you're right."

Clara held up the coat and studied it professionally. "It's new: clean lining, no pulls, tears or wrinkles. Anything in the pockets? No. Well, between the coat and the cuff links and the rings and the wristwatch, this guy is obviously loaded. And he's also got a whole team of people waiting for him out on the street. You won't believe what went on out there."

"Tell me!" Mary demanded.

Clara hung the coat back up, then sat down next to Mary and spoke conspiratorially. "I go down there, right? And there's this huge car parked right out front, painted this gorgeous creamy yellow. I mean, I've never seen anything like it. And the car was on the same level as the coat: it looked like it was brand new or that someone had just washed the whole thing about fifteen minutes ago. And I know it's his because the driver looks Indian with the same kind of headdress that those monks wore, and a long white smock. So I asked for the secretary and this English guy—a white guy, not like him—he opens the door and gets out of the back seat and I asked him for the birth information for Mr. Holkar. Well, that gave them all a good laugh."

"Who, all?" interrupted Mary eagerly.

"Oh, the rest of them. There was another guy from India up front. And sitting next to the secretary was a girl, and she sounded American and looked American. I think it was her birthday he wanted, which was September 9, 1907; I memorized it 'cause I knew you'd want to know. And they were having a whole cocktail party in there. The car had some kind of polished hardwood inside, and the seats were this rich dark brown leather, there were curtains on the windows. It was nicer than most living rooms I've seen. And they had a table and drinks and hors d'oeuvres and everything back there. They were having a regular little cocktail party at the curb while they waited for this Mr. Holkar to come back from his interview with Miss Adams."

"The girl was born in 1907 and he was born in 1890," Mary said. "Could it be his daughter?"

"She didn't look like him, very light skinned, oh, and born in Seattle, too. So I don't think so. A lady that looked like she could be the girl's mother sat on the other side of her. She was maybe in her forties, kind of like a chaperone."

Mary was concerned. "She's seventeen years younger than he is, but could it have been a girlfriend?"

"It seemed more like that. She kind of blushed when the secretary asked for the birth date. But her mother seemed very pleased about it all."

"OK, so now we know a lot more than we did before. This Holkar's a real swell. He's from India and he has a young American girlfriend who he's asking Miss Adams about. And we suspect he could be connected with the Maharaja of Indore and maybe Jesse as well."

"That about sums it up," Clara agreed.

"Oh, and I think he's a womanizer. He looked you up and down like you were a piece of meat."

"Really? *Me?*" Clara was pleased.

"I wouldn't take it as such a compliment. He's dating a much younger girl and he's still looking around. It says something about him."

"I don't think you can jump to that conclusion," argued Clara.

"Anyway," Mary continued, "we know more but we don't really know anything important yet. Maybe we'll learn something if Miss Adams has me do an astrological report for him."

Mary's phone rang and she answered it. Dorothy was on the line as usual. "Mary, that Mr. Dodd the editor called again, but Mr. Jordan said not to put any calls through. He may also be gone by now, I don't know."

"Yeah?"

"Well, he's getting a little testy. He wants to talk to someone and find out what's happening with the manuscript."

"The manuscript is finished. I gave it to Mr. Jordan over a half hour ago. He said he was going to review it and have Jesse bring it over. I guess you can tell him that."

"OK, thanks."

Mary hung up the phone. She needed to relax. The detective's visit had been stressful and on top of that they had the book deadline and Mr. Holkar. But the Wendel twins were coming after Holkar left and she'd have to be businesslike and efficient—or at least pretend to be. Mary took a deep breath. What had happened to that feeling of utter peace and contentment that she experienced when the monk spoke to her? And what about the journey of the mind that he'd promised? Listening to the Wendels drone on and squabble certainly didn't fill the bill. It was going to be a long day.

Chapter 11

Jeannie stepped into the elevator with the dogs on their leads. She wasn't quite sure how to hold the three leather leashes, but had settled on holding the more assertive Lover with her right hand and Sonny and D'Artagnon together with her left.

Todd, the elevator operator, said, "I see you've got them OK."

"I'm a little nervous," Jeannie admitted.

"What's there to be nervous about? I've walked them myself. They're good dogs. If they try to get away with anything, just snap at the leash, that's all. You'll do fine." The elevator arrived at the lobby and Todd let Jeannie and the dogs out. "Remember," he called after her, "just snap the leash if they act up."

Jeannie walked through the lovely lobby. The floor was a light gray marble with little flecks of sparkling green and brown all through it. There were big domed lamps on the ceiling, and daylight streamed in from the two glass entrance doors and a large revolving one at the center.

"You must be Jeannie Adler," the gray-haired, uniformed man at the front desk said in a friendly way. "I'm Jimmy, the starter."

"Hi," Jeannie said, stopping. The dogs stopped, too. "How did you know my name?"

"Oh, your mom told me you'd be walking the dogs. She asked me to look out for you."

"That's OK."

"You got it all figured out?" asked Jimmy.

"I think so."

"I'd go slow the first time with them, they can be a little rambunctious if they don't know you."

"Has everyone in the building walked these dogs?" Jeannie asked.

Jimmy laughed. "A lot of us have," he said. "Have fun out there, it's a beautiful day."

"Thanks." Jimmy held the door for Jeannie and the dogs to go out. It was a bright and cool April afternoon, and many people were outside, on their way to lunch, shopping or appointments. Lover pulled on his leash toward the park and Jeannie and D'Artagnon followed. Sonny seemed to be holding back, and when Jeannie looked, she could see he'd been dribbling as he walked, leaving a zig-zag trail from the front of the building. His old bladder wasn't what it used to be. Sonny finally stopped by some nearby planters and lifted his leg.

"No, Sonny, no!" Jeannie yelled. "Mr. Jordan said you're only supposed to go in the street." She tried to pull the dog's small leg down to stop him but her hand was spritzed in the process. Sonny just kept peeing. "*No!!!*" Jeannie screamed. Now Lover and D'Artagnon were also lifting their legs at the same place. "Stop it! *Stop!*" Jeannie yelled. She snapped on the leashes as Todd had said, but only ended up getting her shoes and stockings wet with the dogs' water.

Jimmy rushed out of the building. "Jeannie, here, take my handkerchief and clean yourself off. They know they're not supposed to be using these planters for a urinal."

"Bad dogs!" Jeannie scolded. "*Bad!*" Jimmy took the leashes from her as she wiped herself off with his handkerchief. The dogs, having relieved themselves, were now sitting quietly.

"There's a fountain just inside the park," Jimmy gestured. "Go along and rinse the handkerchief and you can clean yourself up a little more," he said as he handed the leashes back to her.

Jeannie and the Pekingese were on their way once again. Lover took the lead, walking out in front as they made their way down Seventh Avenue to Central Park. The other dogs followed, trotting happily along. They could see the numerous stores across the street, many with awnings open. There was a cigar shop, stationery, a Royal Tailors with a sign saying "Made to Order," Leggett's Drugs, Circle Lunch, a restaurant advertising chop suey, and another which simply called itself Eating Place. Big posters on the sides of some buildings advertised The Best Play of the Year and Chesterfield Cigarettes. They passed a large store called Monroe's Clothes; a sign on the corner advertised billiards; and another touted a Ford Car dealership.

The weather was still cool enough that most people wore coats. There were women with fur at their collars and cuffs, some with pretty artificial flowers pinned to their coat lapels, others in plain wool jackets. Almost all wore close-fitting cloche hats; there were black hats, blue hats, gray, brown, pink and red hats. Some women carried purses and a few had books under their arms. They wore sensible black shoes, smart Mary Jane pumps, closed patent leather shoes or even brocade satin pumps. All revealed silk and rayon-encased legs: shapely, attractive legs; delicate legs; or chubby, curvaceous calves with feet bursting out of strapped shoes; others with older, skinnier legs.

A passing man smiled at the dogs and tipped his derby to Jeannie. Most men wore overcoats and many carried walking sticks or newspapers under their arms. Some wore casual caps; others were topped with a Stetson or Homburg. The street was crowded with motor-cars. The ubiquitous black Ford Model T, open touring cars, burgundy sedans, delivery vans and yellow cabs all made their way along Seventh Avenue, keeping up a regular honking and tooting as they maneuvered through traffic.

The three Pekingese paused obediently for the traffic cop at the wide intersection at Central Park West; they were familiar with the route. The officer soon stopped the bustling motor-cars and beckoned the pedestrians across the broad street. All of the modern buildings and traffic fell away as they approached Central Park. Old-fashioned horse-drawn carriages were lined up beside the park, waiting for customers who wanted a ride. There were winter-stripped trees and broad meadows.

The dogs pulled Jeannie off the path and onto the lawn to do their business. She didn't remember if Mr. Jordan said if it was allowed, but the dogs seemed to have a routine. Jeannie saw the fountain, and when they were finished, she drew them along so she could wash up. But Lover and D'Artagnon weren't really interested in that. They wanted to go in the opposite direction and play.

"No!" Jeannie cried and snapped the leashes. "I need to wash up. You're clean and happy now — I'm not. Come on! Lover! Sonny!" she pleaded. But Lover dug his hind legs firmly into the ground and refused to move from the lawn. Jeannie tugged on the leash but he was surprisingly firm. She could have dragged him along, but didn't want to hurt the small creature. Lover sat down, and Sonny and D'Artagnon followed suit, sitting silently beside him. They once again took on the impassive look of statues and seemed unmovable.

"Hey! *Come on now!*" Jeannie urged. "We'll walk more later." She pulled at the leashes repeatedly, but the little Pekingese troop was rooted to the spot. "I want to wash up now!" she pleaded. For a moment the dogs appeared to go along with the idea, as Lover moved ahead of Jeannie once again and the other two dogs followed. But then Lover changed directions and they all began dancing happily around her. Jeannie tried to change her grip on the leashes and step out of the way, but the three Pekingese had already wrapped the leads around her legs.

"Hey! Lover, *cut it out!* You're hurting me." Jeannie scolded. But the dogs either didn't understand or chose not to listen.

"Stop it! *Stop it, Lover! Bad dogs!* Sonny, *stop!* Jeannie tried to move forward and free her legs, but she lost a shoe in the process, although one stockinged foot was now free. As she tried to pull her left foot loose, the dogs again ran around her. Jeannie lost her balance and fell on her backside on the lawn.

"Why are you being so bad?" she shouted as she threw the leashes down, losing her temper. She stayed sitting on the lawn, one shoe off. "I was nice to you! I made you scrambled eggs — it could've been *crappy kibble —*" she enunciated the difference. "That would've been a lot easier for me. You don't even deserve kibble. Go and eat the grass for all I care," Jeannie said bitterly. She ran a hand through her disheveled hair. "And you can just go ahead and get home on your own. I hope a pigeon bites you." She started crying and covered her face with her hands. The dogs once again came together, sat down next to her and watched closely. "You're just bad dogs! *Very bad.* And I'm not gonna do this anymore." She looked at them angrily. D'Artagnon crept over on his belly and licked her hand and the others followed. Jeannie grabbed them to her and hugged them. "Please be good," she whispered earnestly. "Please be good," she repeated and cried a little more.

Chapter 12

"Here we are again, Mary," Ella Wendel announced gaily as she walked through the office door and sat in a chair opposite Mary's desk. "Another six months have passed." She sighed as she put down her umbrella and carefully removed her black gloves. Ella was in her sixties and her clothes were at least twenty years out of date. She wore an old-fashioned travelling suit with an ankle-length skirt and high button shoes. Her blouse had a high collar with lace at the front. A bonnet with a single feather was perched on top of her head, and beneath it, her gray hair was done up in a bun. Everything was black, except the feather, which was purple.

Where did she find these items? Mary wondered. Was an ancient dressmaker using a decades-old pattern for her? Were the clothes stored in a closet years ago and never worn? She remembered the classic advice to dress conservatively for an interview. But this was not that kind of an interview.

Mary smiled as genuinely as she could. "Yes, it does seem like you were just here."

"New dress?" Georgiana Wendel asked crisply as she came in. "Very nice." She plumped herself down next to her sister. "How've you been?"

"I can't complain. Miss Adams keeps me busy." Nearly an hour of their bickering lay ahead. Mary inwardly groaned. The twins generally spent much of their visit arguing with one another. Adams never became impatient with them, as she was keenly interested in their personalities and their astrological similarities and differences. For Mary, it was a different story.

Ella's sister Georgiana was also dressed completely in black. But while the twins looked very much alike in face and form, their attire was completely different. Unlike her sister, Georgiana had assertively kept up with the times. She wore a smartly cut V-neck dress in a rough-weave silk with a pleated skirt just past her knees and graceful Mary Jane pumps. Her bobbed hair was set in a lovely marcel wave and showed not a streak of gray; its chestnut color looked so natural that Mary would not have imagined it was a dye job except for her twin's older appearance.

Ella was the elder by about fifteen minutes, and while their rising signs, Moon signs and the rest of their horoscopes were very much the same, Ella's Sun was actually in the sign of Capricorn and Georgiana's, Aquarius — a rare occurrence. The two women lived together in an ancient Fifth Avenue home that was now squeezed between high-rise buildings on every side. Their father had made countless millions in real estate — if the papers were to be believed — but they kept mainly to their own circle and never spoke to reporters.

"What do you see in Toby's horoscope?" Ella eagerly asked. Georgiana crossed her arms and gave her sister a disgusted look.

"You'll have to ask Miss Adams about that; she should be ready for you shortly," said Mary. "But I have his horoscope chart right here."

"We want you to write everything down," Ella continued. "Everything Miss Adams says, especially about Toby."

"Oh, you know I always do, Miss Wendel." Mary turned to the intercom box on her desk, pressed the lever and leaned forward. "Miss Adams, the Misses Wendels have arrived."

Mary looked at the chart in front of her. She didn't care for Toby. She had been hearing about him for years, but had never met him. Even Ella Wendel's praise made him sound spoiled, willful and misbehaved. Toby would now be seven years old and he was an Aquarius. He had once accompanied the ladies to their consultation and had been so disruptive, teasing the Pekingese and chasing them around the room, that he was no longer permitted to the readings. Evangeline generally favored Sun-sign Aquarians like herself, but this was not the case with Toby.

Miss Adams appeared at the door to her office and invited the ladies in. Mary took her steno pad and followed them.

"I don't think you've met D'Artagnon here," Evangeline began. "He's been with us less than six months. Of course you know Sonny and Lover." Mary placed the charts for the Wendels and Toby on Miss Adams' desk and sat down.

"My Toby has learned to use the telephone!" Ella immediately began. "When we were out in Great Neck last week, I phoned our man, Phipps, and Toby began howling when he heard my voice on the line. I told Phipps to step away from the telephone box so that I could speak to Toby directly. He said that Toby put his paws right on the table and listened carefully. Then he ran off to get his ball and placed it before the instrument! How clever he was."

"Why don't you tell her the story of how Toby picked up your false teeth and came to bring them to you, Ella?" Georgiana asked sardonically. She turned to Adams and Mary to include them. "I looked up from the morning paper and there he was, standing in the doorway with the teeth in his mouth, as if they were his own—grinning like a clown." She burst out laughing at the recollection. "What a sight that was! I'll never forget that image as long as I live."

"Oh, hush, now, he was only trying to help me," Ella scolded.

"Now for Toby," Miss Adams began as she studied his horoscope, "This is an important year. He's seven years old and Saturn demands that he develop some discipline. I know it's a difficult topic, but perhaps you might hire a trainer to help him."

"Oh, no, Toby would never like that," Ella instantly replied. "He doesn't want anyone coming into the house; it disturbs him too much."

"Well perhaps in the yard then?" Adams inquired.

"Why not the yard, Ella?" Georgiana asked. "It sounds like a good idea to me."

"My Toby will not have anyone invading his territory," she assured them.

Evangeline sat back and pushed her glasses up on her nose. "I'll tell you a story," she began kindly. "As you know, Miss Mary Pickford is a client of mine and she consults with me regularly. Some years ago, she adopted a wire-haired terrier named Zorro, who was exceedingly troublesome. She had to settle one lawsuit after another because the dog was routinely biting people he came into contact with." She paused then added, "I tell you nothing confidential, his behavior was in all the papers. As it happened, when Miss Pickford and Zorro were in town a few years ago, Zorro bit a carriage horse in the park and was kicked in return."

"Toby doesn't bite . . ." Ella hastily interjected.

"Zorro was never properly trained," Adams continued. "And no one dared correct the animal because Miss Pickford is a wealthy star. Out in California, she would bring him into the studio with her, but of course she was busy working, and Zorro was left to roam free and piddled wherever he chose. Time went on, and Zorro was seven years old, just at this Saturn juncture that Toby's coming to now." She tapped the dog's chart, then folded her hands on her desk. "Well, they had a lot of lighting equipment at the studio that required electricity. Miss Pickford described a large outlet called a spider where the technicians could plug in a dozen instruments. Zorro took it to be some kind of bush or tree, I suppose. He raised his leg and began to make his water on it, and received a tremendous electrical shock in return. Threw him across the room." Evangeline stopped to look intensely at Ella Wendel. "Stone dead," she added gravely.

"We don't have to worry about that," Ella quickly replied. "The house is lit entirely by gas."

"The point I'm making," Evangeline continued gently, "is that if you don't discipline him, the Universe might."

"One day he's going to have a run-in with me," Georgiana muttered. "He's not even housebroken."

"Of course Toby's housebroken! What a thing to say, Georgiana."

Georgiana turned to Adams. "Toby pooped on my bathroom floor just the other day," she said drily. "Waltzed in there as nonchalant as you please. He's learned how to open the doors now. I stepped out of my bath and right into his pile. And Toby's poopy pile is not petite, I can tell you that."

"We all make mistakes," Ella said defensively. "No one's perfect. You surely don't think he did it on purpose, do you?"

"If he can't be trained, he should stay in his crate," Georgiana growled. "Or keep him in the yard," she said dismissively.

"You know the streetcar bell bothers him so!" Ella turned to Adams. "He's a highly-strung, exceptional creature. Georgiana doesn't appreciate his finer qualities."

Miss Adams continued. "Now, as I say, this year there could be questions of discipline for Toby."

"I don't have the heart to make him so uncomfortable, to go against his wishes!" Ella cried.

"I'll do it!" Georgiana flared. "*I* don't mind making him uncomfortable."

"You will not! *You leave him alone!*" her sister shot back.

Evangeline calmly continued. "The astrology indicates that he needs to become more mature or he could run afoul of the authorities. It's the same with any child. He wants to be independent, but he must learn to accept the rules of society. Everyone has growing pains from time to time. "

Ella changed the subject. "We saw Mr. Holkar outside the building just now . . ."

"Oh, yes!" Georgiana added enthusiastically. "He was very pleased he had such good news from you."

Mary was stunned to hear the name and was instantly at attention. She kept unobtrusively writing to be sure she jotted down all the gossip and information about Holkar.

Ella continued: "Nice young man, I'm sorry for his problems. Such good manners. It's becoming rare these days even among the better class of people."

"We met his new lady friend," Georgiana stated bluntly. "Young. American, from Seattle, I believe they said."

"Oh, yes, very young," Ella interrupted. "Her mother is closer to his age, wouldn't you say, Georgiana?

"It's disgraceful. The girl is probably half his age," Georgiana complained.

"Still, he cuts a beautiful figure," Ella offered. "So cultured. Such good taste."

"Good host," Georgiana grudgingly conceded.

"Oh, yes, very good host." Ella agreed. "Can't argue with that. And his first wife is lovely."

Georgiana leaned forward conspiratorially. "We saw that other woman they talk about in London a few years ago." She paused for effect. "Common."

"Oh, yes, very common," Ella agreed.

"Common as a tack." Georgiana confirmed.

"There's no accounting for it," Ella went on. "Such good taste, and then . . ." She trailed off.

Georgiana cut in derisively. "He trades up for a new model, just like his motor-cars."

"Don't be so cynical, Georgiana," her sister chided. "Not every man is a monster."

"He's the same as any American man except he doesn't divorce them, that's all."

Mary glanced at Miss Adams who was listening to the twins with interest and occasionally making her own notes.

"Wealthy Indian men are expected to collect wives, you know that," Ella countered. "Whatever have you got against marriage?"

"I didn't choose to get married, did I?" Georgiana again crossed her arms. "I had opportunities. I chose not to. I don't see that the institution works very well, that's all. Here or elsewhere."

"He supports his wives; the first one still had her own wing in the house. What more can you ask? Love doesn't last forever," Ella said realistically. She again turned to Adams. "His estate is like a little city onto itself. Beautiful."

Georgiana agreed. "Oh, yes, lovely estate. Got to give him that."

Ella continued. "We were in India that year. When we first saw Mr. Holkar at the Delhi Durbar. Remember, Georgiana?"

"1911," Georgiana added. "Fifteen years ago already. He was almost a boy."

"We had very good seats, right before the dais," Ella shared. "They said there were half a million in attendance."

"Oh, I can believe that's true," Georgiana added. "Tremendous amphitheater. English, Indian troops, marching, on horseback, incredible pageantry. A sea of turbans in the audience: yellow, red, blue. A sight you'd never forget."

"There sat the King and Queen," Ella continued, "and each of the local men were to go up, one by one, to bow before them. Magnificently dressed, one more richly adorned than the next. I think Mr. Holkar wore more jewels than the Queen herself."

"Jackie Baroda didn't," Georgiana added pointedly. "He was in white cotton trousers and a plain shirt, just to show them where he came from. Good for him, I say. He turned his back to the King. He gave them his own. You wouldn't see me catering to them, playing by their rules."

"He had a different background from the others of course, more the common man," Ella recollected. "Caused quite a stir, though, I can tell you that. There was a gasp from the crowd."

"Bully for him!" Georgiana concluded.

"And then Mr. Holkar," Ella went on, "Well, he was still a very young man then, with all the confidence of youth. You know his family always had political complications. But he was too sophisticated to make a public display."

"Do you remember his cane, Ella?" Georgiana asked.

"My, yes, that cane," Ella said, remembering.

Georgiana set up the story. "Mr. Holkar was standing to one side, waiting for his presentation. He was young, he looked fabulous and he knew it. He carried a golden cane and he shifted it back and forth as he waited and even twirled it a bit as he stood there. It had a large gem at the top and the entire thing was studded with countless precious stones. The effect as it caught the light was dazzling. And he was dazzling, too. He wore a lovely wide-brimmed hat, dripping with gemstones, that reflected the light as well. There were so many well-dressed people there, but he almost seemed possessed of some special power. We were all a little hypnotized," Georgiana admitted. "I couldn't take my eyes off him."

"No one could," Ella replied. "You almost forgot the royal couple."

"There was an aura about him as he walked up to the dais," Georgiana recalled. "Well, you thought, here's someone to be reckoned with."

"Oh, yes. I saw it, too," Ella echoed. "So much promise. And then, of course . . ." She shook her head sadly. "Poor Mr. Holkar!"

"Oh, yes." Georgiana picked up the story with relish. "You see, just at the moment when he stepped before the royal couple, with a million eyes upon him, all the top people in the country, what happens? His cane breaks! Shattered into several pieces. And in probably the most public moment of his life, he stumbled. Fell right down on the ground in all his finery. He looked for a moment just like a crumpled old heap of brocade and silk. He was a young man, of course, got right back on his feet, made his bow and collected his dignity."

"Someone ran out and picked up the hat and the pieces of that remarkable walking stick," Ella added. "But what a shame, what a shame. Poor man."

"Then we met him again several years ago in London. When was it, Ella? He had a whole floor at the Savoy."

"Oh, he has his entourage, you know, when he travels," Ella said. "I believe that was in 1921, right after Mother died," she confirmed. "We saw that woman they talk about when we were there. Not this American; her predecessor, I suppose. They say she had an affair with someone on his staff. In his own house, no less. He educated her, supported her entire family. That's how she repaid him."

"We don't know her side of the story," Georgiana interrupted.

"He can't respond publically, of course, not a person of his class. He's not in a position to speak to the press. Poor Mr. Holkar!" Ella seemed genuinely sorry for the man. "This situation he's in now . . . I'm afraid he'll lose everything."

Georgiana cut her short. "He hasn't lost everything! They let him go with a fortune in jewels. He got a free pass as far as I'm concerned."

"There was something about a treaty he was involved with, I didn't understand it all," Ella said, vaguely waving her hand. "Political problems, you know. They made a big to-do about this girl to force him out. His friends said that he let her go."

"You don't know the whole story, Ella," Georgiana countered. "He had something to do with it."

"I don't say he had nothing to do with it. I'm just saying I'm sorry is all. He seems like such a nice young man."

"His wife told me otherwise. And that was five years ago. A lifetime in terms of his relationships it appears," she added sarcastically.

"Obviously he was involved with the girl," Ella retorted. "She was on his payroll. But those people attacked and killed? I can't imagine he had anything to do with it."

Georgiana raised her voice. "When you break the law, you take your punishment. Acting like she was stolen property. *Ha!*" They all sat for a few moments in thoughtful silence.

Miss Adams finally got in a few words; she was able to review the twins' forecast for the coming months. "Now for both of you, we have some very nice Jupiter transits coming up, especially this summer. Good time for a trip, to ask for a favor . . ." The sisters always became restless during this phase, preferring to drive the meeting themselves. Before long, Georgiana interrupted.

"When will my lawsuit be over?" she asked crossly.

"Well, you could have some good news, things should be going your way in a few months," Adams told her.

"They want to put me away," Georgiana said angrily. "They think they can get hold of my property, those bastards. They've got another thing coming."

"Don't worry," Evangeline soothed. "I think it will all work out. Everything will be all right. Have your lawyer move forward soon, that's all."

The little alarm on Adams' desk softly trilled. She and Mary stood up.

"So nice to see you both. Mary will send you your report as usual."

Ella turned and waved goodbye as she left the room. "Lovely to see you again."

"We'll see you in the fall—if we're all still here," Georgiana joked as she followed her sister out the door.

• Chapter 13 •

Evangeline Adams closed the door to her office as she often did in the afternoon, instructing Mary to take messages if anyone called, while she meditated and returned to the day's correspondence. Many clients who couldn't make a trip to New York wrote to request personal chart work and forecasts by mail.

Mary sat at her desk and began to wind a sheet of paper into the Underwood to transcribe Miss Adams' advice for the Wendels and Toby. She paused to be sure that Adams had returned to her desk, turned to Clara and lowered her voice.

"The Wendels talked about Tom Holkar," she began. "It sounds like he's a major leaguer in India, but he seems to have had some problems. He was supposed to be introduced to the King and Queen but he was showing off and fell down right in front of them. It also sounded like there was some scandal or some problem with a woman he was stuck on. Everyone knew about it and it got him into trouble. It sounded a little creepy."

"Yeah, there was something like that in the article I read you in the paper this morning—" Clara began.

"No, I'm not talking about the Maharaja. I'm talking about Mr. Holkar. Something happened because of some woman and it sounded like he lost a lot of money or something. Maybe in a separation agreement, I don't know. He's had more than one marriage. The Wendels saw him in India and said that he was dripping in jewels."

The phone rang and Mary picked it up and wrote down some instructions. She turned back to Clara. "That was the Fiskes' butler. They're having the wake at their house and they're inviting Miss Adams. She might want to go."

There was a knock on the hall door. Mary and Clara looked at each other. Someone was once again ignoring the sign to go down the hall to reception. They heard Mr. Simon call out, "Mary? Clara? It's Robert Simon. May I come in?"

Clara said, "Let's let him in, he may know something." She got up and unlocked the door and the landlord stepped into the inner office.

"Miss Adams can't be disturbed right now, Mr. Simon," Mary said, "But I'll let her know you stopped by."

"Oh, no, no, no, don't worry," Simon said, lowering his voice. "I understand, I don't want to intrude." He looked eagerly toward Evangeline's office. "I was just speaking with Jimmy in the lobby and he said that Tom Holkar was here. Is she in with Mr. Holkar now?"

"Why is everyone so interested in this Mr. Holkar?" Mary blurted out.

"Oh, he's a very important man," answered Simon. "Very important. He's the one that was selling the ruby elephant. You know, the one that disappeared."

"The missing jewel?" Clara asked.

"Exactly. So I'd like to get in a word with him if I could. You girls wouldn't mind, would you? On his way out? I can just wait here quietly until they're finished, I wouldn't interfere with your work." He sat down in one of the client's waiting chairs and made himself comfortable. "Just pretend I'm not even here."

Mary tried to process what Simon was saying but it didn't make sense. She looked up at him. "I thought Mr. Fiske was selling that jewel," she said.

"Yes, he was," Simon answered, "Henderson Fiske was handling it for Tom Holkar," Simon said in a confidential tone. "Fiske was the broker. This Holkar fellow is apparently selling a lot of jewelry and gave it to Fiske to sell for him. He's some kind of prince from India but he appears to be on the outs with them at the moment and left the country. They're also not too keen about his relationship with an American girl, I hear."

"What do you mean, 'some kind of prince'? Mr. Holkar is royalty?" Mary asked. "From India?"

"Yes, yes, there are a lot of princes over there, different levels, but Holkar was ruling a very big state," he said, still careful not to be overheard. "I'm afraid I don't recall his title right now. Something like a Nawab or something like that, I'm not that familiar with those foreign titles. Maybe a Raja? I can't recall."

Mary and Clara looked at each other and said at the same time, "The Maharaja of Indore?"

"Yes, that's it! That's it. The Maharaja of Indore, I remember it now," said Simon, pleased with himself.

Mary was astonished. "But Mr. Holkar is the Maharaja of Indore? How could that be? His name is Tom Holkar."

"Maharaja is his title, but Holkar is the family name. And Tom is probably just a nickname; you know how it is with these foreign royals."

"Actually, we don't," Clara said.

"Well, they all have a lot of long names and they often have nicknames, too, that's all,"

"Mr. Simon," Mary asked. "Why would that detective want to see Miss Adams? Just because Mr. Holkar is a client? She sees a lot of people, it doesn't mean she's involved with them."

"Why, she's the elephant lady! That's why I was here. And she knows everyone in town. Henderson Fiske told me he was showing it to her. He used to do that, to let you know there was competition. He probably said the same thing to a lot of other people. It's a sales technique to make everyone more interested and raise the price. But now that he's gone, of course, it's a different story . . ."

"Did he mention any other names to you? Other people that might be interested?" Mary eagerly asked.

"Oh, the same people he always did. I guess it doesn't really matter now that he's gone. Charles Schwab. That psychic, or medium, what's her name? Juliet Pontin. Evalyn Walsh McLean, of course, she's always interested in any large stone. It doesn't mean they were really interested, of course. They were probably just the people he was going to telephone next. To see who might be interested."

Simon paused. "So, when do you think the interview will be over?"

"What interview?" Mary asked.

"The one with Mr. Holkar," he looked at Mary inquiringly. "And Miss Adams. How long do you think it will last?"

"Oh, I'm sorry Mr. Simon, I didn't understand. Mr. Holkar left over an hour ago. I'm afraid you've missed him."

"Oh, dear, I'm very sorry too." The landlord stood up, clearly disappointed. "Will he be back?"

"He may be back for another appointment someday, but we don't expect to hear from him soon."

"Well, can you at least tell me where he's staying while he's in town? He must be stopping at one of the big hotels."

"I have no idea. He didn't ask for a typed report, so there's no address to send it to."

"A pity, a pity," Mr. Simon said, almost to himself. "You'll let me know if he returns? I'm just a phone call away, you know. And I'm usually in my office upstairs during the day."

"We're really not supposed to talk about the clients, Mr. Simon. But you can ask Miss Adams when you see her."

"Yes," Simon said thoughtfully. "Yes, I may very well do that." Then he was once again all charm and lightness. "All right, girls, thank you for your time. Have a good day." And Robert Simon left as he had come in.

Clara jumped up to lock the door. "Mr. Holkar is the Maharaja of Indore? No wonder he had such a nice coat."

"It's a real Mercury retrograde thing, that we completely misunderstood," Mary said glumly. "What did that article say? That he was deposed or something? Where's your paper?" Mary asked.

Clara grabbed up the newspaper from the side of her desk and leafed through it excitedly. "Here it is," she said, reading: "*Former Indian Ruler to Peddle Fabulous Gems. Maharaja Who Lost Throne over Dancing Girl Visits New York . . . ready to sell precious stones in order to make up for the revenue he has had to surrender . . . abdicated in order to avoid an official inquiry into his share of the murder of the Bombay merchant Bawla, and the attempted abduction of Mumtaz Begum.*"

Clara looked at Mary with excitement. "He's this guy? And he was sitting right here?"

"I can't believe it either," Mary said. "What the heck does 'his share of the murder' mean? And 'attempted abduction'?"

Clara continued reading, "*The value of the jewel collection which the ex-ruler must dispose of . . . is understood to be almost fabulous.*"

"Clara, this is not good," Mary said hurriedly.

"Why? What difference does it make? If he was really guilty, they'd have taken him in by now."

"I don't know about that. But I'm talking about the office. All these people are already coming here because Mr. Fiske was murdered and that elephant is missing. And now it turns out that the Maharaja is a client and his story is all over the papers, too. It's just going to bring more people here, snooping around and asking questions."

"I'm sure it'll blow over. They'll find this jewel and that'll be it."

"But what if they don't? Miss Adams gets very upset about these legal problems; she's not herself. And these detectives are not the brightest bulbs in the chandelier. They're obviously looking to pin the murder on her. What if they do? Then we'll both be out of jobs. I really like my job; I don't want to leave here. And I couldn't do Miss Adams' job if she weren't around."

"You're right, Mary," Clara agreed. "I've been here over two years. I feel like I've worked my way up. I don't know any other astrologers we could work for."

"That's just it. And I don't think we could make this kind of money anywhere else."

"The only other job I ever had was doing the books at my Uncle Frank's deli," Clara remembered. "It was OK, but when they were busy, he'd ask me to work the counter and he always wanted me to put my thumb on the scale. Plus the pay was a lot lower."

"So we're going to have to find out what's really going on so we can put Miss Adams in the clear."

"I can go along with that."

"Maybe we can give the cops another suspect or solve the crime for them."

Evangeline Adams opened the door to her office and stepped into the room, very pleased. "I just got off the telephone with Coco Chanel, the fashion designer. She wrote me to say that she's in New York and that my forecast for her was singularly correct. She had asked for my timing for the release of a new line, and it's been enormously successful. Now she has an idea for a simple, affordable black silk sheath, and she wants me to again select the release date. I feel that it, too, can't help being a success since it's absolutely appropriate for Saturn in Scorpio this year."

"Congratulations," Mary said sincerely.

Evangeline changed the subject. "Mary, I'd like to send Mrs. Fiske a flower arrangement. Can you phone the florist and order something appropriate? Nothing too elaborate; the same as we've done for other clients before."

"Sure, I'll call them right away. And Mrs. Fiske's butler called to say that the wake will be tonight and tomorrow."

"All right. I think I'll go this evening, then, so it would be nice if the flowers could arrive this afternoon."

"I'll see what I can do. I did have one question, though," Mary said. "I kind of feel the office has been involved in this situation more than usual, and I wonder if Clara and I could accompany you to the wake? We don't want to intrude, but if you think it might be appropriate . . ."

"Oh, my dears, that would be lovely," Adams agreed with enthusiasm. "Yes, of course you can come. Let's think about it now. I'll plan to leave here shortly after seven. How would you feel about meeting me back at the office then? We can all take the car together. Will that leave you enough time to have some dinner and return?

"Absolutely," Mary said.

"Yes," Clara agreed.

"It's a plan, then. And I'm sure Mrs. Fiske will appreciate the gesture."

• Chapter 14 •

Mary returned to the office after a light dinner to find her space in complete disarray. Wires and tools were strewn across her desk and on the floor. She looked with dismay at a large black wooden box standing in her waiting area. There were heavy wires connecting it to the power socket and an item on her desk that looked like a small fan. The thing had a Bakelite base, but where the blades and cage of the fan should be, there was only a metal ring connected by springs to a disk-shaped metal object suspended in the center. Mary was flabbergasted, dreading that Adams had invited some off-balance psychic investigator to test the surroundings; she seemed to attract eccentrics.

"Is that you, Mary?" Evangeline called from inside her office.

"Yes, it is," Mary responded as she opened the door. "What's all this stuff out here?" she asked, concerned.

"I'm afraid it's our friend Jesse Bauer." Evangeline said. "That's a microphone on your desk. Jesse was working with Mr. Jordan so I could practice speaking on the microphone before my radio appearance this month. Jesse thought it would be a simple task, and as you can see, that's not quite true. They couldn't arrange it before Mr. Jordan left. Why he's decided to do so now, I can't say. He was supposed to be clearing it away. Do you mind, Mary, straightening things up a bit while we wait for Clara? I'll be a few minutes myself."

Mary turned back to her desk and began coiling the wires and placing them with the microphone on the amplifier box. Clara soon arrived.

"Don't even ask," Mary advised. "Just help me. I'll tell you about it later." The two women gathered the tools and wires together and moved the box towards the outer office door.

"Miss Adams will be out in a few minutes," Mary said, lowering her voice. "I've been thinking about the wake. I want to get into the Fiskes' sitting room upstairs to see the scene of the crime."

"I picked up the evening paper," said Clara. "It has an obituary on Mr. Fiske." She finished coiling her wire and picked up the paper from her desk, turning a few pages. "Here it is: *The City was shocked to hear of the brutal slaying of investment broker Henderson Fiske, who was found murdered in his West 9th Street townhouse early this morning. Fiske, 52, first came to prominence at Kidder, Peabody & Co. in Boston. Once he had amassed a vast fortune, he moved to New York to open his own brokerage firm. In recent years, Fiske specialized in negotiating exclusive deals for wealthy and socially prominent clients.*

"*Detective John Sterling of the New York City police force reports that they are investigating all leads, but refused to comment further. Anyone with information related to this heinous crime is asked to contact the Sixth Precinct immediately.*"

"OK," said Mary. "I'm sure we'll find out more when we get to the house. But we have to come up with a plan. I thought I could pretend to be his long-lost cousin from Hoernerstown, Pennsylvania. If the parents didn't speak, they wouldn't know me."

"But Mrs. Fiske knows you," Clara said.

"This is for the butler or the housekeeper. We speak to Mrs. Fiske as ourselves, then act like she sent us to the room and ask for help."

"Who can I be?" Clara asked. "I don't look like your sister."

"You can be my maid."

"Your *maid*?" Clara asked, appalled. "I'm not going to be your maid," she said firmly.

"All right, you'll be my assistant, then. That's what Miss Adams calls me when I travel with her."

"You know that part better," Clara countered. "You can be the assistant. *I'll* be the cousin."

"But, Clara, you don't even look like them," Mary argued. "How could you be his cousin?"

"That's the whole point! We're assuming that Fiske's uncle married someone the family didn't approve of. They were different. That's why they're not talking anymore. I'm the black sheep," Clara said, very pleased with herself.

"You just want to be a sheep because you're Aries," said Mary. "The ram."

The phones all rang, and repeated regularly. Dorothy had left for the day and the night switchboard was turned on. Calls were automatically put through to all of the office phones at once.

"Mary, would you answer that, please?" Miss Adams called from inside.

Mary picked up the phone. "Evangeline Adams' office."

"Oh, hello," a man's deep voice said, hesitating a bit. "Eh . . . this is Leo, Alexa husband," he said in heavily accented English.

"Oh, hi Leo. This is Mary speaking. How can I help you?"

"Alexa say maybe work late? Not home."

"I don't think so, it's after seven. The office is closed. But hold on, Leo, and I'll check." Mary put the phone down and dashed over to open the door to the outer office. All the lights were off and the place was deserted. She came back and picked up the telephone again. "No, there's no one there. Alexa must be on her way home. Maybe she stopped at the store or something."

"Must be. Thank you. Goodnight." Leo rang off.

Mary turned back to Clara. "Just be my assistant," she said.

"I don't want to be your assistant!" Clara replied, becoming agitated.

"But Clara, you *are* my assistant in life!"

"That's the whole point. It's no fun doing something that's the same as in life."

"We're not doing this for the fun of it. We're doing it to figure out what happened to Mr. Fiske. How about this?" Mary proposed. "I won't introduce you at all unless it seems like I need to. You just come along with me and probably no one will ask any questions."

"All right," Clara agreed.

Miss Adams soon came out and the three of them greeted the driver waiting downstairs and climbed into Evangeline's motor-car. They drove down Fifth Avenue with its tall bronze signal towers controlling the traffic. The signal lights had made the Avenue much less congested and it only took them about half an hour to get to the Fiskes' home.

The driver dropped them off in front of a lovely townhouse on West 9th Street. The three-story brownstone had bay windows on the third floor and was surrounded by a black wrought-iron fence. Gas jets in front had already come on. The property was well kept, with trees by the street and potted plants on the stoop. The three women climbed the stairs to the main entrance. A butler immediately opened the door and took their coats as they stepped into the Fiskes' home. "They're all inside, ladies," he said in a somber voice, gesturing them ahead. They stood in a large entryway with the living room to their right and a tall, carpeted staircase before them.

Mary, Clara and Adams walked into the large, sedate parlor done in rich shades of chocolate and beige. There were gas sconces on the walls as well as electric lamps inside. A fireplace along one wall served as the focus for a grouping of chairs, a couch and coffee table, where a few guests softly chatted. At the back of the house Mary could see the open coffin placed before closed curtains. There were several rows of black folding chairs in front of it for the visitors. Many people were already there, sitting and speaking quietly. Mary recognized a few of them as clients from Evangeline's office.

"Let me see if my flowers have arrived," Miss Adams said as they all signed the guest book. Miss Adams immediately caught Mrs. Fiske's eye and walked back to talk to her. Mary and Clara looked around them.

On the near wall, there was a wedding photograph, taken about thirty years before. "Is that Mrs. Fiske?" Mary asked, looking at the pretty young woman in a long corseted dress from the turn of the century. "I don't recognize her." She wore leg-o-mutton sleeves with expensive-looking lace at her collar and cuffs, and a long train. Her hair was piled high off her forehead and the hint of a smile remained on her lips.

"It looks to be," confirmed Clara. "And that must be the dead husband." Mr. Fiske stared out of the tintype picture with no hint of emotion. He sat stiffly in an armchair, and his wife stood behind him with a hand on his shoulder. He was hard looking, with close-set eyes and a strong jaw. Despite his youth, it wasn't a particularly flattering portrait.

"Look at this spread!" Clara whispered to Mary as they walked towards the main room. There was a punch bowl and hors d'oeuvres. A maid was pouring drinks and a footman walked through the room, clearing napkins and empty glasses.

"There's Mrs. Fiske," Mary said, inclining her head towards the back of the room. Mrs. Fiske stood near the casket as she spoke with Evangeline. She was dressed all in black and Mary thought she actually looked younger, but also more fragile, as it was clear that she was not well. All signs of her previous self-assurance were gone and she appeared rather distraught. She seemed almost in a trance, with no signs of animation, and she grasped the back of a chair from time to time to steady herself.

Clara leaned forward and whispered to Mary, "I think she's been drinking. That's what my Uncle Frank used to look like after a big bender."

"Could be," Mary responded. "She's been under a lot of strain." She scanned the room. "Oh, no," she said, scowling. "Look who's here, in the corner." Mary had spied Detective Sergeant Brophy and his assistant.

Clara drew in her breath. *"What are they doing here?"*

"I don't know. But I don't want to go near them. No one's by the coffin—let's go in and look at Mr. Fiske." They walked down the aisle. Clara kneeled by the luxurious casket while Mary stood beside her and bowed her head. They both said short prayers for Mr. Fiske.

"This casket looks nicer than most furniture I've seen," Clara commented *sotto voce*. "What is it? Maybe cherry wood? Something expensive. What a shame to put it all in the ground." She paused as they examined the body. "Mr. Fiske looks awfully pasty."

"Of course he's pasty, he's dead!" Mary whispered. "They clean them up and put on cosmetics for the presentation."

"Should I feel for the bump on the back of his head?" Clara asked.

"Clara," Mary said between her teeth. "*Do not touch him!*" She tried to be firm while retaining the posture of a prayerful mourner.

"Then what are we here for?" Clara asked, looking up from her kneeling position.

"I don't know. Let's study the body a little more to see if anything jumps out at us."

They observed Mr. Fiske for a while longer.

"Nice suit," Clara said. "He looks better in the picture on the wall, though."

"That was a long time ago. And the photographers always make them look good because that's how they make their living."

"Do you think they'll bury him with that tie pin and cuff links? They look like diamonds. It'd be an awful waste."

"I guess they can afford it." They looked at Fiske some more.

"Well," Clara finally said, "he didn't chew his nails. I don't think they could change that."

"You're right, that's something. Not a nervous person, I guess. And I think he dyed his hair," said Mary. "Not many businessmen dye their hair. What do you think?"

"It's not a completely natural color. So maybe he was vain or trying to look younger," Clara added. "What else?"

"Well, I remember Miss Adams saying that detached earlobes mean that someone is generous. He has almost no earlobes, so I guess — not generous. Although we pretty much already knew that."

"Oh!" Clara exclaimed. "I have detached earlobes," she said, feeling them.

"Let's move on," Mary said, noting other friends approaching the coffin. They turned toward Mrs. Fiske.

"Look out, Mary, that detective is heading right toward us," Clara said out of the side of her mouth.

"Hello, ladies." Detective Brophy's supercilious assistant greeted them in a falsely friendly tone as he stepped up. "Remember me? I'm sorry we weren't introduced. I'm Detective Jack Sterling."

Mary regarded him coolly and only said, "Hello."

"May I get you a glass of punch, Miss Adler?"

"It's *Missus*."

"Oh, is that so?" he asked a little sarcastically. "Then why does your mother have the same last name? Coincidence?"

"Have you been *spying* on me?" Mary asked him incredulously.

"We look into all parties of interest. And I find you *especially* interesting," Sterling said baldly.

"That has nothing to do with me," Mary said automatically.

"We've made the standard inquiries. We do have to do background checks on all the people associated with this case."

"We're not 'associated with this case,' as you put it."

"Oh really? Well, then, why are you here?"

Clara quickly cut in. "We're supporting Miss Adams and she's supporting Mrs. Fiske. It's a terrible thing to happen . . ."

Sterling interrupted her: " — and it can happen to anyone at any time if they're not careful and associate with the wrong kind of people," he said smugly.

Mary looked him straight in the eye, annoyed. "Excuse us. We have to pay our respects. Please let us have a moment to pray," she said abruptly, turning Clara around by the shoulder and walking toward Miss Adams. To her chagrin, Sergeant Brophy was now directly in their path. They quickly changed direction and sat down on some of the black folding chairs.

"I guess that scratches our plan to pretend to be the black sheep cousin," said Clara gloomily.

"I'm sorry I invited us, Clara. It's all a waste of time and now they're spying on us." She looked around. "Who do we know here?" She didn't see anyone at the moment that she could put a name to. She leaned back in her seat. "I'd really like to see the scene of the crime, but I don't see how we can arrange it with the two charming officers here." She looked up as someone approached them.

It was Adams' landlord, Robert Simon. "Why it's a pleasure to see you here, Mary." He sat down beside her. "Clara—how are you?" he asked pleasantly.

"Oh, Mr. Simon!" replied Mary. "It's nice of you to come." He looked debonair in a beautiful black pin-striped suit and gray silk pocket square.

"We knew the Fiskes socially. Such a sad tragedy." He sat back thoughtfully for a few moments. "Mary, let me confide something to you," he said, straightening his pants leg. "I find myself in a bind. My wife, it turns out, is very eager to have this ruby elephant. I could've bought it, but I didn't like to make the first offer. And of course I hadn't even seen it. But now that this terrible story is in the papers, Mrs. Simon is determined to have it. And when Mrs. Simon wants something," he exhaled a little heavily, "she can make things very uncomfortable until she has it." He paused again, then smiled. "So I'd appreciate it if you would pass along any information you'd happen to come across."

"Mr. Simon, believe me," Clara blurted out, "we know less than you do."

Simon calmly raised a hand to object. "Now, don't rush to assume you won't learn anything new later on," he said genially. "Someone may call and try to sell Miss Adams the jewel. A client might talk about it. You never know. If you two keep your eyes and ears open and report any news to me, I'm sure I could make it very much worth your while. Please keep it in mind."

Mary sat still, feeling uncomfortable and not knowing what to say.

"Who's that big man talking to Evangeline?" Simon asked. "He seems to be making her quite cross," he observed.

Mary looked over to see that Detective Brophy had now cornered Miss Adams and appeared to be pressing her for information.

"That's Detective Sergeant Brophy," Mary quickly replied. "The other detective was bothering us, too. That's him, Jack Sterling, behind Brophy. They already interviewed Miss Adams at the office this morning."

"Oh, that's not right at all." Simon frowned. "Mr. Fiske would be very unhappy about that. In his own home, no less." He clicked his tongue and shook his head in disapproval. "And Mrs. Fiske too weak to object."

He was right. Mrs. Fiske, they could see, now that they were closer, was draped in old-fashioned black crepe, and looked almost attractive without her usual layer of cosmetics. But she also looked completely exhausted. Her face was ashen, and she couldn't seem to keep her eyes open.

"Let me take care of it." Simon got up and bowed graciously to Mary and Clara. He took Mary's hand. "You'll remember what I said, won't you?" he asked while smiling a bit sadly. He strode over to the detective and Mary could hear most of his very firm but reasonable words.

"Pardon me, Detective, this is no place for you to be speaking to the guests," he said evenly. "I'm sure you've already paid your respects to the deceased. Don't you think it's time to take your leave? We don't need a scene, do we?"

Sergeant Brophy began to protest, but Mr. Simon had already taken him by the elbow and was gently but insistently leading him toward the entryway. There he hailed the butler who immediately got the detective's hat and coat and saw him out. When Simon returned for Sterling, the younger man avoided the escort and hurried away to join Brophy.

Mary looked down. She had something in her hand. "Oh, my God, Clara, look." She opened her palm to reveal a large gold coin.

"Where did that come from?" Clara asked.

"Mr. Simon must've passed it to me when he took my hand. I was so distracted by the detectives, I didn't even notice."

"So we both got tips today," Clara said, laughing.

"You got a tip. I got a bribe. This is a $10 gold piece — that's a lot of money."

"Oh, it's just a gift," Clara said.

"Clara, he was asking us to let him know if we hear about the jewel. And telling us that he'd make it worth our while. This is like the down payment."

Their boss, extricated from the detective, now approached. "I'm afraid we should leave. Detective Brophy seems to have turned this family gathering into an open interrogation. Let's get our coats before he decides to return." They went to the entryway and the elderly butler gave them back their things. "Perhaps I should thank Mr. Simon for his assistance?" Evangeline asked as they all turned back to see him in an animated discussion with another guest. "Oh, well," Adams concluded. "Looks like he's hobnobbing."

"Miss Adams," Clara asked as they stood in the vestibule putting on their jackets. "Are they allowed to do that? Come into her house like that during a wake?"

"They probably asked Mrs. Fiske for permission. They'd want to see who turned up — as it might provide some clues. Although I'm sure she didn't expect they'd be speaking to any of the guests. The effrontery!"

"We were surprised, too," Mary shared.

"Everyone becomes a suspect," Adams added grimly, then changed the subject as they walked out onto the front stoop.

"Did you observe Mr. Fiske's thumbs? You know, I practiced hand reading for many years, and I couldn't help but notice them. They were short, thick and clumsy-looking in the extreme. I'd developed a picture of Mr. Fiske over the years that his wife had talked of him. And those thumbs fit perfectly with what I surmised. That kind of coarse finger shows a brutish man with animal instincts." She considered it a bit. "Of course, anyone may have similar thumbs. But unfortunately, nothing in Mr. Fiske's physiognomy compensates for it or suggests an ability to overcome this limitation. All of his fingers are thick and heavy, with short, flat nails, confirming his coarse nature.

"I'm not an expert, mind you, but face reading can also tell you much about a person as well. Mr. Fiske's eyes were set very close together, suggesting a narrow and calculating individual. His nose area was the largest part of his face, making him self-involved, ambitious and driven. But at the same time, the chin was unusually broad, which gives toughness to the character and a need to have his own way. His thin upper lip makes him secretive, but with a thick lower lip, he could nevertheless be a charmer and persuader when he chose to be. Not a nice man," Evangeline concluded.

They stepped down the stairs and saw the detectives standing by the curb smoking. They turned and walked a few doors down in the other direction toward their waiting car.

"I appreciate you two coming," Evangeline added as they approached the auto. "Shall I give you a ride home in the motor?"

Mary opened her mouth to agree, but Clara interrupted her. "Oh, no, Miss Adams. We're going to take some air and Mary said she'd come with me to visit my cousin at the new hotel across the street on Fifth Avenue."

"Well, that's just lovely. Good night, then. It was very sweet of you two to accompany me. We'll see each other again in the morning."

Clara took Mary's arm and drew her further away along West 9th Street. "What are you doing?" Mary asked, shaking her off. "I would've liked to get a ride!"

"I thought you wanted to see where Mr. Fiske was killed," Clara said.

Mary stopped and looked at her. "But now we can't. I don't want to go back in there with some pretense while those two are still hanging around."

"I have a cousin who works at the Presada on the corner and she's met the Fiskes' housekeeper several times."

"*What?!*"

"Sure," Clara said with a wave of her hand. "We were talking about Mr. Fiske the other day and she mentioned that she knew her. All we'd have to do is go downstairs and ask. I don't think she'd mind showing us the room."

"But why didn't you just say so? Why go along with pretending to be the cousin?"

"It actually sounded like a lot more fun. And either way, we get to see the murder room."

Chapter 15

Mary and Clara walked down to the end of the block, then crossed to the other side of West 9th Street and turned back in the direction of the Fiskes' brownstone. It was dark now, but they could still see the two detectives waiting out front.

"Let's sit down and figure out what to do," Mary said. "They can't stand there all night."

They walked down a few stairs and sat on the steps near the service entrance of another building, somewhat concealed, though with a view of the Fiskes' house. It was a beautiful evening, almost serene. The sky was clear and a few stars had appeared here and there. They no longer heard the traffic from Fifth Avenue, and the West 9th Street homes were quiet, with gas or electric lights on in front.

"It's a little chilly," Clara said, wrapping her coat around her knees.

"I know," Mary agreed. They sat quietly for a while. "I was just trying to remember what Swami Puri told me," she said. "I was supposed to have something like an adventure of the mind, whatever that is."

"That sounds interesting," Clara commented hopefully.

"I have enough adventures keeping Jeannie out of trouble, and with all the crazy clients we have. But I liked that monk. When he was communicating with me, I felt like we were all part of a big family and that was nice. It was a really warm feeling, kind of like my birthday when I was a kid."

"I felt the same way," agreed Clara. "Do you think he could have hypnotized us? He said something to me, too. I thought it was just my imagination."

"What did he say?"

"Just that I should listen to my mother," Clara said, a little annoyed. "I guess he could be right. Ordinarily, I wouldn't like anyone getting inside my head like that, but it was such a peaceful feeling. And I guess I do argue with my mother too much. Maybe I should just take the prune juice like she says. I don't know. I don't really want to. But maybe she's right." Clara thought a little longer.

"He also seemed to think I should learn astrology," Mary said.

"Oh! I got that, too," Clara added. "That's OK; I like astrology a lot more than prune juice."

"Miss Adams says that Mercury retrograde is a good time for all the 're' words: research, review, rethink, revisit. Let's try to use that. What do we know? Mr. Fiske was killed and the jewel is missing, but it didn't sound like they had a lot of other evidence to go on. Why else would they be bothering us?" Mary turned toward the Fiske house; some guests were leaving, but the detectives still lingered in the front yard. "Miss Adams seemed to know a lot about Mr. Fiske from his appearance," she said.

"Yeah," said Clara. "He's self-involved, a brute . . . what else?"

"Ambitious and calculating. But he could also charm people," added Mary. "And it sounds like the Maharaja actually gave Fiske the jewels to sell for him."

"I'm glad we didn't know he was the Maharaja when he came to the office," Clara shared. "I would've felt uncomfortable."

"Me too," said Mary. "He probably likes to keep it quiet or people act funny. But I wonder what happened to all the other jewels. It sounded like he had a lot, but only this one elephant piece is missing. They didn't ask Miss Adams about anything else."

"You're right."

"You know," Mary continued, "I wonder if there's a chance the killer might be someone in the Fiskes' household. It could be anyone, but that would make the most sense to me. Someone who would know all about this ruby elephant, when Fiske would have it out, where it would be. Someone who would ordinarily be in the house at night and wouldn't have to break in."

"We don't have to worry," Clara replied. "There are lots of guests in the house right now. They wouldn't try anything if they could be caught so easily. And we'll be with the housekeeper anyway. She'll take care of us."

"But what if the housekeeper is the killer?" asked Mary.

"Nah. I don't think so."

"Why not?"

"My cousin knows her, it just doesn't sound right."

"We don't really know." They were quiet once again for a few minutes. "Oh, and Miss Adams said that Jesse left that mess in our office."

"*What?*"

"Mr. Jordan wanted him to set up a microphone for Miss Adams to practice for her radio appearance."

"He's involved in this, I'm sure of it," Clara said in a low voice.

"We still don't know why he had Mr. Holkar's — the Maharaja's — chart."

"The problem is," reasoned Clara, "it's hard to make sense of anything Jesse does."

"Oh, and Mr. Holkar had a pretty good astrological report," Mary remembered. "Miss Adams gave me her notes to file away. A little Uranus, a little Jupiter, nothing exceptional. There was something with Saturn in November, but he'll probably be out of town by then. And nothing difficult or challenging for the next six months."

"That's weird," Clara said.

"I know," Mary replied. "You'd think with this expensive elephant stolen and all, something would show up in his forecast."

"Maybe they'll find it. Or he'll make so much money selling the rest of the jewelry that it won't make any difference to him."

"Look —" Mary whispered hurriedly as she stood up. "The detectives are leaving." They could see them walk down the block, climb into a waiting vehicle and leave. "Let's go."

The two women quickly returned to the house, but this time, instead of going up the main entry staircase as they'd done before, Clara led them to the service entrance located immediately below, several steps beneath the ground floor. They rang the bell, Clara asked for Marjory, the housekeeper, and they were shown into the Fiskes' home once again.

The lower level was strictly utilitarian, with a black and white parquet floor and household servants bustling about. As they walked toward the kitchen in the back, they passed a tremendous glass-doored cabinet filled with the family's china; another cabinet held glassware. There were two stoves, a large food preparation area, and a great big icebox. Countless pots, pans and other large utensils hung from the walls and ceilings. Several young women were at work preparing more of the hors d'oeuvres they had seen upstairs. Behind the kitchen was a well-kept garden in the rear, accessible through a large windowed door.

A robust woman in her forties with glasses and graying hair pulled back in a bun greeted them. She spoke with a Scottish accent. "So you're Laura's cousin, are you? You look just like her. Laura helped us out more than once in an emergency. They have everything at that big hotel. Mr. Fiske didn't like them building it so close to home, but it's been convenient."

"Marjory," Clara began, "we work for Evangeline Adams, the astrologer."

"Oh, Evangeline Adams! I know who she is. Mrs. Fiske always said she made her feel better whenever she visited her."

"The police are accusing Miss Adams of being involved in Mr. Fiske's murder," Mary said. "So we're trying to find out what happened. Do you mind if we take a look at the room where he was killed?"

"I'll take you there myself. Mrs. Fiske will be downstairs for quite a while with the guests; now's a good time." Marjory turned and opened a small wooden door leading to a narrow staircase with a thin metal bannister winding up through the back of the house. "If we go this way, no one will see us," she said as she led the way through the servant's passage. The stairway was dimly lit, with no decorations; the opposite of the grand carpeted entrance staircase at the front of the house. Marjory opened another small wooden door as they reached the second floor. They peered out cautiously, walked down the hall and stepped into what appeared to be a sitting room.

"This is the Fiskes' parlor," Marjory said, turning on the lights. "The bedroom is through there," she pointed toward curtained French doors on the other side of the room. "Let me close the drapes." Three floor-to-ceiling windows looked out onto the front of the property, with a view of the houses across the street. Marjory pulled the heavy curtains closed.

"Wow," Clara said, impressed. "This must be Mrs. Fiske." They looked at a large canvas portrait on the wall, depicting a striking young woman reminiscent of a Gibson girl. She wore a shirtwaist with a long skirt, and held a boater-style hat jauntily at her side. Her other hand was placed insouciantly on her hip. The whole impression was one of breeziness and vitality.

Marjory came to stand by the portrait with them. "That was how she appeared when I first started working for Mrs. Fiske, over thirty years ago now. And a very good likeness it is, too." Marjory stopped to regard the picture for a few moments. "The artist captured her youth and charm. The whole family was very pleased with it, I recall, very pleased. Of course, that was before her marriage. I'm afraid she's very much changed since then, unfortunately." She sighed. "He wasn't a nice man, Mr. Fiske, but you don't like to see someone killed in his own home. Although I think she'll be better off without him, if you ask my opinion."

Mary looked around her at the luxurious sitting room. There were polished hardwood floors along with rich carpeting and warm, dark wood paneling. Comfortable-looking wing chairs and a sofa were arranged before fireplace on one side of the room. Marjory walked toward them and pointed. "He was lying right here, in this chair, as if he'd been smoking or reading and had fallen asleep. The maid had come running down in a frenzy and I came back with her. At first I thought she must be wrong, there seemed to be nothing unusual. Except, of course, that when I got

closer I could see he wasn't napping at all but was dead."
Marjory closed her eyes and shuddered at the memory. "Oh,
it was a terrible sight. We've never had a death in the house.
I can still see him lying there, though there wasn't much
blood to speak of. Whoever hit him must've known what he
was doing, to fell him with a single blow. The policemen said
they thought he'd been struck with some kind of a blunt
object. But they couldn't say what. The fireplace pokers were
in their normal places, by the side there. They haven't been
used very much in recent years since we got the gas."

Just then, one of the radiator pipes started banging softly.
"I must call the plumber tomorrow morning to take care of
that," Marjory said, making a mental note. "It bothers Mrs.
Fiske terribly."

"Marjory," asked Mary, "we have the same problem at
our office. The people in the building don't seem to be able to
correct it. Can you recommend someone?"

"We have a very good man, his name is Bill Westbrook.
He needs to bleed the pipes from time to time and it always
helps. I don't know if it would be the same in a larger
building, but you can always try. If you telephone me
tomorrow, I'll give to you his number and address."

Marjory continued her description of the murder. "Now,
Louise had come up here as she always does with their
breakfast on a tray. She placed it on the table by the door as
she went inside to wake them up, and discovered Mr. Fiske,
lying there, just as I told you. She ran back downstairs and
we phoned the police straightaway. Mrs. Fiske was still
sound asleep. It fell to me to wake her and break the bad
news." She looked away from them. "My goodness, that was
a terrible moment. One of the hardest things I've had to do in
my life. The poor lady! How she screamed and cried and
carried on. It was all I could do to get her up and dressed
before the investigators arrived."

Mary asked, "Did Mr. Fiske often bring jewels into the
house?"

"Not very often. He generally worked more with
investments and real estate," she said as she straightened a

pillow on the couch. "But once in a while there would be quite a lot of jewelry. Sometimes he'd see a client after-hours down in his study, and they might leave some items with him. But he almost always brought them to the office the next day."

"And what about Mr. Holkar, the Maharaja? Was he ever here?"

"Oh, yes, Mr. Holkar was here, on more than one occasion. Some of his men brought in a heavy box one afternoon, and they went into the study. This was maybe a few weeks ago. The next day, Mr. Fiske had the driver bring the box in to work with him."

"And what about this jewel that's missing—the one that everyone's talking about?" Mary asked. "It's an elephant carved out of a ruby? Did you ever see Mr. Fiske with it?"

"I did see it. He had it with him here in the parlor one evening. Sitting on that low table, right there where he was found. Which was unusual. He generally didn't bring anything from the office up to this room. I don't know if he might've wanted it for himself or a friend was planning to take a look at it. It was a beautiful object, I can tell you that, the way it caught the light. A lustrous red, smaller than a half-pint Mason jar, I'd say. Not a very practical sort of thing, but I can understand why someone would want to steal it. They said it's worth a fortune and I can well believe it. The detectives, of course, asked about that, too. Very suspicious of all of us, they were. We had to sit around the kitchen table, not speaking, under guard of the detective, while the Sergeant called us in to my office, one by one, to get our stories. Very off-putting. But none of us had anything to say, really. We'd locked the house like we did every other night. Didn't see anyone come or go, heard nothing in the night. Nothing else was stolen. Mrs. Fiske keeps quite a bit of jewelry in the bedroom. The more expensive pieces are in a safe deposit box. She hasn't worn them in years, doesn't go out in society very much these days. It's very mysterious, but that's all there is to it. Louise found the body, we called the police, and that was that," Marjory shook her head, remembering. "The elephant was all that was taken."

"And the way they went after Mrs. Fiske, too! How I felt for the poor soul. Here she was with her husband dead and they'd be hounding her with questions and insinuating comments. Suspected her, too, if you can believe it. Sent us all away then and searched the entire house," Marjory recalled. She clicked her tongue in disapproval. "How they tore through all of her closets and drawers. No consideration. None whatsoever.

"I hope they find the killer soon. We haven't a clue." Marjory paused again as she looked around the room and turned off the light. "She'll close the house down now, Mrs. Fiske. He'd bought it anyway, her husband; it was never her affair. She never especially wanted to live here. I don't know where she'll go now, but she has family and friends and enough money to do whatever it is she wants to do with her future."

Mary and Clara thanked the housekeeper and soon found themselves back on West 9th Street. "Having met Marjory," Mary said as they walked toward their streetcar and elevated train on Sixth Avenue. "I guess it's obvious she had nothing to do with the crime."

"And everyone seems to agree," added Clara, "that Mr. Fiske was not everyone's favorite kind of guy. No one but Mrs. Fiske seems upset that he's gone."

They walked in silence for a few more minutes. "What I want to know," asked Mary, "is why did Mr. Fiske keep the elephant in the house, and why couldn't the police find anything?"

• Chapter 16 •

Mary arrived at work the next morning to find Miss
Adams already bustling about her office. "Oh, Mary, I'm
glad you're here. I'm afraid we had a bit of a situation here
last night. When I returned to my apartment from the wake,
the dogs were barking excitedly, and making every effort to
get down to the office. I opened the adjoining door and they
dashed down here. It appeared that someone had gotten in
somehow. They may have fled when they heard the dogs.
The lights were left on, my elephant lamp had been knocked
over, and one of the drawers of my desk was open. It looked
as if they were searching for something. And my door to the
inner office was open, too. You know, it's my habit to always
lock it before turning in for the night."

Mary was glad the Pekingese had frightened the intruder
away; they were small and could easily be hurt. Now,
though, they sat in their usual places in Evangeline's office as
if nothing at all had happened. Sonny was gently snoring
under the sofa. Lover was sitting on top of it, quietly resting,
while listening to the conversation. D'Artagnon stayed near
Adams and cautiously sniffed the floor from time to time.

Evangeline continued looking around her office to see if
anything else was out of place. She sat down at her desk and
placed D'Artagnon on her lap. "I don't think anything was
taken. Perhaps someone simply wanted information. My
astrological notes from Dr. Smith are still in my drawer,
thank goodness. I'm checking my figurines, but the display
case does not seem to have been tampered with. And all the
elephants on my desk are still here."

Mary looked toward her own desk area, which, aside
from the remains of Jesse's radio activity from the previous
night, also seemed to be in order. "Let me go through my
things to be sure nothing was taken," she told Evangeline.

"Yes, please do. It's very tiresome. And disturbing. I'm
afraid the dogs didn't get much sleep and neither did I," she
said as she stroked D'Artagnon. "And I'll have to station
them down here tonight, just to be sure this doesn't happen

once again. Oh, and Mary," Evangeline continued, "Please call Marco and have him come up and change my office lock as soon as possible."

"Did they break it?" Mary asked.

"No, and that's what worries me. No damage was done." She paused as she stroked the puppy, then looked at Mary with her intense gaze. "Someone apparently had a key."

A wave of anxiety passed through Mary's body. Her shoulders tensed and she found it hard to breathe. Nothing like this had happened before. To think that someone—whoever it was or whatever their motive—had gained entry when almost no one was there, was frightening. It was a violation of the basic ground rules that were part of the stability of working for Evangeline. Even more alarming was the fact that Adams had been home alone and could have easily been hurt. Mary swallowed. "Miss Adams," she asked cautiously, "do you think we should call the police?"

"I don't know," the astrologer said truthfully, pushing her glasses up on her nose. "I've been giving it a lot of thought. I'm afraid that if we do so, the detectives will soon be harassing us once again, which I'd prefer to avoid. Let's first do a thorough search. If anything valuable is missing, then perhaps they should be called in. If not, well, the dogs will be on guard tonight, which I'm sure is more than the police would do for us. But please call Marco right away."

Mary closed the door and returned to her desk. She immediately phoned the building manager, who assured her that they'd send Marco to change the lock. She sat down at her desk and looked around. The fact was, there was nothing much of value here. She'd already mailed out the astrological reports for the Wendels and Anita Stewart, who'd been there the day before. She quickly went to the filing cabinet and pulled out Mr. Holkar's horoscope chart. No one had disturbed it further, though Miss Adams had added a few illegible handwritten notes during their session the day before, along with her notes on Holkar's forecast. Mary looked around the room. Jesse's hulking equipment still lay by the door where they had left it the previous evening. All the filing cabinets were closed. She sat back down and looked at her desk. Stapler, pencils and bond paper were all where they should be.

Then Mary noticed that there *was* something missing. The office kept a good supply of paper horoscope blanks: horoscope wheels to fill in with the clients' personal planets and signs. There were inexpensive pads for their own work. But the ones printed on good cotton bond paper were for Miss Adams' interview clients, friends and other special individuals, and they were gone. Mary usually kept some near at hand, on her desk, but now she couldn't find them. She looked for the larger supply in her desk drawer, but there were none there, either. That was certainly strange, and Mary really felt afraid that something was not right.

Clara came into the office. "Sorry I'm late. There was a problem with the subway. I was waiting on the platform and the guy standing next to me kept coughing; I've never heard a cough like that in public." She hung up her jacket and hat. "I wanted to say, 'I hope you're going to a doctor,' but I just moved away. Everyone else did, too. And then when the train came, we couldn't all fit in that car and I had to wait for the next one." She sat at her desk and continued. "When the next train came, I got to sit down, but I was scrunched between two people who wouldn't move. And the woman on my left kept digging into her bag: her elbow kept jutting out at me over and over and I thought she was going to jab me." Clara enacted the movement, then leaned her head on her hand. "Finally they both slid over like they should've done in the first place and I could breathe again." She looked up. "What's the matter?"

Mary filled Clara in on the break-in. She concluded, "I think it may be someone looking for that elephant that was stolen from Mr. Fiske. I don't want to get you worked-up, but Jesse was in here setting up that radio thing before we left last night."

"He did it, then," Clara instantly responded.

"I just have a hard time understanding why he'd have to steal them. There's probably several reams of chart blanks in the supply cabinet; he could've taken them all if he wanted to."

"But if he went into Miss Adams' office, he was probably looking for something else," Clara said. "Like the elephant. He might have done this just to spite us — or to pin the blame on us."

"The other thing is that Miss Adams thinks that whoever broke in had a key. And Mr. Jordan gave all the keys to Jesse before he left. I don't think he ever had the key to Miss Adams' office before."

Clara whistled low. "It's getting a little scary," she said.

"I know."

"Now what's become of my manuscript?" Evangeline Adams asked brightly as she stepped out of her office an hour or so later. "Was it delivered to the publisher? I believe the deadline is today."

"Mr. Jordan said he was having Jesse or Richard take it over personally. I'll check and find out when it was done," Mary said, making a note.

"Good. And who do we have coming to see us today?"

Mary looked at her scheduling book. "Mrs. Fiske has the first appointment."

"Oh, yes, poor Mrs. Fiske. That's fine."

"Ramini Rahman at one," Mary continued, "Evalyn Walsh McLean at one-thirty, then Carmel Snow and Arthur Hopkins."

"Mary, you've dealt with Mrs. McLean before, haven't you?"

"No, ma'am."

"I suppose she hasn't been here for a few years." She leaned forward confidentially. "Just be on your guard. She means well, I think, but she's very difficult and accustomed to having her own way. We cannot bend to her wishes. She'll be asking about the elephant stone, no doubt. One of her grand passions is collecting remarkable gems and she must imagine I could be helpful to her, you see? I don't want to become more involved in this affair. She's here for a reading and that's all, as far as I'm concerned. We are not to give her any information about the detective, Mrs. Fiske, or any of it, all right?"

"Of course."

"She's a Leo, with a strong personality, and she can be very persistent. Clara? If she addresses you, you know nothing."

"Oh, no, I don't know anything about it anyway."

"And let me remind you both. We should never feel obligated to tolerate clients who are rude, insensitive or otherwise try to take advantage of our kindness and generosity. Be businesslike and professional. If you're inclined to do them a favor, fine. Otherwise, it's not part of your job. All right then. Let's do some letters." Evangeline turned back into her office and Mary followed her, sitting in the client's chair across from her desk with her steno pad and pencil in hand.

"This is to Mrs. Charles Raymond in Lakeline, Ohio," Adams began. "Her address is on the envelope. *Mr.* Raymond has the effrontery to suggest that I actually had their apartments burgled!" she declared, unbelievingly. "But I will not stoop to his level.

"Dear Mrs. Raymond:

Your husband has written me a most angry letter that I don't believe merits a direct response. As you are a longstanding client, however, I would like to put the issues before you. I note the following series of events:

1. Due to Neptune afflicting Jupiter in your horoscope, I suggested the possibility of loss in March and April and advised caution as to your possessions. Please see enclosed mimeographed page that was supplied to you with your reading, especially the part I have underlined in blue pencil, which begins, 'all care should be taken with any valuables as we are apt to be careless at this time. We may also be more susceptible to loss. Take the more cautious path in trusting others and cultivate skepticism.'

2. You left several valuable pieces of jewelry in your hotel room in Palm Beach in March, all of which were stolen.

3. Your husband has the temerity to suggest that I sent 'henchmen' (his word) over 1,200 miles to break into your room and remove your jewelry, all in order to prove my prediction correct.

If this were the case, would I have gone out of my way to suggest caution? Is that logical? Is it logical that I could imagine where you and your husband were vacationing out of state and exactly when you would be away?

Astrology forewarns us. We may not always be able to avert loss, but we can lessen the impact if we are aware of the astrological weather forecast. I predicted rain. I advised taking an umbrella. You did not heed the warning. Unfortunately you suffered the consequences and I am sorry for it. Your husband, it seems to me, is a thoroughgoing skeptic who would suggest almost anything to avoid admitting the power of astral influences.

Faithfully yours, Evangeline S. Adams

"What can we do with people like this? It's all terribly distressing. And here's a poor woman who's very upset that her husband lied to her." She handed over the original letter and continued dictating.

"Dear Mrs. Edwards:

I am sorry to learn that your husband has misled you by providing you with incorrect birth information. Of course our report was based upon that information and will therefore be incorrect as pertains to your husband.

Since the error was no fault of your own, we are enclosing the correct report and hope it will be helpful in understanding your relationship in the future.

"Have Clara put a report together for her and try to get it out today. Or you can do it if you have the time. This is the type of thing that undermines all of our work; we must try to correct it whenever we can."

There was a light knock on the open door and Mary turned to see who it was: Jesse Bauer. Actually, she realized, she had smelled him before she saw him, as she could immediately sense the excessive use of what seemed to be bay rum. Mary regarded him critically once again. There was something that indeed seemed out of kilter, but she still couldn't figure out exactly what it was. His hair was flat and slicked back in an ordinary style, but there was so much Vaseline in it that she wondered what his pillowcases must look like. The off-center part did seem in keeping with his unbalanced personality. His flannel trousers and vest were nice enough, as was the plain light blue shirt he now wore rolled up at the sleeves.

"Excuse me, Miss Adams," he said as he stepped in.

"Oh, Jesse," interrupted Evangeline, "Just the fellow I wanted to see. You'll clear away that microphone equipment and all of those wires, won't you? I'd like to have it all out before the clients arrive today."

"Oh, I'll take care of it—don't you worry," Jesse promised.

"Thank you. We'll try it again when Mr. Jordan returns from Boston," Evangeline assured him. "Oh, and Jesse," she added more earnestly, "you were here yesterday evening. Did you happen to notice anything unusual?"

"How do you mean?"

"There has been some confusion in the office these last few days and I wondered if you noticed anything peculiar. Was there anyone here after hours, for example?"

"Well, I was here setting up the microphone and of course checking that all of the doors were locked, just like Mr. Jordan asked me to do." Jesse paused. "Anything unusual," he said, searching his mind. "Anything unusual," he repeated as he looked toward the ceiling and rubbed his chin. "I will tell you this," he bluntly declared as he looked straight at Adams. "When I came into the inner office with the equipment, Alexa was there, which seemed suspicious to me."

"Suspicious? Alexa?" Evangeline asked.

"Sure. She doesn't belong there. She had no reason to be there."

"Perhaps she was looking for Mary or Clara or me," Adams suggested.

"Well, I'll tell you, Miss Adams," Jesse said emphatically, drawing out his words and becoming more expansive. "I had my suspicions. So I just asked her what she was doing." He waited.

Mary and Adams looked at him, expecting more information. "And?" Mary urged.

"Oh, she said she was looking for some chart blanks for a report and Mary had already left. So I told her she could just wait until tomorrow and ask Mary then."

"Very good, Jesse. That's all for now," Evangeline said, wrapping things up.

"Ah, Miss Adams," Jesse began again, holding his ground, "Mr. Jordan said that while he was away, if I needed his office, it was OK to sit there. Is that all right with you?"

"Whyever do you ask me?" Evangeline replied a little briskly, not understanding.

"Well he's not here . . ." Jesse trailed off and looked at the floor.

"Oh, by all means," Evangeline warmly assured him. "That's all right. Do whatever Mr. Jordan has instructed you to do," she said pleasantly. "Thank you, Jesse. That's all for now."

Jesse nodded and left the room. Evangeline looked after him and said, almost to herself, "Odd young man." Then she added more openly to Mary, "I always feel that learning astrology can help anyone. But in his case, I'm not so sure." She paused again thoughtfully, then returned to business. "Where were we, my dear? Oh, yes. Our letters. You get started on those and we'll do some more later. Thank you."

Mary left Adams' office and closed the door on her way out. She turned to Clara. "Did you hear?"

"Of course I heard." Clara said disgustedly. "Now he'll have his own office and pretend he's the boss. Just wait and see."

"At least we'll be rid of him for a while," Mary replied.

"Don't count on it," Clara said decisively.

"Oh, shoot!" Mary exclaimed, annoyed. "I forgot to ask him about delivering the manuscript. *And can you believe it?*" she added, exasperated, "He promised to clean up this mess and he's ignored it again!"

"See what I've been dealing with?" Clara said, raising her eyebrows and giving Mary a significant look.

Chapter 17

Marco, the building superintendent, knocked on the door from the outer office as he walked in. A clean-shaven, humorless man in his mid-forties, he wore gray coveralls with his name embroidered in red on one side of his chest. "I'm here to fix the lock," he said. "Which one?"

"Oh, hi Marco," Mary said. "It's Miss Adams' office. Just let me tell her you're here." Mary knocked on the door; as she opened it, Adams eagerly approached.

"I'll replace the lock," Marco confirmed. "This one, right?" he asked.

"Yes," Evangeline said. "Thank you for being so prompt. There may have been a break-in last night and I want to take precautions."

Marco ignored her, unrolling a fabric kit with tools and laying it on the floor. He opened a small box with a new lock. "Ten minutes, I'll be out of your hair," he said bluntly, standing up.

"While you're here, Marco," Evangeline began pleasantly, "We hoped you'd also check my radiator again. It continues to make all sorts of noises."

"Miss Adams," Marco said intensely, "Three times, four times, I don't remember how many times I've come here and fixed that radiator for you."

"Yes, and I always appreciate you coming. But Marco, it's not fixed. The banging always returns."

"It's not fixed because there's *nothing wrong!*" he said pointedly, and counted with his fingers. "I gave you new vents. You also got a new radiator. I put in a new valve – and that's a big job. A very big job. It's not easy to do. Everything works fine. You have heat. It's working."

"Yes, we have heat. It's working. But the banging in the pipes continues, Marco. What's causing that? It's very disruptive. I don't think it's a local problem because my husband downstairs hears it, too. It seems to me it's system-wide."

"No one else complains," Marco said dismissively. "There are twelve floors here," he continued, putting a hand on his hip and gesturing up and down. "If the problem is the system, everyone would have it. You're the only one to complain," he said stubbornly.

"My husband hears it, too—downstairs. And I hear it upstairs, though not as loud. That's three floors." Evangeline retained her composure.

"Miss Adams, I don't know what to say," he added, aggravated. "I'll check it again. It's not a complicated thing. There are no moving parts. I've done all I can do. Mr. Simon asked me to look, so I'll look. I'll give you another new vent. But if no one else hears the banging . . ."

"I understand," Evangeline assured him. "But it doesn't make sense."

"No, it doesn't make sense," confirmed Marco, somewhat hotly. "But I will try—*again*—to help you." He looked toward the radiator. "You keep the valve open all the way?" he asked, striding into the office, removing the radiator cover and trying the valve himself. D'Artagnon trotted over to watch; the other dogs were so accustomed to Marco's visits that they virtually ignored him.

"I no longer touch the valve. Last time the new air vent helped for several days. But then the banging returned," Adams explained.

"It helps—it doesn't help," Marco said, standing up and wiping his hands. "I don't understand why you have this problem." He spread open both hands, indicating the absurdity of his situation. "We have 170 studios. I can't spend all my time in this one."

"All right, Marco. You're here now; let's see what you can do. I appreciate your help."

"I'll start with the lock if that's all right with you," he said, not waiting for an answer.

Later that morning, after Marco had completed his tasks, Miss Adams once again closed her office door. Mary turned to Clara.

"Listen—Jeannie told me that she found an invitation to a party for the Maharaja on Miss Adams' kitchen table yesterday."

"Really? Do you think he gave it to her?"

"I don't know. But she hasn't mentioned anything about it. She hasn't responded to it one way or another."

"Huh. It may mean nothing. He saw her. Maybe he's inviting everyone."

"That's true. But I'd like to know if she's going."

Clara interrupted her: "Can you hear it?" she asked abruptly.

"Hear what?"

"Ssh! Listen." There were noises from below; someone was banging around and talking loudly on the phone. "Mr. Jordan's office is just below us, right?" Clara asked.

"I think it is."

"Guess who's moved in? Jesse Bauer. He's already down there! Sounds like he's settling in," Clara said angrily.

"What difference does it make?" Mary asked. "Aren't you glad he's not standing out in the hall? And you don't have to sit next to him anymore, either."

"But I can't escape his big fat mouth no matter where I go."

"Just focus on your work. Don't you have some reports to put together?"

"He's got his own office now!" Clara grumbled. "He can use the private bathroom. I resent him moving up."

"He's not moving up! As soon as Mr. Jordan comes back, he'll be right back where he started."

"He has the nerve to make things happen for himself. I could never do that."

"Well, you shouldn't. It's all a sham."

Clara moved toward the wall and placed her ear against it. "I can hear him on the phone." She listened. "Sounds like he's talking to someone." She moved to the radiator riser pipe, put her ear to it and listened for several seconds. "*Oh, my God!*" she exclaimed. She turned back to Mary. "I think he said something about an interview. I wonder if he's looking for another job! Mary, Mr. Jordan's out of town. If he gets a call for a recommendation, please, please give him a good reference."

"You're getting ahead of yourself. Things don't move that quickly. Mr. Jordan will be back and they'll probably just write him a letter."

Clara turned to the pipe again and listened for a while. "It sounds like he's talking to a girl." She listened some more, then turned to Mary. "He's bragging. I think he told her he got a promotion . . ."

Mary, intrigued, came over and put her ear to the radiator pipe just above Clara. They could both hear Jesse rather clearly.

". . . I'm in charge now. I have my own office . . . Come up anytime, doll . . . Why don't we go out Friday night? Last time you wouldn't dance with me . . . Pos-o-lutely, I'll have more money . . . I just told you, I got a promotion." He was quiet for a minute as he listened. "Oh, I have a gun . . . and I know how to use it," he said teasingly. "And it is *loaded*. With *live ammunition*." He laughed raucously.

"Who would fall for that?" Clara demanded, whispering. "He makes me want to vomit."

"Excuse me, ladies," Miss Adams interrupted as she appeared by her office door. They started and turned around. They'd been so focused on Jesse, they hadn't heard her approach. "Whatever are you doing?"

"Ummm . . ." Mary faltered.

"Oh," Clara began, haltingly, "We're conducting a scientific experiment," she vamped. "Trying to figure out what's causing the knocking in the pipes that's been bothering you so much."

Evangeline clapped her hands together, enormously pleased. "You two are wonderful. You take such good care of me. Very kind. We'll figure it out together, don't you worry. It makes me feel so much better about the whole thing, that you care enough to try to help. Thank you. Carry on!" she called after them as she returned to her office with a beatific smile on her face.

Clara made for the pipe again but Mary stopped her. "That's enough, Clara."

Clara sat back down. "I can't believe the nerve—telling her he's 'in charge.' Where does he come off?"

"Clara, it's Mercury retrograde. Don't misunderstand him. You know he's just making it up."

"*Of course he's making it up!* But he believes it and he's convincing some poor girl that he's a real he-man." She looked down at her desk sullenly.

"Clara, he's a nut—you said so yourself. And anyway, you're the one that got the promotion."

"I didn't really."

"Yes, you did. You're going to be doing more for Miss Adams; I can easily use the help. And he's mad because he wanted your job. Now it's completely out of his reach." She paused. "Does he really have a gun?" she asked seriously.

"Of course he has a gun! He was in the army. He talks about it all the time."

"Well," Mary wasn't sure how to ask the question. "Do you think he's dangerous?"

"Of course he's dangerous! What do you think I've been telling you for the last six months? *He's dangerous!*"

"I mean, do you think he'd actually shoot someone?"

"*Shoot someone?*" Clara asked, taken aback. "I don't really know." She thought about it. "He used to mention that he killed people in the war. But it always sounded made-up to me."

"He's *killed people?*" Mary asked, her neck tensing. She could feel the skin on the back of her head crawl.

"Well, he said he did. I never believed it. He just tossed it off, no details. Not like my Uncle Frank, who really *had* to kill people in the war. People like that, they don't want to talk about it. It's not something they brag about. And if you ask, they act funny."

"Clara, think about it," Mary asked, dead serious. "Do you think Jesse could kill someone?"

Clara had to consider it. "I think he probably has a gun, yes. And he can be very aggressive at times. But I don't think he could plan out a crime, if that's what you're asking. Although sometimes he's capable of some very insightful things. His mind is like twenty percent reality and eighty percent completely made-up. Sometimes it's obvious which side of the equation things fall in. This? I don't know. If he was pushed to it, maybe. What do *you* think? Is he capable of murder?"

Mary didn't like the word "murder," but that was what they were talking about. "I don't know him as well as you do. But let's be on our guard. Look how easy it was for him to insinuate himself into Mr. Jordan's office. He still has a certain boyish charm when he wants to. He might just as easily have insinuated himself into Mr. Fiske's study."

"*You think he could've killed Mr. Fiske?*" Clara asked. "Or stolen the elephant?"

"I think it's possible. No one knows what Mr. Fiske was killed with. He could've been hit over the head with a gun."

Mary's phone rang, three long times, the signal from Dorothy that something urgent was going on. Mary grabbed it. "What?" She listened. "*Oh, no!*" She dashed to Adams' office. "Miss Adams!" she called, while knocking loudly and opening the door. "Sergeant Brophy is on his way back here again. Dorothy tried to keep him out but he pushed right past her!"

Evangeline stood up from her desk, angry. "I'm going to give him a piece of my mind." She came to her door just as Brophy and Sterling entered the inner office.

"Our encounter at the Fiskes' last night wasn't sufficient?" Evangeline demanded, glaring at them. "Are we to have you here *every day?*"

Mary sat at her desk while Brophy took off his hat and settled himself in one of the client waiting chairs with a show of nonchalance, wafting the scent of cheap cigars all around him. "Miss Adams, we've just discovered that you haven't been completely honest with us," he said as he placed an unlit cigar in his jacket pocket.

"Whatever do you mean? Of course I was honest. I'm always honest."

Sterling, lounging insolently against the door to the outer office, answered. "We learned today that the Maharaja of Indore is a client of yours and that you saw him only yesterday."

"It looks like you were withholding information," Brophy added pointedly.

"As I told you gentlemen the other day," Adams stated firmly, "My client consultations are completely confidential. I have no intention of informing you of anything regarding any of them. I neither confirm nor deny a visit from the Maharaja."

"Miss Adams," Sterling cut in, "We'd also like to speak to your husband. But there's a strange fellow in his office who's not making much sense."

"That's probably his assistant. Mr. Jordan is away in Cambridge for a few days, attending a seminar."

The detectives looked at one another. "Left town, eh?" Brophy asked suspiciously.

"My husband has absolutely nothing to do with the Maharaja, *or* Mr. Fiske for that matter," Miss Adams said defiantly. "He knows nothing whatsoever about this whole affair."

Sergeant Brophy crossed his leg, brushed off his pants casually, sat back in the chair and gave detective Sterling a significant look.

"Miss Adams," Sterling began, "Where were you on the night of Monday, April 5th?"

Evangeline was stunned. "You dare to ask me my whereabouts as if I were a suspect?"

"You *are* a suspect," Brophy said plainly, leaning forward with his elbows on his knees with his hat in his hands.

"Then I'm afraid this interview is at an end," Adams said decisively.

"Miss Adams," Brophy began, "I advise you to cooperate with us. The Maharaja had an appointment with you. Mr. Fiske had an appointment with you. You're involved with the family. You have elephants parading all around your office. You know more than you're telling us. Frankly, it looks like you're involved."

"And now your husband skipped town," Sterling finished. "It doesn't look good."

"No, it doesn't look good," Brophy echoed, shaking his head.

"Mary," Evangeline said, "Call my lawyer and put him through to me as soon as he's on the line. These gentlemen can see themselves out. And you're not to communicate any further with them, either." She turned and disappeared into her office, closing the door loudly.

Mary picked up the phone and asked Dorothy to put the call through to Walter Clark, Esq. "She's ringing him," she informed the detectives. She listened again, "No, put him right through to Miss Adams," she told Dorothy and hung up. She looked at the detectives. They looked at each other. Brophy sat up, resignedly. He put on his hat, put the cigar back in his mouth, and opened the door.

"Good day, ladies," he said. "We'll see you again, I'm sure."

"We're watching you," Sterling confirmed as they left and closed the door behind them.

Mary ran to her boss' office. "They're gone," she told Evangeline.

"These men are *completely disruptive*," Evangeline fumed. "Mr. Clark says I need *not* cooperate. If they had any evidence against me, they'd arrest me and take me to the precinct. He's absolutely right; I know it from my previous experience with the law. As it is, they're just making inquiries. My goodness!" she added and exhaled sharply. "Be a dear, Mary, and make me a cup of chamomile tea?"

Chapter 18

As Mary settled herself back at her desk, after preparing the tea upstairs for Evangeline, there was a soft knock on the door of the outer office and Alexa came quietly in. She lowered her voice but spoke intensely. "Detective here again for Fiske? I saw story in paper yesterday. Any news on killer?" She sat down in the chair next to Mary's desk.

Mary responded, also *sotto voce*. "He just accused Miss Adams of the crime, but left when she called her lawyer. And they think it's suspicious that Mr. Jordan is out of town."

"Jordan," Alexa said meaningfully. "I am suspicious, too. Not nice man."

"He's a real jerk," Clara said.

"Oh, no. More than jerk," Alexa continued, first looking around to be sure no one else could hear her. "Now he is suspect, I tell you everything." She crossed her legs and sat back in her chair. "How you think I get job here?"

"Well," Clara recalled. "You said you were rehearsing at a Carnegie Hall studio and Mr. Jordan was there and he was looking for secretaries."

"Is all true. Rehearse here, meet Jordan here. But I also meet Jordan before. Remember I was in show at Cosmopolitan Theater on 58th Street last year?"

"Sure," Clara answered.

"George Jordan stage door man," Alexa said simply.

Mary listened, horrified. Her eyes opened wide while Alexa continued.

"Yes, Jordan stage door man," she repeated matter-of-factly. "Same as others. I have dinner. Boring, nothing special. No Ambassador Hotel, that is sure. Few weeks later I see him again here in lobby. Offer me job—I type, good with figures. Is good job for me, regular pay."

"So Jordan skips around behind Miss Adams' back?" Clara asked, surprised.

"No surprise to me," replied Alexa. "How old is Miss Adams? Sixty years? Jordan maybe forty. Men all same. Probably marry for money."

"I guess it doesn't surprise me either," said Clara. "He's a real creep all around."

"Big creep, yes." Alexa agreed. "After I am here, Miss Adams very good to me. Does horoscope for baby. My job is very good. Jordan one day call me to office downstairs." She paused and looked at them both significantly. "Has gin, entire office smells. Wants me to dance for him, sit in lap. Big difference to dance, sit in lap at party. Alone in office? No. I say no, he say get out, no more job." She gave a short disgusted laugh. "I say, no more job? *I tell Miss Adams whole story.*" She paused for effect.

" —And then?" Mary asked impatiently.

"And then nothing," Alexa replied, shrugging her shoulder. "Jordan not want wife to know his business. I stay. He says nothing, does nothing, ever since. But still, creep. Tries to get something for nothing. He is also jealous of Henderson Fiske. At dinner I mention Henderson Fiske and Ambassador Hotel. George Jordan does not like. Says Fiske is thief, only interest is money," Alexa concluded. "Leo says good situation. Is security that I know Jordan has secret."

Mary was stunned by the levels of manipulation she was completely unaware of, right in the office. But the mention of Leo interrupted her thoughts.

"Alexa," Mary remembered. "I forgot—Leo telephoned you yesterday."

"Leo? Here?" Alexa was instantly provoked. "Dorothy doesn't tell me."

"He called after hours. We came back to go to Mr. Fiske's wake with Miss Adams. Around seven o'clock."

"Seven o'clock Leo calls me *here*?" Alexa asked angrily.

"He said you told him you were working late. He sounded worried that you weren't home yet."

"That man controls me like dog on leash," Alexa barked out. Her anger gave her a toughness at odds with her lovely outfit and beautifully made-up features; she suddenly looked care-worn and hard. "I tell him I work late. Instead I buy few things for baby. If he knows I have money, he takes everything. I hide sometimes."

"So you weren't even here?"

"No, I leave after work, go to department store."

"Alexa," Mary said. "I don't like to bring this up, but Jesse told Miss Adams that you were here looking for chart blanks last night."

"Yes, one time Jesse right. I use up blanks. About five o'clock. You are both gone. He is here fooling with big box and wires. He says to wait for tomorrow. Then I find blanks in paper closet today when I come back. Is problem?"

"No, no problem," Clara said genially, brushing it off. "I think Jesse just wants to get us all in trouble."

"I think, too," Alexa said. "Jesse and Jordan good partners. Both lie, cheat, try to get something for nothing."

"Thanks, Alexa," Mary said. We'll see you later."

Mary waited a few minutes after Alexa had left the room to turn to Clara. "Do you think she was here?"

"Sure, she said she was here."

"You don't think she took the chart blanks?"

"Why would she take them?" Clara asked a little defensively. "She has no reason to. There's always more in the storeroom. And what would she do with them, anyway?"

"But why would Jesse take them?"

"Just to annoy us. And now to pin something on Alexa 'cause he's mad that she won't let him blackmail her."

"I don't know if he's smart enough to put something like that together so quickly," Mary said.

"Look, it's the most natural thing in the world for Alexa to ask me questions. That's what we did on the other side. And when she came by, Jesse always made some kind of crack about how good she looked, trying to get her to go out with him, and she always ignored him. She just assumed we were still here."

"All this stuff about Alexa and these men, and Mr. Jordan trying to blackmail her? I don't like to think it's true."

"She and Leo are both dancers. It's more of a bohemian lifestyle. And they're foreigners. They don't know how they're supposed to act. I've worked with her for nearly a year now and she's really very nice."

"But the whole point is," Mary argued, "would she try to break into Miss Adams' office? They seem to need money and it sounded like she also had cash that Leo doesn't know about."

"How would she get in?" Clara countered. "She has no keys. I don't even have the keys for that matter. If I get in early and Dorothy's not here, I have to wait outside."

"That's true," Mary realized.

"And you said nothing was taken from her office, right?"

Mary nodded.

"I feel bad for Alexa," continued Clara. "They have the baby and she's working practically every day and looking for dancing jobs at night. She works very hard. She doesn't cut corners. Leo won't get a regular job. He thinks he's an impresario. And it sounds like he's completely controlling."

"Is he Leo?" Mary asked.

"Yes, Leo. That's who we're talking about."

"No, I mean, *about* Leo. Is he Leo? The zodiac sign?"

"No, I think she said he's Taurus. She's Scorpio. They're opposite signs, but they're supposed to be complementary."

"I didn't know she was Scorpio. No wonder she got involved in these intrigues. They're supposed to be good at understanding the power structure." Mary said. She also wondered if Alexa was telling them the whole truth.

Clara changed the subject. "But why are we talking about Alexa? We should be talking about Mr. Jordan."

"You're right," Mary agreed and exhaled loudly. "I always suspected he might have a woman on the side, though it was just a feeling, I never had any real proof. But this is almost worse, picking up strange dancers after a show, even if it was Alexa."

"And not even giving them a nice dinner!" Clara cut in. "He's so cheap."

"All that Emile Coué stuff," Mary added. "Miss Adams said it's basically about getting what you want. It's not like a religion that gives you guidelines on how far you can go. So if you don't have that already, it could be very selfish."

"What's their relationship, anyway?" Clara ventured. "Miss Adams and Mr. Jordan."

Mary thought a bit. "I think it was more of a legal thing. They live together, but it seems like it's mostly about the business."

"I don't know why she even likes him. She's so nice and he's so —" Clara searched for a word.

"Not nice." Mary concluded.

"Yup."

"She says they have a spiritual relationship."

"He's not *spiritual!*" Clara cut in.

"I agree. But you know, a lot of those Theosophical people talk like that."

"Yeah?"

"Well," Mary continued, "I've heard her use the word 'slime' to describe people who are only interested in a physical relationship. And she's forever telling young clients to wait until after the physical attraction has worn off to get married, to be sure they get to know each other first. It's not bad advice; I wish I'd heard something like it before I married Jeannie's father."

Mary's phone rang: Dorothy had a caller on the line. "Mary, it's that Mr. Dodd again, the editor," she said with her usual calm southern inflection. "He'd like to speak with Miss Adams. He hasn't received the manuscript yet and he's becoming a little impatient. He wants to visit her later to pick it up."

"*Tell him no!*" Mary instantly responded. "Miss Adams asked me to track it down for her. Where's Jesse?"

"He left the office a little while ago, it seemed like he was going downstairs. He asked me to put all his calls through to Mr. Jordan's office."

"Patch me through to Jordan's office. Put Dodd off and tell him we sent a messenger with the manuscript yesterday and that we're trying to find out what happened."

"All right."

Mary held the phone while Dorothy rang Jordan's office. She turned to Clara. "Do you hear him down there?"

Clara got up and put her head to the pipe. "It's quiet now."

Mary hung up her telephone. "Dorothy thought he went out. That editor keeps calling and Jesse was supposed to deliver the manuscript. Obviously he didn't. And he's still got all his garbage to clear out of here!" Mary said, flaring up. She picked up her phone again. "Dorothy: Jesse didn't answer. Has he been on the telephone at all?"

"I haven't put any calls through for him either way. But Mr. Jordan has three phones, and one line goes through the main building switchboard. Miss Adams has one set up that way, too, in their apartment. They're separate from our system. So he could be in there and on the phone and I would never know it."

"Can you put me through to the main switchboard?

"Why, certainly."

The operator came on the line. "Carnegie Hall Studios."

"I'd like to speak with Jesse Bauer, please."

"Mr. Bauer is not available."

"George Jordan, then."

"That's the same exchange, ma'am. No one is available. Please try your call again later." The operator disconnected her.

"Mr. Bauer is *not available!*" Mary repeated for Clara's benefit, fuming.

Evangeline Adams buzzed on the intercom. Mary depressed the lever to speak. "Yes?"

"Mary, would you order me up some lunch please? I'd like a pastrami on rye with coleslaw and a fruit cocktail."

"Right away." She turned to Clara. "I'm getting hungry, too. Do you want anything?"

"Nah, I brought a sardine sandwich. Thanks anyway."

Mary placed the order and added a roast beef sandwich for herself. As she was putting down the phone, she noticed that Clara had stopped what she was doing and was staring at the hall door. They could hear noises: someone was trying to get in. This still happened from time to time, despite the sign saying, "Private. Please enter at Room 1003," with a drawing of a hand pointing toward the entrance down the hall. But now they heard the doorknob being tried repeatedly to no avail. And then the unmistakable sound of keys jingling and someone repeatedly trying a key in the lock.

"Should we open the door?" Clara asked.

"*Sshhh!*" said Mary, waving her hand. They could see a hulking shadow on the other side of the frosted glass window.

"Mr. Simon?" Clara whispered.

"He knows how to get in and expects courtesy," Mary whispered back. "He would have called out to us. And he wouldn't be fooling around for this long."

Evangeline stepped in just as the visitor appeared to stand back and reconsider the situation. "Who is that, Mary?" she asked bluntly. "Ignoring the sign."

"I don't know but it sounded like they were trying to use a key."

Without waiting for further information, Evangeline turned the bolt and opened the door while blocking the doorway. Mary could see a middle-aged woman outside in the hall.

"Mrs. Pontin," Miss Adams addressed her formally. "Whatever are *you* doing here?"

"Hello, Evangeline. Well, I'd like to request on behalf of a certain person . . ."

"And who might that be?" Evangeline cut her off.

"I'm not at liberty to discuss—surely not out here in the hallway. May I come in?"

Adams stood aside a few feet and allowed Mrs. Pontin to enter. She was a somewhat stout, pretty woman of medium height, wearing a rose-colored tea gown, with a matching turban tied across her forehead. Over her dress was a long strand of pearls and a flowing robe in an ancient Greek pattern. It had wing sleeves that fluttered as she walked, in the vague look of an Attic goddess. Mary thought she knew who it was, a woman that Adams had mentioned from time to time, always disparagingly.

Mrs. Pontin looked about her, very self-possessed and obviously pleased to have gained entry. "Well!" she stated. "Things haven't changed here very much, have they?"

Evangeline clearly did not want a discussion, though she continued in a curt but businesslike manner. "Yes, and who were you saying it was that sent you?"

"I'm sure you could guess," was all that the lady replied as she stroked the sleeve of her robe.

"If I have to guess, I certainly don't know, do I?" Adams responded testily.

"I can't share that information as this person prefers confidence. But actually she expressly desires *not* to be mentioned in any way in your biography. She—or perhaps *he*—prefers no publicity."

"I see," Evangeline said a little ironically. "But if I don't know who it is, how can I tell you if they're mentioned or not?"

Pontin smiled. And it was a reptilian smile, Mary thought, looking somehow like a snake on a Grecian urn. "She, or he—perhaps *he*—" Pontin continued, again smiling slightly, "thought you would know."

"It's out of my hands," Evangeline replied briskly. "The book is already complete and at the publisher's. Good day, Mrs. Pontin. Next time if you'd like to visit us, please make an appointment and we'll see if we can accommodate you."

"Oh, I know how it is. I'm finishing up my own memoir right now," Pontin bragged as if she hadn't heard what Adams had said, and actually sat down in one of the client waiting chairs. She gave another of her peculiar little smiles as she abruptly changed the subject. "I received a call from Mr. Ziegfeld this morning. He's looking for a jewel—a lucky piece—and I thought you might have it."

"Ah, yes. Well, Mr. Ziegfeld already called here last week, didn't he, Mary?" she asked, turning.

"That's right, ma'am," Mary answered. "Friday afternoon, I think it was."

"So you see, Mrs. Pontin," Evangeline continued with composure, "Mr. Ziegfeld knows how to use the telephone and doesn't need to pay a finder's fee for you to visit us on his behalf. Now if that's all," the astrologer concluded, holding the door open for the uninvited guest.

"Well as a matter of fact," Pontin countered, once again ignoring Evangeline's obvious suggestion to leave. "Hazel mentioned that the Maharaja of Indore was a client of yours. And Miss Wendel said she met him here just the other day. Perhaps as a professional courtesy you might put me in touch with him?"

Evangeline Adams looked at her competitor and her eyes took on a steely cast. "Mrs. Pontin," she began tersely. "If you had behaved in a professional manner when you left my employ, I might entertain your request. If you had behaved professionally when you appropriated my office manager, I might consider treating you as one astrologer to another. But I'm afraid you're not that much of an astrologer either, are you? You needed to bribe our Hazel away to cast charts for you, didn't you? You had just as much opportunity to train and learn as Hazel did. More, really, given your background and education. Of course, with your horoscope, I understand why you behaved as you did. You are obviously incapable of the focus and attention needed to do the mathematics, something which Mary and Clara here, as well as numerous secretaries in the outer office, easily mastered."

Mary took some small pleasure in the praise. But she had never seen her boss act this way before. She'd been told that Hazel moved on and that Miss Adams was thinking of letting her go anyway, as her work was getting sloppy. Pontin finally seemed insulted into silence. Evangeline continued to vent.

"I understand your limitations. But you didn't have to be so underhanded about things, did you? You needn't have treated me as a competitor when I believe I always treated you as a friend." Pontin did not move or speak. Adams took a deep breath and spoke slowly and distinctly. "Now: I'd like you to raise yourself from my chair and take your spirit guides or whomever is advising you on how to behave these days, and *leave this office!*"

Mary and Clara both stood up and came forward to support their boss. Pontin looked around and blinked. Slowly, she stood up. "Well, if I knew I'd get this kind of a reception, I would never have come . . ." she said coldly.

"And well you shouldn't have," Evangeline interrupted as she held the door open wider to allow the intruder to leave. "Good day. Kindly don't grace us with your presence in future."

Pontin left, muttering something under her breath.

"The nerve," Evangeline said to herself out loud, as she shut the door firmly and secured the bolt. "The unmitigated gall." She turned back to her employees. "I apologize for that outburst. Mary, Clara, please don't allow her in again." And without another word, Adams returned to her office and shut the door.

"What was that all about?" Clara asked quietly.

"Hazel had this job before I did. They wanted me to start right away, so it seemed like she might not have given much notice. And I think that woman was Juliet Pontin. Miss Adams said she bills herself as a "psychic astrologer," but now it seems like she must've worked here at one time, too, and that she took Hazel away."

"How would she know about the biography?" Clara asked.

"They were already beginning it when I started working here. So Hazel would've known about it. And she might still be in touch with someone in the office," Mary added. "The book's gone through so many revisions that most of the secretaries in the office have probably typed part of it. And Miss Adams has been talking about it herself for years. The Wendels obviously consult with Mrs. Pontin, too. And all they do is talk."

"This woman also thinks Miss Adams has the jewel," Clara commented.

"I guess she's the only person in Manhattan with an elephant collection who also knows all of these society people. But you're right," Mary said, thinking out loud. "It does seem like it's all connected, doesn't it?" Mary searched her memory for something that had been eluding her. "Why were the monks here?"

"You remember, the swami said he dreamed about Miss Adams. And then to tell you that you were going on an adventure and not to be afraid."

"Right," Mary agreed. "And the detective was talking about Mr. Fiske and the Maharaja of Indore." Mary thought. "The Maharaja of Indore. I know I've heard that name before."

"Well, I read you that article in the newspaper yesterday," Clara said.

"No, that's not it." Mary thought some more. "Mrs. Pontin knows about the book. She knows about the Maharaja. Hazel would've met the Maharaja, he came here before." It suddenly came together in her mind, like finally deciphering Evangeline's often-sloppy script. "Clara! How could we forget? The Maharaja's in the manuscript!"

"He is? I don't remember. What does it say about him?"

"He's just mentioned as a client, in a list with other rich and famous people. *Oh, no!*"

"Why, what's the matter?" Clara asked.

"*Don't you see?*" Mary asked impatiently. "Anyone who's read that book—or *will* read the book—will know that the Maharaja of Indore is a client! No one really knows *now* and look at the number of people flocking in. What'll happen when it's published and out there and anyone can read it? And then Joe had to go and add that part about the elephant collection, so everyone will know about that, too."

"Mary, the detectives will find the jewel soon."

"And what if they don't? Look at how Brophy and Sterling have been pestering us. They obviously don't have any real suspects."

"Well, look," Clara proposed, "It doesn't sound like Jesse delivered the manuscript yet, right? Why don't we just delete those things?"

"How could we do that? Mr. Jordan will know."

"Do you think he's ever going to read that thing again?"

"I'm not sure," Mary admitted.

"We've changed it so much," Clara continued, "I don't think anyone could remember what's in or out, ourselves included."

Mary thought it through. "Maybe this could be a Mercury retrograde thing: time to revise and replace. It might work. We can't delete the story about the ivory elephant; Joe just added that and Miss Adams was in love with it. But I guess we can go ahead and delete the Maharaja, couldn't we?" Mary brightened.

"Sure. That's the important thing."

"All right." Mary glanced at the clock on the wall. "You take the carbon." She turned to the filing cabinets to her right, brought out the bulky carbon copy of the manuscript, and gave it to Clara. "Find that page and re-type it exactly the same as before, with a copy for us. Except just delete the Maharaja's name, OK?"

"Got it."

"And then we've got to figure out where that manuscript is and how to replace the page."

Chapter 19

Mrs. Fiske, as expected, arrived on time for her appointment, and Mary once again found herself seated by the window in Evangeline's office with her steno pad and pencil. This time, though, she was no longer pretending to take notes. She was eagerly trying to write down everything Mrs. Fiske said without being too obvious, since Fiske probably knew more about her husband's death and the theft of the jewel than anyone else. The dogs were resting in their usual places.

Mrs. Fiske wore a longish black mourning dress and lifted a short black veil from her face. She looked somewhat pale without her face powder and cosmetics, but as Mary had already observed at the wake, she also looked weak and fragile. As usual, though, Mrs. Fiske talked.

"It has been a trial, I can assure you, but it's also something of a release. To be able to handle things with only my own needs in mind has been much less stressful than dealing with Henderson. Yet of course it's still a tremendous ordeal." As Fiske removed her hat, Mary could see that her hands were shaking. The lady took a deep breath and clutched the hat tightly in her lap.

The radiator next to Mary began to whistle a bit as the steam came up. Soon there was a loud, rhythmic snapping and then a banging noise. D'Artagnon whimpered and Mary reached over and patted him with a gentle "*Ssh.*" The pipe banged again and the puppy leapt to his feet and began whining frantically while pawing at the steam pipe in the floor, then jumped back and barked. Sonny, startled awake by D'Artagnon, barked loudly a few times. D'Artagnon sat back on his haunches and let out a piercing yowl.

Mrs. Fiske shrank back in her chair. "Miss Adams!" she cried. "*Do something, I beg you. I cannot tolerate the noise!*" She put her hands over her ears.

Evangeline stepped over and picked up D'Artagnon, who relaxed in her arms. "Mary," she said quietly, passing the animal to her, "take them upstairs. And bring a glass of brandy for Mrs. Fiske."

Mary carried D'Artagnon and quickly led the other dogs up the staircase to the apartment. When she returned and placed the glass on the desk in front of Mrs. Fiske, the client had already begun her story and was complaining about the detectives.

"They searched the entire house. The servants set it right, but it was an invasion. I was almost in shock at the time. And then to return to the wake! Who would do such a thing? They assured me they would simply stand quietly at the back of the room, but nothing could be further from the truth. I noticed they had accosted you, too, and I do apologize. Your friend, I think, led them away?"

"That was our Mr. Simon," Evangeline assured her. "He's the owner of this building and has had dealings with your husband."

"I thought I recognized him—we've met before. He did me an inestimable service. Thankfully, the detectives seem to have abandoned their suspicions of *me* and have apparently moved on to other suspects." Mrs. Fiske paused and looked down at the hat in her lap.

"Last night the house was so quiet. I woke up in a sweat of anxiety from a terrible dream, and thought I heard Henderson coming to bed; I was relieved he was with me. But when I awoke more fully, I realized that he was lying down there in the living room, all alone." With that Mrs. Fiske's voice cracked and she took out a black lace handkerchief and dabbed at her eyes.

"That's what he feared the most, you know. He made me swear on my life when we were married that I would never leave him alone at night. He so feared death he needed someone in the room with him at all times, to try to pull him back if anything untoward happened. If he fell ill or had any kind of an attack, I was to phone the doctor immediately. Of course, he was a healthy man and nothing ever occurred.

"But he was always a restless sleeper. His work was constantly on his mind. When he was putting together a deal he'd be elated and only slept for a few hours. If things didn't move forward, he'd become despondent and would sleep straight through the night and often until lunch. It became a great burden, keeping up with his erratic sleep schedule. Almost always he snored. At times it would wake him with a great start and he imagined someone choking him. At other times it was only a gentle sawing noise and I could get some rest. I used to be a sound sleeper but it's been so many years, I don't even know what I'd be like anymore.

"We had known each other since childhood, and he had been a lovely boy. Our parents all approved of the match, but he changed as he grew older and assumed his responsibilities in life. He became harder and even, I fear, somewhat ruthless. And he didn't trust any of these young women he became involved with, you know. Afraid they only wanted his money and that once he was asleep, they would rob him. That's why I knew he'd never leave me. We spent every single night of our married life together. He could never totally trust anyone else as he trusted me.

"We were in the habit of going to Europe every year and Henderson naturally took care of some business there. At first it was lovely meeting new people and seeing the sights. But as he became more involved with his business, it turned into a chore. We first met the Maharaja in Zurich a number of years ago, when he asked Henderson to find a buyer for some beautiful pieces of jewelry. Large stones, diamonds, such big pieces! Tiaras, tremendous scarves made entirely of pearls, all almost haphazardly piled up in a box. Henderson sold them successfully as I recall, and the Maharaja was very pleased. The piece that's now been stolen came from the head of a cane, I believe. It was one of the more valuable pieces in the collection and was certainly the most unusual.

"When Henderson first brought it home, I thought it was the most beautiful object I had ever seen. It was a small statue carved from a single ruby, and the stone itself was flawless. But the artistry with which it was made was quite exceptional as well." Mrs. Fiske became more animated as she described the elephant statuette. "Its color, the way it caught the light, the whole piece was engraved with such skill and in such fine detail that it was almost astounding. It was truly a work of art; you could almost see the living, breathing animal that inspired it, about to trumpet.

"But as the days went by, Henderson became more and more obsessed with the thing, and I must admit that I began to despise it. It had small round eyes and the more I saw of it, the more they looked beady and unwholesome. And the way its trunk was upraised, I thought somehow a little obscene. Henderson was torn between selling it and asking for it as his commission on the rest of the sale. It had a supernatural story attached to it, reported to bring renown and riches to its owner, and that was undeniably true for the Maharaja. I don't know that Henderson really believed in the power himself, but he certainly thought others would. He supposed he'd finally found something of potentially limitless value. 'The deal of a lifetime!' he said. 'A king's ransom!' He hadn't even listed it for sale yet; he was so preoccupied with how to maximize its return. I suggested he ask you since you're familiar with the elephants, thinking you might have a potential buyer. "

"I'm afraid I never heard from him," Evangeline remarked. "But you know I don't buy these pieces—they're all gifts. I'm not sure I could have offered any help."

Mrs. Fiske nodded and continued. "Then things took a dark turn." She put a hand to her face as if to shield herself from the memory. "Henderson couldn't be without the thing. He carried it with him everywhere: the dining room, the bathroom, personally guarding it. He talked about it incessantly. And then he even brought it into bed with him at night! I tried to object, but with Henderson—an Aquarius, you know—he could be quite stubborn, and it was of no use. He held it to his chest and never relaxed his grip, even when he dropped off. And of course I couldn't sleep at all. It seemed to me that it glowed, it was luminous. Perhaps in my exhaustion and imagination, it appeared that it was watching me. It made my skin crawl. I know elephants are supposed to be a good thing, and I have nothing against them generally,

Miss Adams. But I felt that it was evil. It wouldn't let me rest!

"The night of his death, I awoke with a start, alone in the bedroom. I heard something and listened. Henderson was in the sitting room, talking to someone. Of course he'd left the door open. Drinking and laughing and carrying on. And then I realized that his companion was that elephant-thing. He said it was his best friend, the best friend he never had. Pouring out his heart to an inanimate object! It was all too much, the thought that I'd have to live with this false idol forever.

"I had taken a sleeping draught so I can't say I was entirely lucid. But I was revolted. It was as if all his past infidelities were caught up in his relationship with that stone, and all of his obsessions with money. I got up and without a word, silently closed the door, and once again fell into a deep sleep. That's all I know. Then the housekeeper was waking me with a look of horror on her face." Mrs. Fiske collapsed into sobs but quickly recovered herself.

"Had I not closed the door!" Fiske reprimanded herself, anguished. "If only I hadn't taken the sleeping draught! I would've heard the intruder and perhaps been able to save him. And if he hadn't kept the thing at home, in the room with him, it wouldn't have happened, either. He was so caught up in his relationship with the elephant that he forgot he was alone, and that it was night. The first time in nearly thirty years!" Mrs. Fiske shook her head at the irony.

"Saturn in Scorpio can represent a complex web of relationships, my dear," Evangeline said calmly. "But things happen for a reason in life. I believe it was his time. You were at a critical juncture with Saturn opposing your Mars, but now the crisis has passed. We couldn't know in advance exactly how the planetary influence would manifest. Astrology only provides the timing and describes the symbolism."

"Yes, I know. And you were quite accurate, I will say that. Lord knows I tried to follow your instructions," Mrs. Fiske replied. She brought out the astrological report that Mary had so recently prepared for her, already well worn. "I've read it over so many times, I almost know it by heart. But reading about frustration and anger and actually having the patience to overcome them are two very different things indeed. And yet when I closed that door, I felt a sense of finality. For once, I was doing something contrary to Henderson's explicit wishes."

"Saturn has now passed," Evangeline advised. "Of course the transition isn't complete, for you have much to do. But Jupiter will be trining your Sun this spring. It makes for a good time for travel and expansion. I hope you'll be able to take advantage of it."

"That sounds just right," Fiske answered as she put her hat back on her head and drew the black veil over her face once again. "I'll be going to stay with my sister in Newport soon; they have a large home. She and her husband return next week from Palm Beach for the season. I'll get some rest. And it will be nice to spend some time with my real family for a change. I have two lovely nieces and a nephew, almost grown now, who I'd like to know better."

"I'm so sorry about your husband, Mrs. Fiske, but I know you'll recover," Adams said confidently. "The Universe often brings about challenges in our lives whether we choose them or not. But we are still here, and alive, and we must move forward. And I think you'll be doing fine," Evangeline concluded as she escorted her sorrowful client out.

Chapter 20

After Mrs. Fiske had gone, Adams returned to her office and closed the door. The next client would arrive soon. Mary felt drained and genuinely sorry for Mrs. Fiske; she had endured a lot. But now she was free. Mary went back to her desk, and sat there quietly for a few minutes.

She turned to Clara. "I feel really bad for Mrs. Fiske. What a horrible marriage."

Clara didn't reply.

"Did you finish re-doing the page?" Mary asked.

"Here's the original. I already replaced the copy and filed it away," said Clara.

"Good. Now we just have to find the manuscript and replace it." She picked up her phone and had Dorothy ring Jesse in Mr. Jordan's office. Once again, there was no response. She hung up and placed the phone back on her desk.

"Do you hear him?" she asked Clara.

"Not really."

"Clara," Mary asked, "what do you think about going down there and checking on the manuscript? I'll give you the key."

"No," Clara said shortly.

"What?" Mary asked, not quite understanding.

"I said no. I'm not going. I don't want to go down there. You just convinced me he could be a killer and now you're sending me into his lair? He could be holed up down there like a bear in a cave. You go in there, he'll lash out, defending his territory."

"How do you know anything about bears and caves? You live in Brooklyn."

"I must've read it in the papers. Anyway, it makes sense."

"We need to see if the manuscript was delivered and switch the page. I'd go myself but I have to wait for the next client."

Clara turned back to her typewriter. "You go down," she said stubbornly. "I can wait for the client."

"I don't think that's the best thing," Mary said persistently. "These people are used to me and some of them need coddling. Just go."

"I'm *not going!*" Clara snapped. "You should've seen the way he grabbed Alexa. I'm surprised she's not black and blue," she said and began typing furiously. "You're turning into Mr. Jordan, you know that? Give you a little authority and you just take advantage."

Mary was taken aback. Clara could be temperamental, but she had never raised her voice in the office like this before; she was over-reacting. Mary got up and gently put her hand over Clara's. She tried to be calm as she asked, "Clara, is something wrong?"

"Yes, there's something wrong. Something is very wrong."

"What is it?"

Clara exhaled deeply. "I'm embarrassed to talk about it."

"You? Embarrassed? At least you can tell *me*," Mary said as she sat on the edge of Clara's desk.

Clara leaned forward with her elbows on the desk and spoke quietly. "When you were in conference with Mrs. Fiske, a call came in on your phone. I picked it up and said, 'Miss Adams' office' just like you told me, but there was a creepy man on the line. I didn't recognize the voice; it was like he was trying to disguise it. But I think it must've been Jesse."

"Why? What did he say?"

"It was a crank call, that's all."

"Clara, it could be important. What did the caller say?"

"Well . . ." Clara hesitated. "He spoke in a low, gravelly voice, like some kind of criminal or something, and he said . . ." Clara took another deep breath before repeating it and lowering her voice even more, imitating the caller. "'The jewel is hidden in your butt crack.' And then he just hung up."

Mary couldn't help but laugh, but she covered her mouth and tried to control herself while Clara continued.

"It's really shaken me up. It was crude and rude and embarrassing, and I don't know why I should be exposed to something like that..." She looked up at Mary. "What, are you laughing? You think it's *funny?*"

"I am not laughing!" Mary said, trying to keep a straight face. "Did you ask Dorothy about it?"

"No, I was too shocked to do anything."

Mary went back to her desk and picked up the phone; Dorothy came on the line. "Is Mrs. Rahman here yet? ... If she comes in the next few minutes, just keep her in reception ... Did you put a call through to my desk? A little while ago ... OK, thanks." Mary put the phone down. "Dorothy says she didn't put any calls through. That's very weird." Mary thought about it a little. "Listen, Clara, aside from anything else, the call was for me, OK? Who could know that you'd pick it up?"

"If it was Jesse, he could easily be listening at the pipe, the same as we were."

"Say it was Jesse. So what? He's not about to do anything, it's just a bunch of childish nonsense."

"... And he obviously knows we're trying to find the jewel," Clara countered.

"I don't think you should jump to that conclusion. The police were just here, everyone knows about the jewel. It's only a prank." Mary got up. "I'm going out to the switchboard to see if Dorothy knows anything else."

Mary stepped out through the communicating door and into the outer office. It was instantly noisier, with several typists working at the same time in the large undivided space. Other secretaries were preparing mail order reports at their desks. As in Mary and Evangeline's offices, immense, nearly floor-to-ceiling windows lined the south wall. Some of the Venetian blinds were raised and a few windows were cracked open.

Mary could see the reception area, enclosed by a low bannister. It was nothing special. There was an old burgundy carpet with several less-than-comfortable looking chairs. Printed brochures on "The Law and Astrology," touting

Evangeline's 1914 victory in the City's fortune-telling case against her, reprints of "Thirty Years of Star Gazing" from a recent issue of the *Women's Home Companion*, and a biographical leaflet on Miss Adams were placed on side tables for waiting clients to read. There were also many framed photos of celebrity clients on the wall, along with a few letters of endorsement, almost a *Who's Who* of the rich and famous. What Mary liked to think of as the theatrical column included Gertrude Lawrence, Isadora Duncan, Eva Le Gallienne and Tallulah Bankhead. The literary wing featured playwright Eugene O'Neill, editor Max Perkins and mystery author Agatha Christie. In the society section were Gloria Morgan Vanderbilt and her identical twin sister Thelma Converse, soon to be the Viscountess Furness. Picture stars Mary Pickford and Douglas Fairbanks smiled out of a large photograph signed by both. Metropolitan Opera stars included Geraldine Farrar and Enrico Caruso.

Jeannie was sitting beside Dorothy at the switchboard, learning to be the relief operator. Both faced away from Mary, intent on their task. Mary paused to watch her daughter as Dorothy was explaining things.

"I first learned at a very large switchboard. There was no talking to each other. A supervisor walked back and forth behind us, and if you even looked around, they'd chastise you. I once sat next to a woman who pulled the plugs out like you'd snap a whip. I was very concerned one would hit me. But they fired her right along anyway for twirling on her stool. We were trained to use a soft, melodious voice," she said as she imitated it. "You won't have to worry about that here," she assured her in her naturally smooth Tennessee tones.

"Now, when a call comes through there'll be a buzzing sound and one of these little lights across the bottom on the left will turn on," Dorothy said. "See here? Miss Adams is on the line. The cord connects her extension up here—" she pointed to a row of female jacks across the middle of her switchboard panel "—to one of these five lines on the bottom. The light at the end of the cord means the party's still on the line." Jeannie nodded. "Each of these lines here has two plugs and this key right in front of them. When you hear the buzzing, you take up the plug that's sitting right in front of the light, and you plug it into the jack just above it." Dorothy demonstrated. Her nails were clipped short for piano playing, but were beautifully manicured, and her long fingers crossed the switchboard with practiced movements.

"Now we're connected to our caller. Of course you'll also have the head phones and the speaking tube on like I do — my glamorous accessories," she joked. Dorothy's curly hair had been straightened into a Marcel wave and the headphones sat across the top of her head. The speaking tube was on a cord around her neck and curved toward her mouth. "So when you plug the cord in, you open the circuit and you go right ahead and say, 'Miss Adams' office. How may I help you?'"

"OK," Jeannie said tentatively.

"Don't you worry — this is only an introduction. You'll watch me do it for a while and then you'll practice while I sit with you. So let's say this lady calls and says she wants to make an appointment, right? Your mom takes care of that. Her extension is up here, right next to Miss Adams, see? Her name is right below it. And we have all the other phones listed across the board, too." Dorothy pointed to each of the female jacks. "Here's Jesse, there's a phone in the back room, and Mr. Jordan has two lines in his office downstairs. See? They're all here. All right. So you have the party on the line with the first plug. You ask who it is and then you go ahead and say, 'One moment please,' and you turn the key in front of the light a half a turn like this," Dorothy showed her. "Now she can't hear you. You've 'split the key,' that's what they call this half a turn. Once you do that, she's just sitting there all by her lonesome. She's still connected to the switchboard, but you've cut her off for the moment from *you*.

"Then you take this other plug, next to the incoming line, and you reach it over to your mom's jack and plug it in. Now we're connected to her and we can talk to her. But she's got to pick up her telephone in order to do it. So you hit this little button below her name and that rings her phone. Give her a little chance to answer, but ring her again if she doesn't pick up. Then you say to her, 'Miss Anita Loos is on the line,' or whoever it is, and she'll say 'Put her through.' So then I turn the key all the way to the right and we're all connected; the three of us could converse if we wanted to. Or you can listen in quietly, but most of these conversations are simply *way* too boring for me to waste my time with that. Now you just say, 'Go ahead please,' and you turn the key all the way back—turn it right on back to the starting position—and the two cords are connecting the two callers and they can talk. They're alone by themselves and I'm no longer connected to them."

Jeannie seemed overwhelmed with all the new information. Mary interrupted them as she came through the low door to their area. "How's she doing?" she asked.

"Well, she's doing just fine, aren't you? It'll take her a few days to learn the system, that's all. You have to expect that."

"I'm doing fine, Mom," Jeannie said crankily. "You don't have to check up on me."

"I'm not checking up on you. I need to talk to Dorothy." Mary turned back to her friend. "Clara picked up a weird call at my desk a little while ago. You don't remember any calls coming through to my line in the last half hour or so?"

"I really don't think so." She turned to her student. "Jeannie?"

"Not since I've been sitting here."

"Could anyone call my phone without going through the switchboard?"

"If someone had your number—it's right here by your name," she indicated on the board. "Each of the office phone lines has its own number. And if they had a dial like I do here, they could bypass our exchange. A switchboard operator downstairs, or anywhere for that matter, could call you direct. Only thing is that we never give out these numbers, so I'm not sure how anyone would know. But they might also have a list of them downstairs."

"Do you think Jesse could have done it?"

"Jesse?" Dorothy thought. "I imagine he could have. He wired up telephones during the war, or so he says. He was supposed to connect another line to Mr. Jordan's office. If he had a dial, or went downstairs to the main exchange, sure, he could've done it."

"When did you see him exactly?"

"Maybe an hour ago."

"Did he say anything?"

"He asked that I put all his calls through downstairs, that was basically it."

"He didn't say anything else? We're trying to find out if he delivered the manuscript."

"Actually he did say something." Dorothy looked up as she tried to remember. "Let me just think about it a little bit. It didn't make much sense so I paid him no mind. Oh, yes, I do remember now. He said he was getting rid of a 'bastard child.' That struck me in particular because it was so odd, but I have no idea what he could have meant. I don't always try to understand him. Different women call him from time to time, personal calls, I believe. I suppose I didn't really like to think about it. A little shameless, if you ask me."

"I wonder if he could be referring to the book."

"The book? As a *'bastard child?'*" Dorothy smiled. "It's not very nice. But I suppose he might have. I guess it could be considered a kind of a bastard child of Miss Adams and those writers," Dorothy chuckled. "You could be right. You never know with Jesse."

"Thanks Dorothy." Mary turned back toward her office but caught sight of Jesse's cohort, Richard, sitting at his desk on the other side of the room. He was working quietly as usual, adding up figures on a calculating machine and pulling the lever to print the results on a tape. Maybe Richard would know something about Jesse and the manuscript, Mary thought.

Mary didn't know Richard very well. He was a mild mannered young man who generally kept to himself. *But he's survived this long sitting right next to Jesse*, she thought. *He must have a great deal of patience—either that or he's completely insensitive*. Richard had a large accounting sheet in front of him and was carefully compiling the day's receipts. With all of the mail order work, there could be quite a lot of entries.

Richard was about twenty years old with plain brown hair parted on the side and brown eyes. He wore tan slacks, a white shirt rolled up at the sleeves, and a light blue wool vest. He simply looked ordinary; he could be anyone. Or no one.

"Hi, Richard," Mary opened. "How's it going?"

"Hello, Mary. I'm just doing the ledger here." He spoke softly.

"Have you seen Jesse lately?"

Richard put his pencil down and looked up. "Not for over half an hour. You might try Mr. Jordan's room."

"I checked already. I can't find him anywhere."

Richard looked at Mary calmly.

"Do you know if he delivered the book to the publisher?" she asked.

"He was going to do it. He took it with him this morning."

"OK, thanks."

"You're welcome," Richard said and smiled slightly as he returned to his task.

Mary went back to her office and spoke to Clara.

"Dorothy thinks Jesse could've made the crank call. He knows something about telephones."

"She's right. That's the one thing he really *does* know something about."

"But she doesn't know where he is, or if he delivered the manuscript." Mary paused, then asked, "What do you think of Richard?" She realized she didn't even know his Sun sign, which would have given them something to go on.

"Richard? I don't really know. He works a lot, always busy doing the books. He doesn't eat much lunch—not that I've seen, anyway. He doesn't go out, and he rarely brings much of anything in with him. He's always pleasant enough but never goes much further. I've got nothing against Richard; he's always nice to me. But he's nice to everyone."

"I know. He's a little too neutral, don't you think? A little nondescript. It's almost as if he's not a real person." Mary thought about it. "It's a little suspicious," she said, and then concluded, "He must be hiding something. What sign is he?" she asked.

"Umm . . ." Clara thought. "I think he said he's Pisces. Does that give us any clues?"

"He could be hiding something," Mary concluded.

"He probably knows a lot," Clara added. "But good luck trying to pry it out of him. He's not one to gossip, to say the least. He doesn't talk much but he'll generally laugh at Jesse's jokes. I've thought that maybe he supports a family. He pretty much wears the same thing every day."

"No, he's probably single," Mary argued. "Most men could care less about buying things for themselves. They eat out and spend all their money that way."

"I used to think sometimes that maybe Jesse had mental control over Richard. Maybe he hypnotized Richard to do his bidding. He does most of Jesse's work."

"Do you really imagine Jesse could have that kind of power over anyone?"

"I guess not," Clara agreed.

"Listen," Mary said, a little more urgently, looking at the clock on the wall. "This client is already late. When she gets here, if she doesn't want me to take notes, we'll go down to see Jesse together. If he has the manuscript, we'll tell him that Miss Adams had a last-minute change. If he's not there, we'll see if the manuscript *is*. "

"But what if we can't find either of them?" asked Clara.

"Well, then, we'll . . ." Mary couldn't think of an answer.

Chapter 21

The elegant Mrs. Rahman stepped into the office and sat in one of the waiting chairs across from Mary's desk. She spoke with an unusual accent, but Mary remembered that she was another client who was also born in India.

Mary wondered how anyone had the time, let alone the money, to manage to look so perfectly put together. At twenty-one, this woman was still very young. She was a foreigner, yes, with a rich rosewood-toned complexion. But it was as if she had stepped right out of the latest fashion magazine. Her helmet of glossy black hair looked like it had been cut that morning, with chiseled bangs across her forehead and ends turning up at her cheekbones. Her cornflower blue traveling suit nicely fitted her slim proportions, and the matching suede pumps were bright and colorful without being overwhelming.

Mrs. Rahman's eyebrows formed perfect arches above her round, expressive brown eyes and long, curling lashes. Her lips were colored a deep rose in the ideal bow-shape; the polish on her long manicured nails appeared to be an exact match. She wore large jeweled rings on both of her hands, as well as a lovely necklace, but the overall effect was not ostentatious or overdone. She seemed to have an unfailing sense of color, proportion and style.

Many wealthy and sophisticated women came into the office every day. Yet as attractive and well-dressed as they often were, each in her own way had natural human flaws. And Ramini Rahman was no exception to the rule. In a bitter contrast to the perfection of her impeccable appearance, there was one tremendous blemish. A livid white scar ran along one side of her nose and its jagged path traced to her forehead, where its beginnings were hidden by the precision of the bangs. Mary tried not to stare, but she wondered what kind of accident could possibly have created such an ugly mark across this pretty young woman's face. It was so striking that no matter what she did to distract from it, the scar, so close to the center of her face, was what caught and held the eye. *What could one do?* Mary thought. *Make yourself up in the hope of overcoming the defect? Or dress down and look like some kind of hoodlum.* Neither worked.

Miss Adams opened the door to her office and ushered the client in. She requested a transcription and soon Mary took her usual place on the sofa.

The women settled themselves and Ramini Rahman began in accented English: "I have a little girl right now and I'm married to a very nice man. We live in India. But I also have an offer from an agent here in this country to sell my story and perhaps to do some modeling. I am thinking that I might like it in America. My husband may not want to come here, but I inherited some money recently and I can do very much as I please. I would like to know, would it be better for me in America than in Europe or India? And what do the stars hold in store for me?"

"Let's look at your horoscope." Miss Adams studied the chart. "You have a number of planets in Virgo, so you are down-to-earth and realistic. That's a big plus for you: you can handle your finances and sort out many things for yourself." Evangeline went on with a recitation of the chart. "Now, it appears that you were born on the day of a solar eclipse," she began as she drew out a large book from the side of her desk and looked the date up. "Oh, yes, a total solar eclipse on the day you were born. You may have a life of some drama, and you can attract the attention of the public. But it will always be important for you to try not to over-react to the outside events of life. Be conscious at all times of taking things in stride. Sometimes you may experience dramatic events, but if you can avoid an extreme reaction—as much as you can, it's difficult, I know—it will help you get through the more eventful times in life."

"Yes, Miss Adams, I agree with you," the client said enthusiastically, leaning forward in her chair. "You have hit upon my experiences perfectly!" But suddenly her face turned ashen and she interrupted herself as if in an apoplectic fit. *"What?—"* Her hands flew to her mouth and she inhaled with a choking sound. Finally she stammered

out, "Where did you *get that* —" she growled with intensity,
" — *that, that elephant?*"

Miss Adams, with her infinite patience, and not
understanding, simply asked gently, "Pardon me?"

"*That elephant!*" Ramini had raised her voice and stood up
as she pointed to a sparkling little jeweled creature sitting on
the desk to Adams' right. "*It's mine!* What are you doing
with it?" she now shouted.

Adams took the precious animal in her hand and said
softly, "Why, this was a gift, as most of them were."

"That's right, it was a gift," the client said sharply. "To *me*.
There's not another one like it in the world." Ramini just
stood there. She clearly wanted to tear the elephant out of
Adams' hand but something about the situation, Evangeline's kind, motherly manner, the desk between them, or the
constraints of the professional consultation, prevented her
from doing so. She fell back into her chair. "Does he control
everyone I have contact with? I wanted to get away from
anything connected with him; I thought I'd make a new life
for myself in America. And he's even followed me *here!* How
could I be so stupid as to imagine that anyplace in the world
was left?" She laughed bitterly to herself, but then anger
overcame her.

"*I'm suing him!*" she shouted shrilly. "I've set up residence
in Switzerland and I can bring a suit against him at any time.
I have the means and I'll pursue it. And if that doesn't work,
he has another home in Paris. I'll do what I have to do.
They're mine! They were gifts. It's small change to him. I
haven't finished with him yet! Look what he did to me!" she
cried as she brushed the heavy bangs to the side, revealing
the full length of the disfiguring scar, which crossed from her
hairline through her forehead before it cut down through the
side of her nose. Adams and Mary looked on, mute. "Don't
you know who I am?" Ramini demanded caustically. "They
call me Mumtaz Begum, the notorious dancing girl kept by
the Maharaja of Indore. Don't you read the newspapers? I
am disfigured for life. *I* should be the one starring in the
motion pictures, not selling my story to them! *I* should be

celebrated in the press, not constantly depicted as some pathetic low-class victim. I had beauty, talent, promise. I was on top of the world. And now what do I have? I can't go anywhere without reporters hounding me, wanting to take photos of my *beautiful face*—" she spat out the words with sarcasm, "so they can sell a few thousand more newspapers. I thought I might escape from it all here. But I'm ruined! *Ruined!* My life will never be the same again. And he will never leave me in peace." She collapsed into her chair, put her head in her hands, shuddered and wept.

"My dear, I'm sorry for your difficulties. If we look at the planetary indications, I'm sure we can sort this out. Calm yourself. Set it aside and move forward," Evangeline soothed. "Mary, get Mrs. Rahman some brandy. And take this away," she quietly added as she handed Mary the little jeweled elephant.

By the time Mary came back, the client was already composed. Her poise and self-control had reasserted themselves and her fashion model persona had once again returned. There was no trace of an outburst. She may have been anyone, wrapping up a reading. She had already put on her hat and was readying herself to leave.

"Mary will send the planetary indications for the coming year to your hotel," Evangeline assured her. "No charge for this session. Good luck to you, my dear. We'll see you again, I hope." And Ramini Rahman left the office without another word.

"I'll take the drink, Mary," Evangeline said, sounding stressed. "Here are my notes for the session. Make her up a nice report, please. Whatever you can do."

Mary returned to her desk.

"What was that all about?" Clara immediately asked when Mrs. Rahman had left.

"That," Mary said pointedly, "was the girlfriend."

"What girlfriend?"

"Holkar's."

Clara was surprised. "That's not the girlfriend," she argued. "I met the girlfriend—the American, in the car."

"She's the new one. This was the old one, the one that's in all the papers."

Clara gasped. "You mean the *dancing girl?* Who made him lose his throne?"

"Uh huh. Did you notice the scar?"

"On her face? Yes."

"She said Holkar did it."

"If he did he must've had a good reason . . ."

Mary cut her off. "Not according to her. She had a conniption when she saw this." Mary brought out the jeweled elephant figurine. It was about two inches long and fit in the palm of her hand. It was cute, seeming to depict a baby elephant. Its body was covered with tiny white diamonds set in gold. The elephant wore golden cuffs on its ankles, a gold tassel on its forehead, and its pearl tusks and toes were all tipped in gold. Its upraised trunk revealed its underside, composed of tiny pink diamonds, as was the underside of its belly. A harness and blanket were in gold with a fine cloisonné pattern in soft tones of leaf green, deep coral and beige. The eyes were polished jet. Mary placed it on her desk.

"Oh! Can I see it?" Clara came over and held it up. It twinkled terrifically in the light.

"Holkar gave it to her."

"So how did *you* get it?"

"Apparently he changed his mind and then gave it to Miss Adams the other day." Mary took the little figurine back from Clara and locked it in her desk drawer.

"If you read the papers," Clara said, explaining, "you can understand why. She ruined him! She's a real gold-digger. She took advantage of the situation and tried to fleece him."

"She thinks he's still chasing her. She came here to get away from him, and now she doesn't know what to do."

"Mary, she's mistaken—read one of the articles—that's *not* what happened."

"Don't defend him, Clara! Didn't you hear her screaming? She's terrified. I thought there was something cold-blooded about him."

"I wouldn't say that at all!"

"I'm beginning to wonder if this Holkar killed Fiske, or had some of his men do it for him. He wouldn't want to take any chance on soiling that expensive coat!" Mary said sarcastically. "He'd be out with his new girlfriend at some party while they do his dirty work and he kicks this one to the curb!" Mary said bitingly, not realizing that she'd raised her voice.

"Ladies, that's enough!" They both turned, surprised. Evangeline Adams was standing in her doorway. "Come in here, the two of you, and close the door," she said harshly. Adams returned to sit behind her desk. "Now sit down, both of you." Mary immediately sat in the client's chair and Clara on the sofa by the window.

"All right." Miss Adams regarded them both sternly as she waited dramatically, her blue eyes taking on a hard, gray cast. "Let he who is without sin cast the first stone." Her two assistants looked down at the floor, ashamed. "Mary? Clara?" She turned to each one of them in turn and paused for effect. "Have you anything of substance to contribute?"

"No," they both replied, barely audible.

"You must understand. A court like that can be full of all sorts of manipulation and intrigue—read your Shakespeare. And if you have a master like Mr. Holkar who can be open and trusting, like an overgrown puppy in some ways, you have to protect him. Then again there are all kinds of people who will take advantage of that and do almost anything to preserve their own position and status.

"There are two wives: he married the first at age five as dictated by the astrologers and chosen by his parents. He married the second in his early twenties, after he'd already been a prince of the realm for ten years. How would either of these ladies take to this woman usurping their husband's affections and upsetting the household? And who may, if things go on as they might, even marry him? Their families have wealth and influence and hers does not. So how will it go for this interloper, do you think?

"I know the story from the London papers and from people who know Mr. Holkar well. Based upon his horoscope, with several planets in Sagittarius opposed to Neptune, he's someone who is kind-hearted and generous and has empathy for others. He's an important person with much on his mind. However his head is often in the clouds and he may not be at all aware of the turbulence he leaves in his wake. And Venus out-of-bounds in Sagittarius loves not wisely but too well. He's probably not the most constant in relationships but that's not considered a liability in his position. He's been surrounded by sycophantic people all his life, who don't tell him the truth. So it becomes a terrific battle, you see, to find out what's really going on."

"But the papers all said that the dancing girl . . ." Clara began.

"No, no, *no!*" Adams interrupted her with a little impatience. "She was not simply a 'dancing girl' as the newspapers call her. Dancing girls are more often slaves and in any event have a much lower rank. Did this woman appear to be a slave to you? On the contrary. The closest word you may be familiar with is a courtesan. Some women of her class are trained to carry on the local traditions. They may be attached to a prince's court; they will perform at official functions and are expected to raise the culture of everyone about them. Apparently this young woman was a favorite of the prince and even travelled with him to Europe.

"Some traditional courtesans are much more independent than other women in India. They can own property and earn an income. They may also be called upon to educate young men in the sexual arts, which is where they run afoul of their British overlords. To my mind, this is probably a useful role in society. So many of my clients complain that they are expected to simply muddle through. Today we have marriage manuals and all that. They lack the personal touch, if you will. I'm not advocating for courtesans, of course, they wouldn't go over very well in this country.

"But I can only imagine what it would be like in her situation. Here I am, a skilled and independent professional.

Say someone like Mrs. Harding wants to set me up in the White House, and pay me a fantastic salary, but I mustn't leave the grounds and I can only read horoscopes for her and her guests. A stifling atmosphere; it can't possibly last. Sooner or later most people will want to get out, no matter how genteel the surroundings. Add youth and an intimate relationship and you can only imagine the complexities.

"I think I can assure you though, that Mr. Holkar is not chasing after this woman as she imagines. Astrologically and otherwise, he's moving on. He once doted on her, showed her off and showered her with affection and fabulous jewels. Then he tired of her; she weighed him down. But what was she to do? It's difficult to leave such comfortable surroundings. Ramini became involved with the commander of the Indore mounted police, which is a dangerous thing in many ways.

"She subsequently bore a child who was either stillborn or was murdered by one of the ladies of the court, perhaps because it was inconvenient or because it posed a threat to someone's position. Ramini leaves the palace and goes to Bombay, where one of the Prince's guests who'd fallen in love with her takes her in. In Bombay, mind you, Holkar has no authority, the British rule absolutely. Mr. Holkar reports to the authorities the theft of a substantial amount of jewelry belonging to his family, presumably taken by this woman. The commander follows her and begs her to return to him and their former life. She refuses. He brings along some of his cronies to abduct the girl and return her to the palace, out of insult to his own pride or the honor of the prince, we cannot say.

"Ramini is out for a drive with her new partner, who is shot and killed, and she very nearly has her nose cut off, a traditional punishment for adultery. But due to a twist of fate, destiny, astrology or what have you, the plot is foiled. Three English military officers returning from a game of golf encounter Ramini's car while the abduction is taking place. They rescue her.

"Everything is then in the hands of a British court and the incident becomes known as the Malabar Hill murder. The commander and another attacker are sent to the gallows. But they cannot arrest the prince, for he must be tried by a jury of his peers. However, they give him a choice: he may face a court of princes or renounce the throne in favor of his son. He does not want to abdicate but the English will force him down sooner or later. This particular incident was the excuse; Holkar had chafed at the bit of his English overlords for too long. As his father had, and as his son also will, I'll wager. Many of them go along with the British; Holkar didn't. He became a political embarrassment to them; he undermined their power. His line is descended from the Sun and he cannot compromise his honor. Of course he is now tried in the court of public opinion by you and everyone else who know nothing about him except some sensationalized story in the press. People with high positions and heavy responsibilities cannot comment on such matters, so the public only gets one side of the story.

"Does Ramini Rahman genuinely believe that Mr. Holkar is personally responsible for the attacks? I don't know. But after witnessing her companion, sitting right beside her in the motor-car, killed at point blank range; frightened, upset and angry doesn't quite capture it, does it? She has certainly been punished in the way the press has hounded her; she's become something of a latter day Helen of Troy. Was she a puppet of the English court? Did she use the British? Did they use her? Both benefitted from their alliance. And remember, she was probably only nineteen at the time, and she'd been in Holkar's household for a number of years. She lost a child. Was it the guard's? Was it killed? I don't know and she may not know either. She may truly believe that the jewels she took were gifts.

"But here's the point," Evangeline concluded as she took off her glasses and rubbed the bridge of her nose. "If you make judgments based on hearsay statements in the press, you're making a very big mistake. You don't have enough information. And if you spend your life expecting every acquaintance or client to adhere to your own code of conduct, you're going to be a very unhappy person indeed.

"Learn to think for yourselves! Most of what you read in the newspapers cannot possibly contain the whole truth; they haven't the time or space. Periodicals are wonderful things. They educate us and take us beyond our physical limitations. But if you don't learn to use your mind at the same time, it's only strengthening the walls that divide you from your fellow human beings.

"Compassion, my dears, compassion! They have both grappled all their lives with Saturn, and Neptune as well. Look at their horoscopes, see what they're up against. People find themselves in many circumstances not of their own choosing. A horoscope gives us knowledge. Use it to better understand others, to help them through the dark forest in which they may find themselves. Don't judge them. I don't know why God intended that they play these parts, but I see that they must." Evangeline looked at them both very earnestly and put her glasses back on. "We may not be able to change their lives or influence their destiny. But if we can make someone's burden a little lighter, if only for a few minutes, we've accomplished a lot.

"Now let's clear our minds and return to work. We must get back on our schedule." She glanced at her wristwatch. "Mrs. McLean will be arriving soon and we'll need to marshal all of our resources to face such a Titan."

Chapter 22

Mary and Clara returned to their desks, chastened. Mary began the report for Mrs. Rahman, while Clara returned to her own reports for mail-order clients. They both worked quietly.

After a while, Clara sat up and listened. "I hear something," she said. "I think he's down there."

Mary stopped what she was doing and listened, too. She looked at the clock on the wall. "We still have a few minutes, but I don't dare go down there now. I've got to wait for this Mrs. McLean, who sounds like a handful."

Clara moved to the steam pipe and put her ear to it.

"I think you've been listening at that pipe a little too much," Mary said. "It's not good for you."

"*Shhh!*" Clara waved Mary to be quiet. "He's down there. Sounds like he's talking to a friend of his. I think he's talking about the office."

"Clara, you were miserable sitting next to him, and now that you've escaped, it's like you want to recapture the experience."

"I know what it looks like. But that's not what's going on. I'm collecting evidence."

Mary turned back to her work. She could vaguely hear Jesse's booming voice coming up through the floorboards.

"He just called Miss Adams an old witch," Clara shared. "And he's telling his friend that Mr. Jordan is in love with him!"

"*What?!*" Mary could no longer contain herself. She got up and went over to the pipe to listen. They could hear Jesse once again, talking on the telephone downstairs.

". . . a whole creepy little tribe, they give me the heebie-jeebies. Like a bunch of big, hairy rats, is what they look like, with their eyes bugging out. Big rats with fluffy tails and long hair. I swear to God."

Clara looked at Mary, deeply disturbed, and whispered, "I think he's talking about the *dogs*! Miss Adams would be very upset if she heard that. I've seen rats down on the subway tracks. They're not *rats*. What's wrong with him?"

Mary nodded. They continued to listen.

". . . pampered pooches. They sit at her dinner table and she feeds them with a spoon."

"That couldn't be true, could it?" Clara asked quietly. Mary closed her eyes, frowned and shook her head while they kept listening.

". . . one of them's completely decrepit . . . he must be twenty years old. He's gonna drown in his own drool one day. They should just put him down . . . Put him out of his misery . . . Euthanize, I think they call it . . . *Euthanize*," he emphasized. "I don't know, Y, O, U, T, H — hey, you're not gonna write it out." He snorted a laugh. "I'd put a bullet through his head if he was my dog."

"There he goes with the gun again!" whispered Clara. "Always with the gun."

Mary stepped away from the pipe. "Come on, Clara. We don't have time to listen to this kind of baloney, and that's all it is. It's mean and petty and — "

"And it's all a bunch of crap!" added Clara. "That's for sure." They both returned to their desks as Mary's phone rang: two long rings, signaling that something annoying was going on. She picked up and Dorothy was on the other end of the line, speaking in the exaggeratedly polite tone she took at times when clients in reception were being difficult.

"Hello, Mary. Mrs. McLean is here with me in reception, along with a rather *large dog*. I've informed her of Miss Adams' policies regarding dogs . . ."

Mary could hear a voice in the background. "It's not just a big dog! It's a Great Dane!"

"Pardon me," Dorothy said. "Her *Great Dane* has accompanied her here to the office today and she's hoping we'll make an exception and let her bring him in when she sees Miss Adams."

"A Great Dane?" Mary asked shaking her head in annoyance. "That's a really big dog, isn't it?"

"You are correct," Dorothy replied pleasantly.

"Tell her she can't bring him in! Miss Adams would have a fit!"

"I understand, and I've informed her of that," Dorothy said calmly. "Mrs. McLean would still prefer to bring the dog. I've also advised her that she cannot smoke near Miss Adams, and that we also ask that she not smoke in reception."

Mary once again heard the voice in the background. It was hoarse and gravelly. "I'm putting it out, see? *See?* And she's nowhere near here! What difference does it make? Mike is very tame; he won't hurt anybody. He just looks like a big bully."

"I hear her," Mary said.

"Yes," Dorothy said. "You understand."

"I'm coming out." Mary got up, knocked on Evangeline's door and opened it.

"Yes, Mary?" Adams said, absent-mindedly, focused on some writing. "Is it Mrs. McLean?"

"Yes, ma'am."

The astrologer put her pen down and looked up. "What's the trouble this time?"

"Dorothy says she's brought along a large dog, and she insists on bringing him in," Mary said quickly. "She was also smoking, but Dorothy got her to put out the cigarette."

"I think I can smell it from here," Evangeline said, coughing slightly. "Very well. I'll see to it." She sighed and remained at her desk for a moment. She almost never went out to reception to meet clients. "Let me tell you something," she said to Mary. "You'll find eccentric people in all walks of life. But when you're eccentric as well as very wealthy, a lot of the boundaries to your desires are removed. For enough money, people will do most anything. So there's a lot of freedom there and it's not always a good thing. And those that go from very poor to very rich, like Mrs. McLean, they enjoy the money while it's there, which means they spend constantly as if the drought is coming tomorrow." She paused and considered.

"Mrs. McLean is married to the publisher of the *Washington Post*. I thank my lucky Jupiter I don't live in that town or I daresay she'd be visiting us every day. She has her own vast fortune as well, and a lot of pull in society. You'll recall that she was a great friend of President and Mrs. Harding. She's used to having her own way. She has the Sun in Leo, it's a fixed sign, and being in the eighth house makes it even more tenacious, and there's always someone she can enlist to do her bidding. We will not enable that pattern here today, I hope. She's a client, we want to help her, but we cannot overturn the office on her behalf. You understand?" she asked, getting up.

"Yes."

Evangeline started toward the door. "I'd like you to come with me, Mary. You may have to help Dorothy restrain the beast."

Mary stood, dumfounded. "But—" she began. She couldn't imagine how she could possibly hope to restrain such a large dog, even with Dorothy to help.

"Come along, Mary, don't dawdle" Miss Adams chided, ignoring Mary's protest and boldly leading the way.

As they arrived at the front desk, they could see the client sitting in reception. Evalyn Walsh McLean was a woman of forty, of medium build, with loosely curling hair colored a striking coppery-red. Her face and nose were both somewhat long. Her companion, a tremendous steel gray hound, sat upright beside her chair, actually a hand taller than his owner. The dog's massive jowls jiggled and he greeted them with a small woof as they approached, pleased for the company. He began to get up but McLean stopped him with a curt, "*Stay!*" The dog moved a little restlessly, fidgeting back and forth with his front paws as he whined a little, but held his ground. Adams and Mary stopped and stood inside the bannister next to Dorothy.

"Evangeline!" McLean cried with a wide smile that revealed longish front teeth. "It's so good to see you again," she said warmly. She had a nervous, highly-strung manner, and her voice was indeed damaged and hoarse. She spoke

with a folksy, rough-hewn western accent. "Your receptionist doesn't want to let Mike here come in."

"I'm afraid that's my fault." Adams coughed a bit again,
waving the air with her hand. "You see, we have a policy
about dogs. As you may know, I have three Pekingese and
I'm afraid they don't take kindly to other animals,
particularly, I imagine, one of this great size. I allowed a
small dog in here once, an Airedale Terrier, I believe. He
wreaked havoc with my dogs; they weren't themselves for
weeks. Mike may wait for you here in reception, if you'd
prefer. That is, if it's all right with Dorothy," she said,
turning to the receptionist.

"Oh, sure, Miss Adams, he doesn't seem to pose a
problem," Dorothy said.

"Though I cannot allow him in," Evangeline concluded.

"But *everybody* loves Mike!" McLean assured her. "He
won't do anything, I personally guarantee it."

"Nevertheless . . ." Miss Adams warned.

"Look at him, who could deny him anything?" McLean
attempted a googly, little-girl voice that was at odds with her
hoarse tones. "He's such a sweetie-pie!" She looked at Mike
and gave him a big kiss on the mouth, leaving some of her
deep coral lipstick on his muzzle. Mike licked his chops and
his immense tongue lolled out; it looked, Mary thought, like
half a boiled ham.

"Whichever you prefer," Evangeline advised firmly and a
little dismissively. "You may come in alone for your
consultation or we can reschedule for another time. The
decision is yours." With that, she turned to go; Mary
followed her.

"No, wait!" McLean yelled, getting up. "I need to see you
now." She again addressed the dog. "You be a good doggy
and stay right there, all right, Mike? Stay." Mike whined a
little at the loss of his companion and fidgeted a bit again,
but stayed in place. "The telephone lady here will watch out
for you, won't you?" She looked up at Dorothy. "You'll call
me right away if he needs anything?"

"Yes, ma'am, I sure will," Dorothy assured her.

Mrs. McLean walked over to open the gate but Adams had now stopped and was observing the dog intently. Mary opened her mouth in surprise. She suddenly noticed that instead of a collar, Mike wore a large necklace around his neck. It featured a tremendous dark blue oval stone, at least two inches long, surrounded by a ring of diamonds, on a chain that was seemingly made up entirely of large diamonds itself. The intense blue of the jewel complemented the dog's coat nicely.

"How can you inflict that stone on such a beautiful animal?" Adams demanded.

"Why, that's the Hope Diamond," McLean said. "Don't you remember? We talked about it years ago."

"If he were Taurus rising, it would be all right; but he doesn't look like a Taurus rising to me. Do you have his time of birth?"

"Hell, no, I don't even have his birthday," the client informed her.

"Well, as I say, he doesn't look like he's Taurus rising. I'd advise you not to let him wear it; it's not beneficial."

"Mike likes it. I don't feel safe wearing it myself when I'm out in the City like this. And people enjoy seeing him in it. The man in the lobby laughed and said, 'Is he guarding you or are you guarding him?' It's almost more fun than wearing it myself."

"As you please," Evangeline said and led them back to the office. "Would you like Mary to transcribe your session?" she asked.

"Of course!" They all stepped in to Adams' office and sat in the usual places.

"When is your memoir coming out?" Mrs. McLean inquired. "Am I in it?"

"Everything you say here is always completely confidential," Evangeline assured her. "Not to worry, you will not be mentioned."

"Why not? Aren't I important enough? Who *did* you talk about?"

"It's my own story; you may read it when it comes out. It's already at the publishers." Adams changed the subject. "Let's continue with the reading."

McLean interrupted her. "I want a full transcription. Last time your secretary didn't get the whole thing down. She only wrote what you said."

"We don't do that, Mrs. McLean," Adams said curtly. "It would take too much time. You're paying for my thoughts, not to hear yourself talk."

"But I *want* to hear myself talk! I want to see how I sound."

"I'm sorry but we cannot accommodate you. Had you alerted me in advance, I would have suggested you bring your own transcriptionist along."

"Mary will do it for me, won't you, Mary?" the client asked. Mary looked at Adams. She certainly wouldn't choose to re-visit this encounter by typing it all out.

"Mrs. McLean," Evangeline said definitively, "You've been here before. You know what my services are. We can only do so much and I cannot make exceptions."

"Just do me this one favor. I'll pay you whatever you want."

"It's not a question of money," Adams said openly and patiently. "Next time you may bring your own transcriptionist," she explained. "Now let's proceed." She glanced at the horoscope chart. "You have Uranus squaring your Ascendant this year, which should awaken many latent possibilities in you. You may find some marked opportunities, but things might not develop exactly as you hope or plan." Adams looked up at the client. "Shall I give you a general reading today or are you interested in something in particular?"

"Yes, yes, that sounds wonderful. What I'd like to do is acquire another jewel. I want to get ahold of that ruby elephant that everybody's talking about."

"A ruby would be much more beneficial for you than the diamond. But everyone that's talking about this one will inform you that it's been stolen. No one has any idea whatsoever where that particular stone is, least of all its owner."

"Mrs. Pontin said that the Maharaja was here and . . ."

"Juliet Pontin," Evangeline interrupted her firmly, "cannot possibly have any direct information about who has or has not been to my office."

"I don't really care if he's been here or not," Mrs. McLean continued hastily, becoming more excited. "I just want to get in touch with him. Can you put me in touch with him?" she asked, agitated.

"I'm an astrologer, not a social secretary. I am running an astrology business. If you're not here to inquire about your horoscope, I can't help you."

"I just want that jewel!" McLean barked, clenching her fists. "My fingers are itching for it. You collect the elephants; the thief will probably contact you. If it comes your way, I'll buy it from you, no questions asked, whatever the price. Name your price," she said impatiently.

"Mrs. McLean," Adams responded, now becoming somewhat annoyed. "I make a good living. My needs are few. There's nothing that could induce me to do something that would demand that 'no questions be asked,' as you put it! I am not a black market tradesman. Now. Do you have any questions about your horoscope? If you'd like to spend the session in gossip, by all means. But don't expect me to join in. I prefer to inform you about the future. We've already lost fifteen minutes. You have fifteen minutes remaining. How would you like to use it?"

"I do have a question for you, yes," McLean said meaningfully. "They're giving a party for the Maharaja on Friday. Could you get me an invitation?—I mean," she corrected herself, "astrologically, how can I get an invitation?"

"Well, as I said," Adams answered professionally, "Uranus is unpredictable. Something may appear from out of the blue; nothing is certain. And you may have to put in some time and effort in order to succeed. Your Saturn square Mars demands it. You must focus your attention and not attempt to evade obstacles. I'd suggest you ask your friends, find someone you know in common, perhaps someone who'll be attending the party, who'll bring you along as his guest."

"I've been trying! I don't seem to know anyone he knows. His girlfriend's family is from Seattle, of all places."

"Jupiter is activating your Mars in Libra on your Midheaven right now. That's very good. I'd say cast a wider net. Make some telephone calls. A polite, influential man might be able to facilitate things."

"I went to his hotel and saw his secretary, but he wouldn't let me in."

"If Mike was your calling card, it doesn't surprise me. You can't expect someone like that to see you right away in any case. He has a staff; there are protocols. And this is in keeping with your Saturn square Mars as well. There could be delays; you can't expect immediate gratification."

"I want to meet the Maharaja!" McLean cried plaintively. "*I want to go to his party!*" she emphasized.

"Mars indicates a man, all right? A man might be helpful; try another man. Uranus will sextile your Neptune in the fifth house soon. Maybe an artist, musician or theatrical person could possibly be of assistance. Someone you wouldn't ordinarily consider. An eccentric of some kind, perhaps. Can you think of someone like that?"

"Maybe . . . I think so."

The timer on Adams' desk whirred. Evangeline stood up and Mary followed her.

"Thank you for coming, Mrs. McLean."

"Wait!" McLean shouted impatiently, not getting up. "I still need to ask you about the Hope Diamond!"

"As I've previously told you, my recommendation is that neither you nor the dog wear it. It's not beneficial for either of you."

"But I might want to hock it, to get the money for this other jewel — that is, when I get my hands on it."

Miss Adams glanced down at the chart again. "This is a good time for finances. Jupiter through your second house should be helpful, and I believe you'll have the liquidity you'll need to accomplish your goals. Much is within your grasp this year. However," Evangeline added, more genial now that the session was ending, "You may be getting ahead of yourself," she said as she started walking towards the door.

". . . and I wanted to get my face lifted," McLean added eagerly as she got up and followed the astrologer. "Can I do that this year?"

"Not this year, my dear, I wouldn't advise it. Not with Uranus. I'll consider it for you next time." Adams stopped at her doorway. "Mary will prepare the report for you in the usual manner. My regards to Mike." Adams bowed her head in parting and the client was shepherded out the door.

When Mrs. McLean had gone and the next client, *Vogue* magazine editor Carmel Snow, was safely ensconced with Miss Adams, Mary again thought of the manuscript and looked over at Clara. "Is he down there?"

"I haven't heard anything lately."

"Are you going to come with me?"

"I don't know, Mary. I don't like it."

"Let's do it. There's no problem. He's probably not even there right now. Do you have the new page?"

"Yeah," Clara said grudgingly.

"I'll take my keys," Mary said, standing up. "Are you coming?"

Clara considered, a little distressed. "I guess so."

Mary looked up at the clock on the wall. "We have twenty minutes before the next client arrives. Get a move on." She strode out to reception with Clara reluctantly following her. They stopped at Dorothy's desk. "How was the dog?" Mary asked, smiling.

"Surprisingly gentle. He looked a little sad after you-all left, so I gave him a salt water taffy and that perked him right up."

"Have you heard anything from Jesse?"

"Not a thing. His mother called a while ago, so I rang Mr. Jordan's office and the back room, but I couldn't find him. I haven't seen or heard from him since this morning."

"OK," Mary said. "We're going downstairs to look for the manuscript. If you see him or hear from him, give us an urgent ring so we can prepare."

"All right. Don't you worry," Dorothy reassured her.

"Oh, and will you ask Alexa to cover my desk, just in case Miss Adams wants anything? She should be in conference for a half hour."

"Sure thing, Mary."

• Chapter 23 •

Jeannie was riding down in the elevator with the three Pekingese. The dogs were sitting quietly at attention, listening to Todd, the elevator operator.

"You just need to show 'em who's boss, see? When I take 'em, I don't let 'em go *anywhere* — unless it's where I want to go."

"But Sonny started dribbling as soon as we left the building. I don't know if he can control himself anymore."

"He can control himself, don't you worry. Don't give in to them. You're in charge, just remember that."

"I'm in charge," Jeannie repeated half-heartedly.

The elevator came to the lobby and Todd opened the doors to let them out. "Good luck, and don't be afraid to snap the leash!" he called after her.

Jimmy the starter was at the door and stopped them, sizing up the situation. "Jeannie, I think they need a talking-to after their behavior the other day."

"We had a long conversation upstairs over lunch," Jeannie told him.

Jimmy squatted down by the Pekingese and regarded them sternly. All three dogs now sat and patiently looked up at him with their dark, intent eyes. "Now, boys, I want you to know that Jeannie here is a very nice girl, very nice indeed," he said. "I want you to behave yourselves with her today. The planter is *not* a urinal," he said firmly, admonishing them with a finger. "You boys know that. Now behave yourselves, or you'll be stuck with me again." He winked at Jeannie as he stood up. "All right," he gestured, "off with you now," and he ushered them out the door.

They walked west on West 56th Street and turned around the broad brownstone front of the Carnegie Hall building onto Seventh Avenue. The air was clear and bracing. Lover took the lead, parading down the avenue with his head and tail held high. He breathed deeply, sniffing at the many passing odors of the busy city street. Sonny, less energized, stayed by Jeannie's side. They all stopped at the corner of

West 57th Street to wait for traffic to clear. The dogs were accustomed to the motor-cars whizzing by and paid them no attention. D'Artagnon spied a stick near the curb and strained at his leash to reach it. Jeannie held him back and kicked it to the gutter. D'Artagnon began yapping plaintively for the stick, now well out of his reach. Jeannie held him in check with a firm, "No, Darty. We're going to the park first. You can play there."

The group crossed 57th Street and continued on their way. The sidewalk was crowded with lively men and women enjoying the spring air, on their lunch hour, or going to appointments. Jeannie and the dogs crossed West 58th street and all at once the view became broader and more expansive as the tall brick and stone buildings gave way to rolling fields and horse drawn carriages. They stopped again for the traffic cop at the corner of Seventh Avenue and Central Park South. Motor traffic continued in both directions, through the park and alongside of it. "We'll be there soon, guys," Jeannie encouraged them, looking toward the country-like vista that seemed miraculously dropped into the middle of the busy city. Light green buds were beginning to appear on some of the trees and the air had the definite scent of spring. As they crossed the street and entered the park, there were birds chirping, and crocuses and hyacinths could be seen popping up in a few places on the lawn.

The dogs seemed eager to get to the grass, and as Jeannie turned toward the pedestrian walkway, a man called out from behind her. "Oh, Miss!" he said, running up to them. "I think you lose handbag." He spoke with a foreign accent, had a big black moustache, and was dressed like a workingman. He tipped his cap as he held out a nice woman's handbag.

"Oh, no, sir, not me!" Jeannie said, as she and the dogs continued on their brisk walk.

"Are you sure?" the man inquired again, following them and touching Jeannie's sleeve. "I think I see you drop it."

Jeannie stopped and said. "I didn't bring a handbag. I have enough to handle with these three guys."

The man bent down and held out a hand to Lover who sniffed him and growled a little. Suddenly, he grabbed Lover by the scruff of his neck and D'Artagnon under his belly. Holding both dogs tightly to his chest, he dashed forcefully off, pulling so hard that Jeannie was tugged along; she staggered behind him. "Hey!" she cried out. "*Stop it!*"

Jeannie held tightly to the leashes and tried to plant her feet on the walkway, but the man was stronger. She pulled backwards with all of her weight, but at the same moment the man had also stopped, and holding the two small dogs like footballs, one in each arm, he gave the leads an enormous tug with his whole body. The leashes were torn from Jeannie's hands and she fell back and down, hitting her head on the ground as the man turned and ran away.

In the next instant, D'Artagnon had wriggled his head free of the attacker's grasp and bit deeply into his hand.

"Ahh!" the man screamed in pain, releasing his grip to try to shake the little dog off.

Sonny now sprang forward, making a flying leap and sinking his teeth well into the seat of the kidnapper's pants. The man fell to one knee as he dropped D'Artagnon and reached behind to dislodge Sonny. Lover immediately broke free and bit the man's other wrist, then jumped down and butted his head sharply into his calf, causing him to lose his balance.

"Get off of me, get off!" the would-be dognapper yelled, standing up again as Sonny released his jaws from his rear end. The three dogs began maniacally barking and biting at the man's heels as he ran off over the lawn and disappeared.

Jeannie lay on the grass and opened her eyes, dazed. She looked around her. The man that had attacked them was nowhere to be seen, but the dogs were all sitting quietly beside her. Sonny had his head on her leg and Lover was calmly washing his face with his paws. When they saw her open her eyes, D'Artagnon yapped happily and came over to lick her face. "Hey, what happened?" Jeannie asked as she sat up and began brushing herself off.

Then strong arms were lifting her upward and a cheery voice said, "You all right, kiddo? Looks like you took a tumble."

Mary and Clara stood in front of Mr. Jordan's office. The glazed glass on the door was lettered with "George E. Jordan, Jr." and "Room 901."

"I don't like this," Clara said, looking down the hall uneasily. "He could come back here any minute."

"Don't be silly," Mary chided her. "We have just as much right to be here as anyone. More, really. That's why I have the key. I'm sure Mr. Jordan never intended him to settle in here." She searched for the proper key on the ring; there were a number of different ones for the various offices and cabinets. "Miss Adams sends me down here sometimes to pick things up from Mr. Jordan."

"Only difference being that Mr. Jordan's not here this time. *And* that Miss Adams didn't send you, either."

"Jesse doesn't know that."

"Mary, what if the next client comes? Alexa doesn't take dictation."

"I know that guy, he never wants dictation. Ah, here it is, I think this is it," Mary said, trying the lock unsuccessfully.

"I don't feel good about this," Clara said. "My heart's beating all fast and I can feel myself starting to sweat." She fanned herself with the manuscript page.

"Got it!" Mary announced proudly as she turned the bolt and opened the door. She faced Clara before entering. "Prepare yourself. It's not pretty." They went in and Mary closed the door and locked it, turning the bolt from the inside, and turned on the light.

"You weren't kidding," said Clara as they looked around.

"Just try to ignore the mess and focus on the manuscript," Mary advised. "We need to get back in fifteen minutes."

No one had straightened the room for quite some time. Jordan's desk was covered with various papers, along with three telephones, one of which had been knocked on its side.

A smaller secretary's desk had a typewriter and Dictaphone machine, but both were covered with a slew of miscellaneous papers and dust. There were new steel filing cabinets along one wall, some with drawers open and unfiled piles of papers inside. Some initial attempt at arranging books on bookcases had been made, but here, too, they were simply stacked on the shelves in batches, rather than put in any kind of order. A closet door hung open, revealing a nice business suit and an extra hat and coat. Boxes were piled on the closet floor and on a shelf above the hanger bar. There was a stale, garbage-like odor in the air.

"The manuscript was tied up with a big red rubber band when I gave it to him, so let's look for that," Mary said. She picked up a necktie from the floor and placed it on one of the extra chairs.

They turned to the desk. Among the phones and papers, there were several ashtrays brimming with cigarette butts. What looked like half a ham and cheese sandwich sat on a white ceramic plate from the deli, completely desiccated. The corners of the ham had gone black and the American cheese was orange and cracking. A mostly finished cup of coffee had become a filmy brown mass where the milk and coffee dregs had congealed.

"Let's try not to disturb anything," Mary warned as they looked through the papers on the desk.

"Look at this—" Clara said. "It's a copy of the art magazine that Alexa posed for."

"Just leave it."

"I don't see the manuscript, Mary."

"Let me look in the desk drawers." She drew the top one open. It was full of supplies: pens, ink, paperclips. The second drawer held stationery, legal pads covered with Jordan's writing, and typewritten pages of individual astrological interpretations for the reports. Mary quickly took them out and flipped through them.

Clara looked in the closet. "*Eww!* An old sock. Doesn't anyone ever clean up in here?"

"Just throw it out," answered Mary. She opened Jordan's bottom desk drawer. "What do we have here?" she said, holding up a bottle. "Boodle's British Gin," she read.

"Doesn't surprise me," said Clara.

"Oh, and there are some glasses here, too. We could have a party," Mary said ironically.

Clara had moved over to the secretary's desk and opened a large green ledger book. She leafed through the pages. "Mary, look at this, it's an account book. It shows what everyone's paid."

"We shouldn't be looking at that," Mary said as she came over to take a look.

"It has everyone's monthly pay listed. Let's see what Jesse makes, since he's such a big cheese." Clara ran her finger down a column of figures. "Here he is: $100 a month?" she asked, surprised at the amount. "Can that be right?"

"Let me see it." Mary nudged her aside. "I guess so. That's what it says."

"That's less than I make!" Clara sang out. "The way he acts, calling himself the manager and all, he makes out like he's such a big earner."

"Now you know the truth. Feel any better?"

"I don't know," Clara admitted.

"Mr. Jordan's cheap, you know that. Here, look at what poor Richard makes—only $75."

"That's not right!" Clara returned, alarmed. "He works *very hard*. No wonder he doesn't go out for lunch."

"See?" Mary asked. "You're luckier than you thought. Now let's focus; I don't want to be away from my desk if Miss Adams calls us."

One of the phones on Mr. Jordan's desk rang three long times: something was urgent. Mary stepped over but couldn't decide which telephone was ringing. She picked up the first one, but there was no one on the line.

The second phone rang once again. But before Mary could answer it, Clara frantically whispered, "Mary, someone's at the door." They could see a form outside the frosted glass. Clara hopped into the closet and called out, "Come on!"

"I'm going to talk to him," said Mary.

"No! Remember the bear and the cave? It's too dangerous. Come in here and we'll listen."

They heard keys jangling and the door began to open just as Mary leapt into the closet with Clara and closed the door. It was a bit of a tight fit for the two women. Mary was squashed against the boxes on the floor and she had to bend over to fit under the clothing rod and shelf. Mr. Jordan's coat was in her face, blocking her from Clara. She slid it down the bar and over her head to the other side. "Are you all right?" she asked softly.

"*Ssh!*" Clara admonished her. "I'm trying to listen."

The phone rang again, three long times. They heard Jesse call out in his booming voice, in no particular hurry. "*Hold your horses*... What is it? Of course, I delivered it! Who wants to know? ... Oh, yeah?" He listened, and then his attitude seemed to change for the better. "OK, put her through."

His voice took on a flirtatious and playful tone as he seemed to be talking to a girlfriend once again. "Well, hel-*lo*," he said in a sing-song-y voice. "Nothing special. I'm coaching the boss for a radio interview. She's going on the radio in a few weeks. I was just practicing with her... Technically she's the boss, but she's just a figurehead. I'm in charge... Um hmm... I just met with the publisher about my manuscript today... of course I wrote it, she's not a writer. They call it a ghost; I'm a ghost. That's right... I also saw the Maharaja of Indore the other day."

Clara elbowed Mary in recognition.

"*Stop it!*" Mary whispered.

"Everybody knew he was the Maharaja but us," Clara complained. Jesse continued talking.

"I'm going to show him around the city. They're having a party for him, he gave me an invitation... At the Plaza, tomorrow night... I suspect every millionaire in town will be there, that's all... Well it says I can bring a guest... I'm not sure yet, you haven't been so nice to me lately... Why don't you stop by? I'll tell you more about it. Room 901. I'll wait for you. Bye."

Jesse must have depressed the switch hook to call the operator; he now seemed to be addressing Dorothy.

"Get me my mother back, will you?" he asked. A few moments later, he had her on the line. ". . . yeah, it went OK. Yes, I *went*," he said a little indignantly. ". . . *I did so!* I gave a really good interview."

"Mary!" Clara cried in a whisper. "He's looking for another job!"

"*Ssh!* He'll hear you." They listened some more.

". . . I don't know. He didn't like me. Probably wanted someone older," he said defensively. Jesse listened for little while. "I give you the rent every month! That was an exception and you know it . . . I can spend my money any way I want! . . . I said I'll pay you back and I'll pay you back. I told you I'd call you, and I'm calling you!" Jesse was becoming excited. He listened a little more. "For crying out loud! I don't *want* to be a mechanic with Dad! . . . No, I'm sick to death of the telephones . . . I'm drowning, Ma! *I'm drowning!*" he cried, anguished. "Don't hold me under, for God's sake." He listened a bit again. "I wish you'd *drop dead!*" he shouted. "Drop dead, you old bitch. That's what you are, just a mean, old, petty bitch." He enunciated each word. "You know the doctor said I have a heart problem, I'm not supposed to get aggravated . . . Well it's your fault for arguing with me . . . You know what? I hope I *do* die! That'll show you! Then you can feel guilty about it for the rest of your life." He slammed the phone back down on the desk. "I need a drink." They could hear him rummaging around for the bottle. "Where do you hide your hooch, Georgie?"

"Now I feel bad," confessed Clara, putting a hand to her chest. "I never knew he had a *heart condition*. I've probably made it worse."

"He doesn't have a heart condition!" Mary said as quietly as she could. "He's healthy. He looks very healthy. He's making it up, just like everything else."

Clara fanned herself with the manuscript page. "He sounded desperate."

"He *is* desperate. He's a desperate character. That doesn't mean he has a *heart condition*."

"I just feel bad, is all. I haven't been very nice to him."

"Clara, he was talking to his *mother*! He told her to '*drop dead.*' I feel sorry for *her*, stuck with a kid like that."

"*Oww!*" Clara exclaimed.

"Be *quiet!*" Mary cautioned her.

"You stepped on my foot."

"I'm crammed against these boxes. Can't you move over a little?"

"There's no more room," Clara answered. "And the page is all wrinkled now. Even if we do find the manuscript, I'm gonna have to re-type it."

"*Sshhh!*" Mary warned again.

Jesse had apparently found the gin bottle. They could hear the clink of glass against glass as he poured himself a drink. There was quiet for a few seconds. And then Jesse exploded in a coughing fit; he must have swallowed too quickly.

Mary and Clara heard a knock at the door. They looked at each other, alarmed.

"Who is it?" Jesse asked, warily. They couldn't hear an answer, but Jesse got up and opened the door.

"Hey, little lady," he said, greeting her warmly. "Come on in. Have a seat. We're alone now," he said, a little suggestively. There was a pause. "So, how do you like the office?" They could barely hear the response, but it sounded like a young woman's voice, speaking shyly and not at length.

"It must be that poor girl he's been talking to on the telephone," Clara said. "She got here pretty quick."

"Be quiet," Mary told her. "I want to hear this."

"This is old Georgie's mess, of course," Jesse continued. "I just took over. I'll have somebody straighten it out for me before you come again." It sounded like the girl had asked a question. "I'm the manager; I run the place. All those typists upstairs are under me." She asked another question. "No, Mary works for the old witch. I don't have anything to do with them, thank God."

Clara looked at Mary and raised her eyebrows pointedly.

"How about a drink?" he said. "I'm having one." They heard him open the desk drawer. He put the other tumbler down on the desk and they again heard the clink of bottle on glass.

"I see you got rid of them, huh?" Jesse commented. There was a soft response. "How's the old man doing? The mangy one. Looks like he's on his last legs."

"Mary," Clara said, apprehensive. "He's criticizing the dogs again."

Jesse was laughing at his own witticisms. ". . . like big, hairy rats, with bugged out eyes, that's what I call 'em." But the girl seemed to take exception to what he was saying and they could hear her voice a little more clearly now.

"Mary . . ." Clara said slowly.

"What is it now?" Mary whispered back, aggravated.

"I'm sorry, but . . ." she hesitated, not knowing what to say. "Can you tell who the girl is?"

"It's that girl—whoever it was—on the telephone," Mary answered.

"I'm not so sure," Clara said.

"It's just some girl he picked up, who cares who it is?"

They heard the girl saying, "You don't know them. They come from royalty. They're something special."

"What?!" Mary gasped.

"I think it's Jeannie," Clara said.

Mary burst out of the closet without thinking, to an astonished Jesse. *"You!"* she shouted, pointing at him. "She's *six-teen*. Get out!" She pointed to the door.

"Nothing was going on," Jesse began defensively.

Mary picked up the glass of gin in front of Jeannie and threw it in his face. *"Get out!"* she repeated. *"Now!"* Jesse sat stunned; he wiped the gin from his eyes, blinking.

"I said *now!*" Mary growled. Jesse practically ran out the door.

"And *you!*" she snapped at Jeannie, still sitting in front of the desk. "What are *you* doing here? Where are the dogs? And what's all that dirt on your sleeve?" Her curls were messed-up and her skirt somewhat awry. "He didn't force you to do anything, did he?"

"No!" Jeannie answered instantly. "He just helped me. I fell down in the park and we walked back together. He seemed like a nice enough guy. The dogs are already upstairs."

"He is *not* a nice guy. He's a very not-nice guy."

"He's not nice at all," Clara added from behind Mary.

"Well, nothing happened," Jeannie said petulantly.

"Did you drink any of that gin?" Mary asked.

"No! He poured it. I didn't *have* any of it!" Jeannie said. "The glass looked dirty."

"Aren't you supposed to be back in school?"

"I don't feel like going back. It's almost two o'clock already, I fell down . . ."

"Get out of here right now and go back to your classes. We'll talk about this tonight."

Jeannie left and Mary tried to collect herself. Clara stood a little uncomfortably, then said, "Gee, Mary, did you have to go and throw a drink in his face?"

"He wasn't moving."

"Think how you'd feel if you thought you were alone and two people jumped out of the closet screaming."

"Don't defend him, Clara!"

"I'm just saying . . ."

"No. He's a sick man. A very sick man. And I'm going to make it my business to get rid of him as soon as possible. I did nothing while he tortured you. I sat back when he threatened Alexa. Now it's Jeannie. If I'd done something sooner, maybe this wouldn't have happened. Had it gone any further, I could never forgive myself."

"But what can you do? You're not his boss."

"No, but Miss Adams is."

"Technically Mr. Jordan is."

"It doesn't matter. She would do something about it. She's a little caught up in her own stuff, not very aware of things going on in the office. I just have to bring it to her attention."

"Mary, you'll get him fired."

"I want to get him fired! He shouldn't be working in an office like this. Look at how much time we've spent over that manuscript, for instance. And that's not counting all the personal problems he's created."

"I just feel bad—"

"You wouldn't feel that way if you were still sitting next to him, Clara. Not so long ago, you would've been quite relieved to get him fired. He deserves it. He's getting *himself* fired, for goodness sakes. But we've got to get back upstairs. Is there anywhere else we should look for the manuscript?"

"No. It's not here."

Chapter 24

Clara returned to her desk, while Mary stopped to see Dorothy in reception.

"Mary, Jeannie came in with Jesse and the dogs about fifteen minutes ago," Dorothy said, worried. "Something was wrong. Her dress was a little dirty. And when I asked Jesse what happened, he just disappeared. Jeannie sat down here with the dogs. I got her some water, but when I asked if everything was all right, she only said that she fell."

"I saw her downstairs," Mary confirmed. "I've got to talk to her later and find out exactly what happened."

"Now, the other thing that's going on is that Frank Dodd, the editor, called again. This is the second time today. He got the book. But he still sounded very concerned and he insists upon speaking with Miss Adams."

"What time is it?" Mary asked.

"Just after two o'clock."

"Is Mr. Hopkins here yet?"

"I sent him in a little while ago."

"Good." Mary was determined to resolve the situation with the manuscript page. She asked Dorothy, "Can you call Mr. Dodd back? I'll take it here. Tell him that Miss Adams is calling." Dorothy soon rang the telephone in the corner of the waiting room and Mary picked it up.

"Go ahead please," said Dorothy professionally.

Frank Dodd's warm, mellifluous voice came over the line. "Miss Adams, it's a pleasure!"

"The pleasure is all mine, Mr. Dodd," Mary said, trying to imitate Evangeline Adams' voice and manner of speaking.

"Why, you're harder to get at than the President of the United States!" exclaimed Dodd.

"I hope that's not true," Mary said. "I apologize for the delay. I understood that a messenger was sent yesterday, so we needed to do some detective work to discover what became of the book."

"I know you're busy," began Dodd. "I did receive the manuscript. But the young man you sent to deliver it was not forthcoming about Mr. Jordan, and told me that *he* was in charge. Mr. Jordan hadn't informed me of any change."

That Jesse! Mary thought. "Thank you for alerting us," she said diplomatically as Evangeline. "We've all had some concerns about that young man, but it's now become obvious that we must address the matter."

"As long as we've got the book, I'm very happy," Dodd assured her. "The manuscript looks wonderful, I've been dipping into it already. You have a fascinating life! I think we may have a best-seller on our hands. And I certainly hope I may have the opportunity of meeting you one day very soon."

"Actually, I do have one more correction that's in typing as we speak. May I bring it along to your office this afternoon?" Mary/Evangeline asked.

"Oh, by all means! How is 5:30?"

"I'll look forward to seeing you then." Mary hung up the phone, exhilarated at having pulled off the charade.

"That's really quite good, Mary!" Dorothy exclaimed after disconnecting the call. "You could go on the stage."

"No, thanks. It's a little more stable here. Though sometimes I wonder."

Mary walked back to her office with a great feeling of satisfaction that she had nearly accomplished her goal. She spoke to Clara. "The editor already has a case on Miss Adams." she said, shaking her head.

"Huh?"

"That Mr. Dodd, the editor? I just spoke with him. He's started the manuscript and he's very interested in meeting Miss Adams. Or actually the character that Joe Mankiewicz and Mr. Jordan created. He's gotten all caught up in this idea that she's some kind of a celebrity," Mary said, dismayed. "And he thinks he's going to meet her."

"She *is* nice. And interesting," said Clara. "I'd like to meet her, too, if I didn't already know her."

"I know, but all those stories. I don't think a lot of them are the most accurate."

"But a book like that, isn't it more of a celebration?"

"I don't know. There's a lot of exaggeration. And it was cobbled together so randomly."

"But it seems like the result must be good. I mean, he's the publisher, right?"

"He's so eager to meet her, I made an appointment after work so we could bring the page. Are you coming with me?"

"What about Miss Adams? You're not going to tell her?"

"What's there to tell? As far as Mr. Dodd is concerned, she had a correction and we dropped it off at the last minute. She's never talked to him, it's Mr. Jordan's project. And then I'll feel like we've done all we can do to keep the Maharaja rumors from dogging us year after year."

Evangeline's door opened and her client, Arthur Hopkins, a theatrical manager, stepped out. "When you get closer to the date, write me," Adams said, "and I'll choose a good day for the opening for you." Hopkins smiled, waved, and took his leave.

"Miss Adams," Mary called as the astrologer turned back toward her desk. "Could Clara and I speak with you? It's important."

"Important, eh?" Adams asked, intrigued. "Personal or professional?"

"Personal," said Clara.

"No, professional," said Mary. "It involves the office."

"Well, then, please do come in." Adams said with something of a twinkle in her eye. She returned to her desk.

"We're having a lot of problems with Jesse," Clara blurted out, sitting down.

"Jesse, is it? I can't say I'm surprised," said Evangeline plainly.

"Mr. Dodd has been calling," Mary began as she sat down as well. "We just found out that Jesse didn't deliver the manuscript until today. Mr. Jordan gave it to him before he left. And when we went downstairs to look for it, we found him trying to give Jeannie a drink."

Clara cut in eagerly. "He took over Mr. Jordan's office and got Jeannie to come down there after she brought the dogs back from the park."

Adams frowned but said nothing.

"Miss Adams," Mary continued, "we really think that Jesse was the one who broke into your office. We know he was here, and Mr. Jordan gave him the keys."

"And he seemed very keen on this Mr. Holkar," Clara broke in. "We're pretty sure he replaced your chart for him with his own."

"I'm quite disturbed that Jesse was plying your Jeannie with drink, Mary," Evangeline said. "But the Holkar chart, that's another thing entirely." She paused. "Perhaps you're unaware of the fact that Jesse had come to me some time ago with a request to learn astrology."

"What?" Mary asked, surprised.

Clara was stunned. "When?"

"I suppose it's been a few months now; Mr. Jordan encouraged him quite a bit. He always came in the evening, after everyone else had gone," Adams explained, sitting back in her chair. "Well, as you probably know, astrology can be taught just like any other subject. But as with a language, mathematics, what-have-you, there's quite a bit of memorization that comes into play at the beginning. And Jesse, who lacks a disciplined mind, like Mrs. Pontin, you'll recall—Mercury in hard aspect with Uranus. They're very bright and innovative, sometimes technologically clever. But Jesse couldn't get past the basics. He lacked focus and was not progressing. He approached me one evening last week, wanting to learn how to connect horoscopes with people in the news, and Mr. Holkar's chart was one that I brought out for him to look at—optimistically, and against my better judgment, I now realize. He spilled his coffee on it and drew up a new one for me. But that experience, of trying to read a full horoscope before he knew the basics, may have put him off the study entirely.

"He realized, on some level, that it was beyond his capacity, I'm sorry to say. Doesn't mean he couldn't do it; he was simply not willing to put in the time or effort necessary in order to overcome his liabilities. He's at a turning point in life with his Saturn return this year, and things are either going to engage him in a constructive manner or not.

"In any event, he has spent a number of evenings in this very room, alone with my books. I have trusted him and nothing has ever been amiss."

"But what about the chart blanks?" asked Mary. "They were missing that night, too."

"Well," said Evangeline, "there I'm not too sure. Jesse had frustrations with his studies, which I believe were expressed in his recent difficulty with you, Clara."

"I think he wants Clara's job," Mary said pointedly.

"Oh, I believe he's more ambitious than that," said Adams matter-of-factly. "I think he wants *your* job, Mary. Perhaps mine, too," she mused. "Though he can't have it. No one would hire him for advice on their horoscope. His aspirations are well beyond the reach of his capabilities in that regard."

"I also overheard him making fun of Sonny," interrupted Clara. "And it was really mean."

"It's very sad, very unfortunate," Evangeline said soberly, sitting back in her chair. "I believe I overheard him saying something very similar myself recently, although I never imagined it was about the dogs." She paused and said firmly, almost to herself, "It's reprehensible." She continued. "I must try to walk them again myself. I think they miss Mr. Jordan. But he'll be back tonight. I promise you both that I'll discuss this matter with him very soon. And we'll resolve it, don't worry. Thank you both for your candor."

The rest of the day passed slowly, with Mary waiting impatiently for it to end so they could keep Miss Adams' appointment with Frank Dodd. Finally, all the correspondence for the day was signed, sealed and stamped. Clara had straightened her desk and was already putting on her hat and coat. They said goodbye to Miss Adams and were soon out in front of the Carnegie Hall building. They crossed

Seventh Avenue to the subway station on the corner of West 57th Street, and went down the long flights of stairs together.

"I guess we've lost our prime suspect," Clara said glumly. "Although I still think it could've been him. Just because he didn't break into Miss Adams' office doesn't mean he didn't kill Mr. Fiske or steal the jewel."

They put their nickels in the coin box, pushed through the wooden turnstile, and walked down the next flight of stairs to the subway platform for their trip on the Broadway local.

"Miss Adams doesn't seem to suspect him of anything," Mary said. "And she's a pretty good judge of character." She thought for a moment. "I don't really think he's capable of it, Clara," she said. "Even Detective Sterling thought he was a joke. The more we learned about the Maharaja, the less likely Jesse's involvement seemed to be."

Clara looked down the track for the train. "So who did it? The Maharaja? For all we know, he could be paying Brophy and Sterling for information. And one of his men took the jewel and killed Fiske," she speculated.

"Miss Adams said he was generous. He has a lot of Sagittarius in his chart. And he seems so rich. Why would he go to the trouble of stealing his own jewel? It was his to begin with, and he was trying to get rid of it."

"Maybe . . ." said Clara. "But let's not cross him off the list."

They stopped talking as the train roared into the station. The steel doors opened and they stepped in, sitting down together on one of the rattan benches. They watched the conductor as he looked down the platform, punched some buttons on a brass plate to close the doors, and then buzzed the motorman to continue.

"So, who do you think broke into the office?" asked Clara. "Who had a key?" She thought a bit, then asked, "Mr. Simon?"

"Not his style. And he has other ways of getting what he wants."

"What about Marco? He has all the keys to everyone's rooms."

"Marco, I think, just wants to stay as far away from Miss Adams' radiator as possible."

"That Mrs. Pontin certainly wanted to take a look around the office. And she definitely wanted to get a hold of the jewel," said Clara.

"But she doesn't have a key, remember?" said Mary. "And we can't assume that the same person who broke into Miss Adams' office also killed Mr. Fiske. The killer took the ruby elephant. Like that Mrs. McLean, the intruder assumed that whoever stole the jewel has put it out on the black market, and Miss Adams will have it."

"Miss Adams really looks like a good suspect, doesn't she?" asked Clara. "She knew about Fiske, she knew the Maharaja, she collects elephants. I can see why the detectives were interested in seeing her."

"I'm very glad we're replacing the page," said Mary, "but once that's done, we're right back where we started. We still don't know who the killer is."

The train pulled into Times Square, 42nd Street. The conductor opened the doors, and a lot of people got off.

"This is where I change for the express to Brooklyn," said Clara, looking out. "There's always a big crowd but I usually get a seat since this is the first stop. Though you have to jump for it. There's always someone more tired than you."

The train continued on its way, stopping at Herald Square and then 28th Street, where Mary and Clara got off. They walked east towards Mr. Dodd's building on Fourth Avenue and 30th Street. Mary hadn't been in this neighborhood for a while and it looked completely different. Whole buildings seemed to have popped up surprisingly quickly. Skyscrapers had grown taller and high-rises looked more exclusive. Shops had upgraded and there were a lot more motor-cars on the streets. Like many parts of the City these days, there was a great movement forward. It was the hustle and bustle of success. In a few minutes they stood on the sidewalk and looked up at the Dodd, Mead building. "He's on the top floor," Mary said. "Eleven."

The elevator operator opened the doors and Mary and Clara stepped onto the eleventh floor. Dodd, Mead & Co. was written in large letters on the big double doors to the left. They opened them into a large waiting room and went in.

The reception area was modern and pristine. Done in soft shades of steel blue and peach, there were Native Southwestern-looking geometric patterns on the tiled floor. The receptionist sat in a pool of light provided by two floor lamps on either side of her desk. Potted plants framed her as well, one on each side. Her large, high desk was cut lower in the center to better communicate with visitors. On the front of the desk was a metal grill with a frond-like pattern that echoed the tile design. It all looked rather chic and new, unlike Evangeline Adams' offices, which reflected a more traditional aesthetic.

The two women walked up to the receptionist. "Hello, my name is Mary, I work for Evangeline Adams . . ."

"Oh, Evangeline Adams!" the receptionist exclaimed, interrupting her. "Mr. Dodd has been waiting to see you. He'll be very pleased that you've arrived." She called him on the switchboard, then turned back to Mary and Clara with a broad smile, having accomplished her task. "He'll be right out."

Mary looked at Clara and raised an eyebrow. "Mercury retrograde," was all she said. Clara shook her head slightly in acknowledgement. Frank Dodd, the editor, presently appeared. He was a genial man in his forties, round-faced, balding and impeccably dressed.

"My dear Miss Adams!" he said, relishing the moment. "Your photograph doesn't do you justice!"

"Oh, Mr. Dodd, there's been a mistake. I'm Mary Adler, Miss Adams' assistant."

"Oh! She couldn't make it?" the editor asked, openly disappointed.

"I'm afraid not."

"She had an astrological emergency," cut in Clara. "She was called on to decide whether one of our clients should try to stick out a marathon dance contest or quit. They'd already been at it for twelve hours."

"Oh?" Dodd asked, surprised.

Mary interrupted quickly. "This is my assistant, Clara Cosentino." Clara dipped her head and curtseyed slightly.

"Well, come back to my office in any case." They turned down the hall and into his office, around the corner from reception. Mary gave him the folder with the new page. "I'll be sure to substitute it," he said, placing the folder on his desk.

"Uh, Miss Adams asked us to bring back the old page," Clara interjected.

" —If you don't mind," Mary added quickly.

"A stickler for detail, eh?" Dodd said, chuckling. "It's right here." He turned to a shelf behind his desk and moved the manuscript, still bound in its big red rubber band, to his desk, expertly switching the pages. "Page 83. Done." He handed the old page back to Mary, who felt a wave of relief as she folded it and put it in her purse. "Sit down, please," Dodd suggested.

Mary could see the sparkling of his gold cufflinks and tie pin as the late day sun streamed through the high windows. Frank Dodd sat down, shot out his cuffs, and folded his hands on his lap, relaxed. His pink cheeks glowed with enthusiasm. "I first encountered Miss Adams in an article in a newspaper many years ago. She talked about the Cryder triplets and how they all became engaged at the same time to very similar kinds of men. I found it fascinating, and I began to think that there must be something to this astrology business. Ever since, I guess you could say I've been following her career. I scan a number of newspapers every day and from time to time I find a news story about her. I'd love to schedule a consultation some time."

"Miss Adams charges $20 for a reading," Mary said professionally. "She's very concise. I'd be happy to help you set up an appointment."

"What about these predictions of hers? Do they really work?"

"It's hard to keep track of," Mary said. "But the clients keep coming back."

"Do you have any personal experience with it your-selves?" the editor asked eagerly.

Clara spoke up. "She told my aunt that one of her Pekingese could be a champion and he was."

"Do you mean to say that she does horoscopes for animals, too?"

"Yes," answered Clara. "Then again she said the same thing about another one and it didn't work out."

"I see," said Dodd thoughtfully. "I once read that Enrico Caruso never crossed the Atlantic without first consulting her for a favorable journey."

"Yes," said Mary, "that was before my time, but I think that story is true."

"Have you read the book?" Dodd asked.

"Many times," said Mary. "Some of her more interesting forecasts are in it."

"I haven't completed it yet, but it's simply delightful!" enthused the editor. "The court case! The famous clients! Thank Miss Adams for me once again for such a wonderful memoir," he said, standing up. "And tell her that I'll hold her to her promise to meet with me some time."

"I will. And Mr. Jordan should be back in the office tomorrow afternoon if you have any questions for him."

Mary and Clara were soon on the sidewalk headed back to the train. "Now there'll be no record that the Maharaja ever had dealings with Miss Adams," said Mary with great satisfaction. "When this blows over, everyone will forget all about it. Thank goodness."

"Well, it's still in the papers," stated Clara.

"But no one keeps the kind of paper that would cover it," answered Mary.

"Maybe at the library —" Clara started to say.

" —and if they do," interrupted Mary, "it'd be yellow and crumbling in a year. Those scandal sheets are printed on cheap paper and they'll disintegrate."

"I guess you're right," agreed Clara somewhat reluctantly.

"Of course I'm right," responded Mary. "This is the best thing we could have done."

Chapter 25

The next morning, Clara arrived at the office and hung up her hat and coat. "We were crammed so tight in the subway there was nothing to hold onto. I put my hand on the ceiling. But I was held there anyway by the people crushing into me on all sides. It's an awkward situation, being that close to people. One woman's skin was very nice but the ears, ugh! Let's just say I was reminded that I hadn't scrubbed inside my own for a while." She sat down at her desk and continued talking.

"I sometimes think, when I'm on the subway like that, what's keeping us all in here without going nuts? It'd just take one person to lose control and then the whole car would go wild and start a stampede before anyone could get off at the next stop. But it just doesn't happen, and I've never even read about anything like that in the papers. And then at every stop, there's always someone else who has to get to work and most of the time they manage to squeeze themselves in. It's weird. Sometimes I feel like I want to run out screaming but I don't. I wait it out and then people start getting off and I'm OK again.

"One time going home, I was standing there holding the strap and we were crammed together pretty tight. Some guy who's standing behind me thinks he's anonymous and I don't know where he is and he runs his hand up my side towards my chest. It was this ugly, hairy hand, too, and it was so instinctive, I just screamed and shoved my elbow back into his stomach really quick-like. Built up some momentum, too, in bringing the arm down from the strap." Clara demonstrated the quick jabbing action that disabled the would-be groper. "And I must've hurt him because he let out a grunt and I said, pretty loud, too, 'You try that again, buster, and I'll get the whole car on you.' But then the train stopped, which I guess is the way he planned it, and I've never seen anyone cut through a crowd so quickly. Kind of a little skinny guy but I didn't see his face. And then everyone just went back to standing there, like we were before. Anonymous.

"Although I think they would've helped me if it came to it. Once I dropped my scarf and there's always someone who'll come calling after you, 'Miss, you dropped your scarf.' You see it all the time." She stopped to think for a moment. "Must be nice to walk, though."

"Most of the time it is," Mary replied. "I can walk by the park. You save a little money and it adds up. I can take a streetcar part of the way if it's really raining or snowing. But then by the time I walk to the car, I'm soaked through already. Once I took the streetcar because the wind was so bad, if you can believe it. But most of the time I like to walk. Yeah."

Mary's phone rang; Dorothy came on the line, saying, "Marjory Buchanan is here to see Clara. She says she's not expecting her."

"Hold on," said Mary. "Clara, a Marjory Buchanan is here to see you?"

"Marjory Buchanan," Clara repeated, searching her mind. "Marjory Buchanan. I don't know who that is."

Mary went back to the phone. "We don't know who she is."

"She says she's Mrs. Fiske's housekeeper."

"Oh, Marjory! OK, send her back." She turned to Clara. "It's Marjory, the Fiskes' housekeeper. What's she coming here for?"

In a few moments Marjory came through the door holding a small basket in the crook of her arm. "I'm at my wit's end," she announced, and looked it. The woman who had seemed so self-assured when they'd met her a few days before, now appeared nervous and distraught. "Those detectives have been watching the house, so I didn't dare come sooner. They stepped away at 4:30 in the morning, and since I'd been up all night, I thought I'd take a chance and leave then. I took the subway and I've been walking around the park all morning, thinking of what's the right thing to do."

"Marjory, sit down," said Mary, indicating the seat next to her desk. Miss Adams wasn't down from her apartment yet; they could speak undisturbed.

Clara came over and asked, sympathetically, "What happened?"

Marjory sat down. "Here's some gingerbread and oatmeal cookies for you," she said, putting the basket on Mary's desk. "They're some of cook's specialties."

"All right . . ." Mary said slowly, not understanding where this was going.

"But that's not what I'm here for. That's just a disguise." Marjory took a deep breath and looked at Mary and Clara in turn. "I hope I haven't made a mistake. I didn't know where to turn. I don't like to go against the police. But I had to protect Mrs. Fiske. And this was the only way."

"The detectives came back?" asked Clara.

"They never really left! Standing out in front at all hours of the day and night. And Mr. Fiske still lying downstairs with the visitors and all." She shook her head in annoyance. "You said that your boss collects elephants, so I thought she'd know what to do."

"But what happened?" Mary interrupted. "Is Mrs. Fiske all right?"

"Mrs. Fiske doesn't even know I'm here. She's as well as can be expected, under the circumstances. But I didn't dare tell her about it."

"About what?" asked Clara.

"It's not really that complicated," Marjory said and sighed, taking an oatmeal cookie from the basket. "I just don't know how to begin." She held out the basket to Clara, who took a piece of gingerbread. Mary declined with a shake of her head. "Do you remember the banging on the pipes the night you two were there, in the Fiskes' parlor?" Marjory asked.

Mary said "Yes."

"I called our Bill Westbrook, the plumber I told you about," she said as she chewed some cookie. "He's a very good man, very thorough. He bled the pipes but he also wanted to clean and check the radiator to be sure there wasn't a problem that was causing the banging. There's a steam pipe that runs through the whole house and connects to the radiator," Marjory said, "just as you have here." She nodded to the radiator and riser pipe against the wall. "In checking the pipe, Bill noticed that the oak flooring beneath the radiator was uneven. And then he saw that a piece of boarding was loose from the floor. Below that wood piece is a cavity. And in the cavity was this . . ." Marjory turned to her basket of baked goods and pulled aside the towel that covered it. Beneath the bread and cookies was a smooth red object about the size of her clasped hand. She took it out. Clara gasped.

"The Maharaja's jewel?" Mary asked.

"The very same," said Marjory, who quickly put it back in the basket and covered it again, taking another cookie.

"How?" asked Clara, dumbfounded.

"Mr. Fiske was a careful man. Very careful, indeed. When they bought the house many years ago, he had several hideaways created. There's a safe in his study downstairs, for instance, where he'd put his cash and other valuables. And under that radiator in his parlor, he had the floor man install a removable board. When it was in place, no one could tell that it wasn't solid oak, all the way to the wall. There's only a few inches visible below the radiator anyway, and if you don't look really close, you wouldn't see it. The police searched the entire house and never noticed. Mrs. Fiske had a small jewelry case for her more valuable pieces, diamonds and the like. And she'd put them down there when she wasn't wearing them, and replace the little door. I've done it myself for her on several occasions. But for the last ten or fifteen years, Mrs. Fiske hasn't been socializing or going to evening parties very much. So she got a safe deposit box at the bank. She hasn't used that cubbyhole in years. No one ever knew about it but the butler, myself and the Fiskes. And I had even forgotten it."

"Do you think the butler did it?" asked Clara.

"Mr. Goodall?" She waved the thought off with the rest of her cookie. "Oh, no, never in a million years. He's been with the family far longer than I even have. I didn't tell him about this, though," she said, nodding toward the basket. "Thought it best. Bill Westbrook hadn't a clue of what it was and I pretended it was just another valuable of the Fiskes'. He seemed delighted at the idea of such a hideaway, though."

"So . . ." Mary hesitated. "Mrs. Fiske?" she asked.

"I don't know," answered Marjory. I don't like to think about it. But seeing as the police have been looking all over for this thing, and that they were so suspicious, I wanted to get it out of the house right away. Sat on a bench in the park to rest myself and dropped off to sleep early this morning. And a policeman woke me with his stick, banging on the bench. 'Move along!' he says. I took such a fright, seeing as I had the jewel in the basket and all. But he only took me for some kind of vagrant. It's a pretty piece, so I judged that your Miss Adams might have a better idea of what to do with it."

"She might know," confirmed Clara.

"As I said, I hope I'm doing the right thing, and I've thought about it long and hard. I think I can trust you. And Mrs. Fiske always set great store by what Miss Adams had to say."

"We'll give it to Miss Adams," Mary assured her.

"Well thank goodness. Thank you both. I shouldn't stop; Mrs. Fiske will be missing me. I left a note for Mr. Goodall, saying that I had a family emergency."

"That's all right. We'll take care of it," said Mary. "You might want to go out the back way, though, just on the chance someone's watching the door. Tell Jimmy in the lobby that you want to take the 57th Street exit."

"I'll do that, and thank you again. I must be off," Marjory said, standing up. "I'll trust to Miss Adams' judgment, whatever it is."

After Marjory left, Mary turned to the basket to examine the piece. Clara joined her, sitting down next to Mary. Mary took out the elephant figurine and placed it on her desk. It did appear to have been carved from a single red stone. It was incredibly smooth, flawless and translucent, in a dark pink-rose. The elephant was perched on a round globe set on a gold base. Mary stood it on her desk. She had never seen anything like it; it was absolutely beautiful. She brushed a few cookie crumbs off its sides. The elephant was realistically portrayed and carved in great detail. Its four feet were drawn together, as if it were balancing on the globe, with its hind legs firmly planted and its front beginning to rise as he reared up. The elephant's ears fell against its back and were smoothly blended to the rest of its body. The trunk was upraised and curled back against its head; the carver must have hollowed out the small empty spaces between the curve of the trunk and the elephant's forehead as well as between its belly and the legs. The tusks lay against the trunk and its mouth was open in what looked to be a joyous greeting. The workmanship was fabulous and the elephant gave the overall impression of energy, vitality and liveliness. Where there were turns in the surface of the stone — the folds of the ears, the wrinkles of the knees, the eyelids, the texture of the trunk — the ruby revealed depth, with gradations of color.

Mary turned the jewel to see all of its sides, and the ceiling lights gave it brilliance and reflected white flashes as it turned.

Clara whistled. "Look at that," she said, impressed.

"It's perfect," said Mary as she slowly revolved the figurine on its base. "Absolutely perfect." They could hear Miss Adams coming down the stairs and Mary took the piece, saying, "We'd better put it away before anyone comes in." She quickly returned the elephant to Marjory's basket and once again covered it with the goodies and towel. They were in a quandary. Here was the exact thing that the police were looking for, but giving it to them would further implicate Evangeline Adams in the murder.

Could silly, self-involved Mrs. Fiske have actually been involved in the death of her husband? Or had someone else hidden the jewel after Mr. Fiske was already dead?

Chapter 26

Mary buzzed Miss Adams on the intercom and heard her say, "Good morning, Mary. What's going on out there so early today?"

"Miss Adams, we need to show you something," was all Mary said, releasing the lever.

"Then come right in."

Mary opened the office door, carrying the basket over her arm, and Clara followed her, closing the door behind them.

"Why, whatever are you up to Mary?" said Evangeline. "You look absolutely breathless this morning. Sit down." The three Pekingese were already seated in their usual places and looked up with watchful, if passive, interest.

Clara spoke first. "Mrs. Fiske's housekeeper came over with some gingerbread and oatmeal cookies," she said, sitting on the sofa next to Lover and petting him.

"And she wanted you to decide what to do about this—" Mary said, placing the elephant on the desk in front of the astrologer and sitting in the chair opposite her.

"Oh, my!" Evangeline exclaimed. "It's Mr. Holkar's jewel, isn't it?" she asked.

"We think so," confirmed Clara.

"What an absolutely beautiful creature!" Adams cooed, turning it around slowly on her desk. "It's a little world all onto itself. Look at the intricate workmanship. And what a brilliant conception!" she announced. "You see, the ruby, the gem of the Sun and the heart, represents life-giving energy. But the rosy hue, I believe, gives it more of an influence toward peace and spirituality, rather than worldly power, as a deep red ruby would do. It reinforces faith, and reduces negative thoughts," she said, turning it. "And then the depiction of the elephant picks up on the spiritual theme. The elephant symbolizes well-being and fulfillment, but also obedience to dharma. With its trunk raised and rearing up, it grants protection and power. So you see, they've combined all of these attributes in this little sculpture. A masterwork," she decided. "A masterwork by a master craftsman."

Adams continued thoughtfully, almost to herself. "So this was Mr. Holkar's stone." And then to the others, "How appropriate for him it would be. Don't forget—the Holkars are descended from the Sun. And the ruby is the gem of the Sun. Clara," she asked, "run and get us Mr. Holkar's horoscope, will you please?"

Clara did as instructed and soon returned with the replacement chart that Jesse had drawn up, the one that had first interested them in Holkar.

"Sagittarius rising, you see? Just like Mrs. McLean, remember?" she asked, pointing to the chart. "But Mr. Holkar has the Sun, Mercury and Venus all rising in the sign of Sagittarius, afflicted by Saturn on the Midheaven. That Saturn is like a heavy weight bearing down on him at all times." Evangeline opened her bottom desk drawer and brought out the folder with Dr. Smith's notes. "Now let's go to the page for the Sun." She leafed through the pages until she found the one she wanted. At the top, it said "Sun—Ruby."

"See, here," she ran her finger down the page. "Sagittarius rising. 'Suitable. Brings honor, power and status.' The ruby will help mitigate the malefic influence of Saturn in his horoscope." She straightened her eyeglasses. "The same would be true for Mrs. McLean, who also has Sagittarius rising. Much preferable to that horrible blue diamond she's so attracted to. Still, it couldn't override the horoscope in Mr. Holkar's case, could it?" she mused. "It's a tremendous jewel and I believe the very same one that the Wendel sisters described in their session the other day. Do you remember, Mary? The one at the head of the cane, that broke as he was presented to the royal couple?"

Mary remembered the dramatic incident of the Maharaja tripping and falling in front of the royals at the Delhi Durbar as a young man.

"It does look like it may have once stood atop a walking stick," Adams said, putting her hand over it. "Very comfortable to hold, too." She looked up at them again and continued. "You can see it in his horoscope, can't you? And in his life story. How Saturn is one of his biggest obstacles to overcome in this lifetime. It frustrates his self-expression, but the ruby supports it. The challenges with authority figures are therefore diminished by the ruby. And the demands and worries that surround him will feel reduced. It's a life of obligation, being born into royalty like that. Your options are very limited. But as much as this jewel might aid his vitality and power, it couldn't overcome Saturn's influence entirely, could it? He still fell—in more ways than one—both literally and figuratively. Saturn near the Midheaven can be difficult. Napoleon, Abraham Lincoln, Oscar Wilde—they all had this placement in their horoscopes and suffered reversals of fortune. Saturn will do that when it's at the top of the sky. Doesn't mean it will happen to everyone; you must always examine the entire horoscope. But it's a danger.

"Of course, to get the greatest benefit, you must wear a gemstone close to the body. But a stone like this, it's much too large for that. And then again, with its spiritual connotations, the stone skews its influence away from material things. The Maharaja fell before the King and Queen. He ultimately lost his throne, but he's gained, one hopes, in freedom and understanding. Now he's released from the oppressive responsibilities of the state. And I think he may find some happiness with this young American woman. They had a nice compatibility between their horoscopes. He told me, you know, that they plan to be engaged after Saturn passes the opposition to his Moon this fall."

"Engaged?" asked Clara.

"That's right," Evangeline said simply. "Everyone deserves a second chance, don't you think? Or a third. Or fourth. Though I'm not certain exactly which one it would be in his case. Let's just say that everyone deserves *another* chance." She smiled and clasped her hands together on her desk and looked at her assistants with interest, then turned back to the ruby in front of her.

"Dr. Smith's notes also contain instructions for authenticating precious stones. I'm eager to try that out. Let's see, where is it now?" She paged through the notes. "Ah, here it is. 'Identification of Genuine Rubies.' There are several tests. Place on a lotus bud—no, . . . place in cow's milk . . . Ah, here's one that should suit: 'When pearls are placed next to a genuine ruby on a silver platter in sunlight, the plate will look black, the pearls will glow red, and the ruby will shine like the Sun.' I think we may have those three ingredients near at hand. Mary, would you go upstairs and fetch me the silver plate that stands on my mantelpiece?"

She hurried upstairs to get it.

Adams unclasped her pearl necklace and removed it from her throat. "That's necessary item number two." She looked out the window. "And I believe old Sol is ready to cooperate as well."

Mary returned with an oblong silver platter and placed it on Evangeline's desk. It had a handle on each end, a timeworn patina, and an intricate filigree pattern etched on its surface.

"From Grandma Smith—supposedly made by a student of Paul Revere. I'm not sure if that's *quite* true." She placed the ruby in the center of the plate. "And now Nanny's pearls." Evangeline put her pearls in a circle around the ruby. "Mary, would you do us the honors?" she asked.

Mary carried the tray over to the window next to the sofa, and Adams followed, standing beside her. Clara and Lover turned from the couch on Mary's other side, Lover standing up with his front paws on the arm of the sofa to see. Sonny now roused himself from his nap and sat up, taking notice. The morning sunlight was already streaming brightly through the high windows. Mary placed the tray on the windowsill. The pearls no longer looked white, but seemed to be reflecting the ruby's red glow, appearing almost like small rubies themselves. And against the brightness of the large red stone, the platter took on a dark, blackish hue.

"I guess it's real, all right," announced Clara.

Little D'Artagnon slipped past Mary and hopped up on the windowsill next to the platter to investigate. He stepped up tentatively and licked the side of the stone. Evangeline quickly lifted him to her and held him in her arms.

Mary moved the tray somewhat so that the ruby elephant fell directly under the sun's beams. It instantly glowed as if an electric light had been turned on inside of it, dazzling in its intensity. It was as if it had come to life. They were awestruck at the way the jewel's rosy radiance appeared to outshine the sun's rays. It didn't shimmer or glitter, but emitted a strong, consistent, deep glow. The elephant now seemed to be even more lifelike and its expression had transformed into one of tremendous beneficence, as if it were giving them a great blessing.

"It's like an eternal flame," Evangeline said wonderingly as she stood back and regarded the jewel. "A little star on earth."

Mary didn't quite know what that meant, but she had a strong feeling that she agreed. She remembered the words of the monk, Swami Puri, saying that she'd be going on a journey. The journey, she now saw, had been about this jewel, and it was nearly over. She felt as if the monk had indeed been with her all along, supporting her, without her having noticed it before. She was aware of a sense of peace and acceptance, and realized that all of this—the jewel, the monks, Mr. Holkar, the Fiskes, Clara, Evangeline Adams and even Jesse—were part of a much larger plan, and that they had each played their parts in the way they were meant to do. She started when Adams spoke.

"We'd best take it off the windowsill, Mary. It's shining such a beacon that if the police are watching the building, they'll be sure to come up here to investigate." She put D'Artagnon down.

Mary once again lifted the tray and placed it on the astrologer's desk, and they all sat down again. Evangeline took up her pearls and put them back around her neck.

"It's precious," she said. "And rare. I doubt there's another one like it in the world. You don't find many stones like this, without a visible flaw. No cracks, no bubbles, no fissures. And who knows how many hundreds—or thousands—of years old it is. A stone like this is ageless; another reason it's considered divine. This one calls to mind the gemstone that Swami Vivekananda spoke about thirty years ago. The legendary Syamantaka stone, do you remember?"

"Right," said Clara. "The guy that hung himself on his own necklace?"

Evangeline nodded. "Legends, myths, ancient stories, they all have a way of being based on something real, and even factual sometimes. Down through the centuries the tale may be embellished to make it more memorable. The story of the Syamantaka might come from the same time as some of my earliest astrological texts, perhaps 1,500 years ago or more. Mr. Holkar or his family had the means to obtain the jewel. The Wendels described him at the Delhi Durbar with almost a supernatural power about him; they were transfixed as he carried the walking stick. That impression might have come from this gem. But just like the man in the story, he was unable to put it to secular use." Adams looked at Mary and Clara with a pensive gaze.

"I think I know what to do with this elephant. Of course I'm tempted to keep it for myself! It seems to have a soothing vibration. But I'd like to sleep on it. I'll bring it upstairs and set the dogs as sentries over it tonight. We'll lock it away for safekeeping for the moment." She opened her center desk drawer, placed it toward the back, and locked the drawer with a small key she wore around her neck.

"Miss Adams," asked Clara, "do you know who broke into the office? Because they might be back, especially now that the jewel is here."

"I do have a suspicion, and I'm sorry to say that it's an obvious one pointing to a member of our staff."

"Jesse?" asked Clara.

"No, not Jesse. Not this time. The morning of the break-in, Sonny found something glittering on the floor by the glass case. It was familiar to me; I knew I had seen it somewhere before. But it wasn't until I saw Alexa sitting at your desk yesterday, Mary, that I remembered who it belonged to." She opened her right-hand desk drawer and brought out a delicate gold necklace, holding it up by its chain.

Mary's heart sank. It was Alexa's pretty little jade elephant charm.

"The catch is broken, you see? It must have fallen off when she was here that night."

"Are you sure?" asked Clara. "Maybe Jesse just planted it here to take suspicion off of *him*."

"And she didn't have the key," added Mary.

"Why don't we call her in and ask her about it so that we can clear this matter up?" Evangeline picked up her phone and asked Dorothy to have Alexa come in to see them. "I'd like you two to stay please, if you don't mind. I know it's awkward, but it will go more smoothly with her friends nearby. Mary, please sit over there on the sofa with Clara. Mercury retrograde continues. Perhaps we'll change our minds about something, and the truth will out," Adams advised.

Mary recalled that Alexa had dated Mr. Fiske and appeared surprised and disturbed by his death. Yet she was a complex Scorpio who had been able to keep her involvement with Mr. Jordan and Mr. Fiske a secret. Could she have played a part in the murder?

Chapter 27

There was a soft knock at the door and Alexa stepped in.

"Good morning, Miss Adams. How may I help you?" she asked in her Russian accent.

"Sit down, please."

Alexa looked inquiringly at Mary and Clara, then sat in the client's chair across from Miss Adams.

"Alexa," Adams began, "Sonny found this trinket on the floor right after someone broke into my office Tuesday night." She held up the necklace. "This is yours, isn't it?" she asked, handing it over to Alexa. "I believe I've seen you wearing it."

"Yes, is mine, of course," admitted the employee.

"And Jesse told me that you were here that evening after hours. Is that true?" Evangeline asked, not unkindly.

Alexa again looked to her co-workers for support. Clara gave Alexa an understanding nod. Mary looked down, feeling embarrassed and conflicted.

Alexa bowed her head into her hand. "Yes, was me, was me. I was here."

Clara asked compassionately, "Alexa, what happened?"

"Is long story," she said uncomfortably, looking at Adams. "I did nothing, really. I looked around. They're so pretty, the elephants. But I didn't even touch anything . . ." She faltered, not knowing where to begin. "Jesse threatened me. I posed for artistic pictures. Nothing bad; is artistic."

"They were in *Artists and Models* magazine," cut in Clara. "She looked beautiful."

"Jesse thinks pictures a secret. He wants money or he tells you to fire me."

"Alexa, you know I'd never listen to gossip or jump to conclusions about one of my staff. It's blackmail, pure and simple. You had only to come to me."

"I know. I know, Miss Adams. I was scared. You are wonderful boss. I like my job here so much, I like the office . . ."

"And Jesse?" Adams asked.

"I said no. I paid him nothing. But I was very angry. Was not first time he made trouble. Jesse is not nice man."

"Mr. Jordan and I will be addressing the issue of Jesse very soon. Go on."

"Mr. Jordan gave Jesse keys. At lunch, I see keys left on Jesse's desk. No one else there. I took them, out of anger, to give him lesson. But then I think, why not make copy? I went to hardware store across street; not expensive. I copy keys, put Mr. Jordan's back on Jesse's desk right away."

"But, my dear, why ever would you do such a thing?"

"Miss Adams, my husband, Leo, is difficult man. Very difficult—stubborn. His sign is Taurus. He is choreographer, stage designer, has many talents. But not good husband. We have baby, is hard for me sometimes. He goes away for work. When he has job in New York, he's sometimes working all night."

"I'm sorry," said Adams. "That must be difficult for you."

"Leo—Leo can be very rough. If I don't do what he says, is hard for me."

Adams made sympathetic noises.

"I talk to Leo," Alexa continued. "Sometimes I say things that happen in office. Leo bought me this necklace for luck," she said sadly, looking down at it in her hands. "I tell him about your elephants. He reads all about Mr. Fiske and the elephant jewel in newspapers, and he wants that elephant from Mr. Fiske. He says, 'Miss Adams will have. She is big lady of elephants in New York. You look and bring home.' I say no! Miss Adams good to me, I don't steal from her. Leo keeps pushing me but still I say no. Then I find keys and I think, well, why not look? I please husband. Not take anything. Say truthfully big elephant is not here. And I can see beautiful elephant collection, too. Is like museum." She looked around her.

"Alexa, you had only to ask, of course I would have shown them to you."

"Jesse makes trouble for me. I also want to make trouble for him. I'm sorry, Miss Adams. I know I was wrong. But he had keys. Anyone finds out, it goes to Jesse, looks like he is the one to break in.

"I come in after work and Jesse is here. He makes same threats again. I pretend to leave, but hide behind switchboard in reception. I hear Jesse leave and then Mary and Clara come in and leave with you again. I come back, unlock office door and go in, look around. I swear, Miss Adams; is whole truth. I take nothing. I do nothing. Dogs bark and I leave. But now Leo knows I have keys, he wants me to take dogs away. I say, no! I like my job here; is not right."

"No, it isn't right," Adams said sympathetically.

"I think sometimes Leo is crazy. All he talks about is big ruby elephant. He comes to office with me yesterday; I don't let him come in. He says he waits outside, follows Jeannie and dogs to the park." She was becoming more excited and angry. "He says he went to park and they chase him! Those three sweet little dogs, they chase my Leo." She folded her arms together and frowned ironically. "He says they're 'wild beasts,' should not be loose in society."

Evangeline smiled lightly to herself.

"Big man, wants to steal big jewel. Ha!" Alexa looked at the others with contempt in her eyes. "What kind of man is that?" she asked derisively. "A coward, afraid of some little animals!" She looked over at the three dogs, who were sitting calmly and observing as usual.

So that's what happened in the park, thought Mary. Jeannie had said nothing about the dogs chasing anyone.

Evangeline spoke again. "Alexa, I understand why you acted as you did. But this is a very serious matter, stealing the keys and breaking into my office. How can I trust you again?"

"Miss Adams, I know. Is bad. I return keys. Please don't fire me—we need money. My Leo is out of work and baby needs food. He can be very rough sometimes," she said as she slid up the sleeve of her dress, revealing an ugly purple bruise on her upper arm. "See what he does to me the other day? Please, please let me keep job." She put her head in her hands and burst into tears. "Let me keep job."

"We'll discuss it later," said Evangeline after a few moments. "That's all for now. Why don't you return to your work?"

"Yes, I will, thank you," Alexa said, wiping the tears from her eyes as she got up to go.

"Alexa," Mary called after her. "Remember I asked you about the chart blanks? Did you by any chance take some from us that night?"

She turned back. "Chart blanks? No. We have plenty in closet."

"OK, just asking."

"Mary," said Adams after Alexa had left. "I believe that Jesse took those chart blanks. Sometimes people behave irrationally. Perhaps he thought it would make him feel like a real astrologer when he knew in his heart he would never be one. Or he was simply angry, like Alexa, and wanted to lash out."

Later that afternoon, Mary was pretending to work while eavesdropping on Miss Adams and Mr. Jordan. Jordan had returned from Boston and was in conference with his wife; he had left the office door slightly ajar.

"But you know I wouldn't have even met you without his parents . . ." Jordan argued.

"I agree, I understand. But I cannot have him in this office any longer," stated Evangeline simply. "I think I can accurately say that he has disturbed the peace of mind of nearly everyone on our staff."

"But a veteran, Evangeline, of the Great War. I'm sorry. I find it heartless."

"That may be. But it's also heartless to see his negative behavior impact on the entire office and do nothing. It's heartless to mock a poor defenseless little creature nearing the end of his life, someone who's only given love and protection to everyone around him." She looked toward her beloved pet. Sonny was sound asleep under the couch, lying on his side. His feet were making little running motions and his head occasionally jerked, as if dreaming of a more lively and active time. "Cruelty to animals suggests larger problems," she said firmly. "I kept still when he upset Clara and the other secretaries. I kept still when he actually mocked me—and you, too, if you'd like to know. No one is sacred. But now he's crossed the line."

"My father practically on his death bed and now this," Jordan said plaintively.

"I hadn't understood the scope of the problem. Do you realize that he was plying young Jeannie Adler with drink?"

"Are you sure?"

"I know Mary to be a person of sterling integrity. She wouldn't make such a charge if it weren't true. Perhaps a different environment for Jesse, where he's more directly supervised, would be best," she reasoned. "He should have never been put in a managerial job, I'm sorry to say."

Jordan did not want to concede. "It puts me in a very awkward position . . ."

"Nevertheless," Evangeline interrupted him.

"I don't like it one bit," he replied.

"Mr. Jordan," Evangeline began, adamant. "If I've learned anything from astrology, it's that things change. He's experiencing his Saturn return; you know he's at a turning point. This environment is no good for him and he's no good for anyone else about him."

"But I run that office and I'm satisfied with his work!" Jordan whined. "It should be my decision!"

Adams became stubborn and spoke distinctly. "George, I love and respect you. But in this instance you're simply wrong. I've managed this business for nearly thirty years and have done quite well, thank you. You're well aware of how much I appreciate all that you've done, and well paid for it, too, I might add. I've taken a *laissez-faire* attitude toward most everything you do. But here and now I draw the line. He's undermining everything we do. So let's move on with our more pressing business, shall we?"

George Jordan looked at her for a moment, exhaled deeply and said nothing.

"Write him a good reference letter, if you'd like," Evangeline said lightly. "Whatever you feel is fair."

Jordan began to leave, but with his hand on Evangeline's office door, he turned back to her and said, "All right. But you owe me. Next time it's *my* way."

"Yes, my dear, next time," Evangeline stroked him with her voice as she returned to her work with an amused look on her face. "Next time."

After Jordan left, Miss Adams called Mary into her office. "Would you telephone these people please and decline the invitation? The party is tonight and I won't be able to attend." She handed Mary a card and continued. "And where is that little diamond-studded elephant from Mr. Holkar? The one I asked you to take when that young Indian woman was so upset. I want to send it to her at her hotel — Mrs. whatever-her-name was."

"Rahman."

"Yes, Mrs. Rahman."

"She's staying at the Ritz-Carlton. The elephant is locked in my desk drawer."

"Excellent. I don't think I should keep something of such controversial energy, do you?" Adams asked, not waiting for an answer. "And her heart seemed so set on having it back. You could probably consider most of these elephants second-hand, before they found a home here." She gazed at her collection in the glass case against the wall. "But I'm generally not privy to their histories, I'm glad to say. In this case, it just doesn't sit well. She seemed absolutely apoplectic about losing it; it might affect her health with all of the Virgo in her horoscope. Perhaps Richard can deliver it for us today. Or tomorrow if he's busy."

"Gee, Miss Adams," said Mary. "Are you sure he's trustworthy? It must be worth a lot." She remembered both his low salary and her feeling that he had been hiding something.

"Of course, of course. Don't concern yourself. I'm sure it will be fine."

"All right. I'll ask him," Mary said, making a note of it on her pad as she closed the door and left the office. She remained suspicious. Jesse may not have the capacity to accomplish anything more than the theft of some papers, and certainly not a murder. But Richard, she sensed, had more depth and purposefulness. And she had no idea what he was capable of.

Mary closed Adams' door, sat down, placed her papers on her desk, and turned to Clara.

"Miss Adams wants me to ask Richard to deliver that little diamond elephant to Mrs. Rahman." She unlocked her desk drawer, brought out the beautiful jeweled figurine, and turned it in her hands. "It must be very expensive. I don't really trust Richard, but she insisted."

"I don't *not* trust him," said Clara, "but he has that Pisces way about him: you don't really know where he stands."

"I know," agreed Mary, putting the elephant away again. "And here's the invitation Jeannie saw, to Holkar's party."

Clara immediately stepped over and picked up the card. "Beautiful paper," she said, holding it up to examine it. She read, "*Mrs. John Miller of Seattle requests the honor of your presence at a reception to be held for His Royal Highness Tukoji Rao, Maharaja of Indore, Thursday, the eighth of April, nineteen hundred twenty-six at half after six o'clock in the evening at the Plaza Hotel, Fifth Avenue and Central Park South.* That's tonight, Mary. Is she going?"

"No, she wants me to call and say she can't make it."

"Let's go then," Clara instantly replied.

"*What?*" Mary asked, appalled.

"Let's go," Clara said calmly as she sat down next to Mary's desk and leaned over conspiratorially. "You can pretend to be Miss Adams again. And see? It says here at the bottom that she can bring a guest. So I can go, too."

Clara, we can't go," argued Mary. "I don't want to be a party crasher. This invitation is for Miss Adams, not us."

Clara turned the card over and studied it more carefully. "I don't see her name on it anywhere . . ."

"You're doing that Aries thing again!"

"What Aries thing?"

"Jumping in," stated Mary flatly. "And asking questions later. We need to think it through. Miss Adams would probably know a lot of people there, it's not like the publisher where she'd never met him before."

"Look," Clara said sensibly, "all we need to do is get in the door. After that, we can just be ourselves and make apologies for Miss Adams."

Mary exhaled audibly. "I don't know," she said.

"It's perfect," Clara exclaimed, leaning back in the chair. "We'll see if Jesse's there . . ."

"He won't be there," Mary snapped. "You just want to see Mr. Holkar again."

"Mary, I personally don't really care about Holkar. But it's our chance to see what the situation is."

Mary thought about it. "We have the ruby elephant, but we still don't know who killed Mr. Fiske."

"And if the detectives come back," added Clara, "and find that jewel in Miss Adams' office, she'll be in even more trouble than before."

Mary realized she was right. If they found her with the jewel, Evangeline would definitely be arrested. "Maybe we could pose as waitresses," she suggested. "Could your cousin get us some uniforms from the hotel?"

"I am *not* going as a waitress. If we're going, we're going as guests. Everybody wants to go to this party, and look at how easily this invitation practically fell in your lap. I have a nice dress I can wear and I'm sure you do, too."

"But maybe we should ask Miss Adams—"

"Don't do that!" Clara shot back. "What if she says no?"

"That's exactly why we shouldn't go."

"Mary: what have we got to lose? The worst they can do is turn us away at the door. And they won't do that because—" Clara held up the printed card with a flourish " – *we have an invitation*," she said triumphantly as she placed it in front of Mary.

"I don't see how attending this party is going to help us. Mr. Fiske might've hidden the jewel in that cubbyhole himself for all we know."

"Yes, but the ruby and the murder are linked, somehow, I'm sure of it. And there are a lot of people who want that jewel."

"That's true," agreed Mary. "Mr. Simon, of course. Mrs. McLean. That psychic, Mrs. Pontin." She thought a little more. "Florenz Ziegfeld. Though somehow I don't especially see *him* committing the crime," Mary said wryly.

"No, but we don't know enough to really know. I don't see Mr. Simon as the violent type. And I guess he's too successful to stoop to murder."

"You're right. And we could say the same for Mrs. McLean. Although she sounded desperate for the ruby and she seems very resourceful. I'll bet she's managed to wrangle an invitation."

"What about Holkar himself?" asked Clara.

"I think if he had anything to do with it, he would've left town by now."

"That'd be a little too risky," countered Clara. "And he has important social obligations; he's moving toward an engagement. Marjory said he'd been at the house a few times. He could've had an argument with Fiske that got out of hand. Or it could've been his secretary or someone like that. We need to go and see who looks suspicious."

"*Looks suspicious?*" asked Mary critically. "What exactly does that mean?"

"I don't know," Clara brushed off the thought. "But if we go, we'll learn more." She stared at Mary steadily, with a determined look in her dark eyes.

Mary began to relent. "If we go, we have to be unobtrusive. We'll just stay on the outskirts and look around. I don't want to have to talk to Holkar again."

"Mary, everyone who'll be there wants to talk to Holkar, you'd have to fight 'em off to get to him."

"Well . . ." Mary considered it.

"The Plaza: Fifth Avenue and Central Park South at 6:30 p.m. Shall we be fashionably late and meet there at 7:30?"

"We'll see." Mary picked up the invitation, put it in her purse, and snapped it shut.

Chapter 28

At 7:30 that evening, Mary stood on the corner of Central Park South and looked across the street at what appeared to be an enormous French chateau. The light-colored stone of the nineteen-story Plaza Hotel dominated the block. The lower floors were strikingly lit in the growing dusk, casting a golden glow around the huge structure.

A few motor-cars pulled up to discharge fancy-dressed guests. A uniformed doorman opened the back door of another car, and out stepped a woman in a cloak of ostrich feathers that surrounded her like a cloud. She strode smartly up to the doorway and disappeared inside.

Mary caught sight of Clara hurrying toward her from Fifth Avenue. She looked vibrant, in a sleeveless red voile dress that showed off her figure. The full skirt fell below her knees and bounced as she walked. She wore several strings of faux pearls around her neck and a matching beaded headband.

"You look beautiful," Mary exclaimed.

"So you did have a party dress," smiled Clara. "Fancy that."

Mary's dress was of dark blue satin that nicely complemented her auburn hair and fair complexion. It had cap sleeves and embroidered sunbursts of silver on the skirt. "Miss Adams bought it for me when we went to London last year. She likes to take me to some of the society dinners and I needed something that was nice enough. She thought it had an astrological theme."

"Well it looks great."

"We can still change our minds," suggested Mary.

"Not on your life," replied Clara as she took Mary firmly by the arm and led her across the street to the hotel. As they approached, the doorman tipped his hat and opened one of the heavy gilt doors.

"You see?" Clara said as they passed inside. "When you dress the part, nobody asks any questions." The hotel lobby was a riot of marble and gold, with a huge burgundy rug on the floor before them and a massive crystal chandelier above, reflected back in a wide mirror behind the solid marble check-in desk.

A clerk greeted them as they advanced: "How are you tonight, ladies? Having a good evening?"

"We're here for Mrs. Miller's party," said Clara confidently and somewhat casually, imitating what she thought was an upper-crust accent.

"Just down that hall and to your left," the clerk said, indicating the way.

"Let's not play games, Clara," Mary warned. "Just be inconspicuous please."

"He didn't even ask to see the invite," said Clara, greatly pleased with herself.

They stepped inside the doorway into a bright and spacious anteroom. "*Here's* where they're going to check it," said Mary, concerned. There were gray and turquoise marble walls, gilt-edged decorative archways, and another large chandelier. A long table stood in the middle of the room, decoratively covered with floral arrangements; it blocked the entrance to the ballroom beyond. Several well-dressed men sat and stood behind it and intercepted a middle-aged couple as they entered, apparently checking their names off a list.

"I don't know if I can do this," said Mary, as her mouth went dry and her stomach churned.

"Where's your sense of adventure?" asked Clara. "What happened to the spy who broke into Mr. Jordan's office?"

"That was different and you know it. We had a perfectly legitimate and good reason for being there," Mary said.

"And anyway," Clara said definitively, "I know that guy: the one on the end is Holkar's secretary. I met him in the car the other day." The secretary was a middle-aged man dressed in a tuxedo, who stood at the side of the table.

"Come on," Clara urged, walking up to the secretary. Mary followed.

"Hello," Clara said warmly. "I believe we met the other day in the yellow phantom."

"Oh, yes," the man said politely, nodding. "Nice to see you again."

"This is Evangeline Adams," Clara said.

". . . and this is my assistant, Clara," Mary added.

The man repeated their names to an Indian fellow with a large moustache, seated beside him at the table, who consulted his list. "We have you right here. Thank you," he said, smiling graciously.

"Oh, Miss Adler," called a familiar needling voice from behind them. "What a coincidence to see you."

Mary turned back toward the door and felt a twist in the pit of her stomach. It was Detective Jack Sterling. And he had said her real name. They'd been so close and now they were caught. "Let's just go," she said to Clara under her breath, wanting to run away.

Clara took immediate action, leaning toward the secretary with an affected tone. "Pardon me," she announced. "That man by the door over there is bothering us."

The secretary instantly stepped toward Sterling. "Detective, we've already asked you not to interfere with our guests," he said firmly. "If you can't follow Mrs. Miller and the Maharaja's instructions, we'll have to ask you to leave the hotel."

"Thank you, my good man," Clara said, laying it on a bit thick.

The English secretary turned back to them, "I'm awfully sorry you were disturbed, Miss," he said, then looked at Mary, "Ma'am. They're investigating something that has nothing to do with us, of course," he said apologetically. He ushered them into the ballroom door with a sweep of his arm and Mary and Clara quickly went in.

"I need to sit down," Mary said, exhaling deeply. They had entered an intersecting corridor and Mary took a seat just inside.

"See, Mary, I told you," Clara said triumphantly. "That's it. We're safe." She laughed and sat down next to Mary. "I never imagined Sterling would be *here*."

"Sergeant Brophy's could be hiding behind a door," Mary added, looking around. "We'd better get it over with before he comes after us," she said, getting up.

"Let's get something to drink," said Clara, agreeing, "and then we'll stand to the side and study the situation."

They entered a vast, ornately designed ballroom. Striking marble columns ran along the walls, with gilt sconces at their tops and mirrored archways running between them. The tremendous classically inspired ceiling featured geometric designs in rust and gold, along with a colorful floral motif. At the corners and in several places below the ceiling, were round, gilt-edged paintings of angels and cherubs. The room was lit with electric candelabrum high on the walls, but most striking were six impressive chandeliers that were hung along the length of the room. It was gorgeous, yet at the same time a little overdone.

Dozens of tables were arranged around a shining hardwood dance floor. A large dais stood at the other end of the room where the guests of honor appeared to be seated. People were chatting and laughing and having a good time. The men were dressed in tuxedos and the women dazzled in a rainbow of colorful, sparkling dresses. A twelve-piece band, complete with a grand piano, strings and saxophones, stood on the left-hand side of the room, playing soft jazz versions of popular Broadway tunes from a raised stage set in an alcove. A number of couples were dancing.

They stepped inside. Mary took one look and said ironically, "Just three hundred of their closest friends." To their left was a long table with beverages and a bartender. A large rack, fully stocked with sparkling glassware, stood behind the bartender, who had chiseled features and jet-black hair. Dressed in a black vest and bowtie, with a spotless white shirt, he blended in seamlessly with the tuxedo-clad men in the room.

A huge block of ice had been hollowed out and was decorated with flowers and greenery, and a large bowl of punch was set in its center. There were dozens of bottles of soft drinks and pitchers of juice, as well as several spritzer bottles set before the bartender on the table.

"Hey, Clara," he said good-naturedly, "how did *you* get in this fancy joint?"

Clara laughed. "*I* had an invitation. This is my friend, Mary."

"Hi Mary," the bartender said. "What can I get you?"

"Some punch, please," said Mary.

"How about a glass of the house champagne?" joked Clara. "Actually, make that two."

"Coming right up," the bartender said jovially, playing along with a wink as he poured some fizzy drinks into tumblers.

"We have to mingle," Clara told him. "See you later."

"Right-ee-oo," responded the bartender as he turned to the next guest with a smile.

Clara gave a glass to Mary, who took a deep, thirst-quenching gulp. Suddenly, she sputtered and spit some of it out: it was burning her mouth and throat. "*Clara, this punch is off!*" She felt like she'd bitten into a sour lemon.

"Didn't you hear me ask for champagne?"

"They'd really serve alcohol in a public place like this?"

"It's a private party," announced Clara with a shrug, sipping her drink, "and it's awfully good. Try it again."

"We shouldn't have anything to *drink!*"

"Why not? You're not allowed to buy it or move it. But you can drink it or give it to someone. My Uncle Frank makes wine in his basement every year. It's copacetic if it's only for your family. We're not doing anything wrong. And you could use a little—it might relax you."

They stood to one side and looked around, sipping their champagne.

"Who was that man—the bartender?" Mary asked.

"Oh, him? That's my cousin Luigi."

"Your cousin? How many cousins do you have?"

"A lot."

"And he just happens to work here? Did you know he'd be working tonight? "

"How could I know that? He freelances." Clara paused as they continued to look around, then exclaimed, "Look over there, at the end of the room. I think that's Holkar's girlfriend and her mother; I saw them in the car the other day. It must be the Millers, the ones throwing the party."

Mary and Clara moved closer to the wall and studied the situation. Miss Miller, presumably the one whose birth date Holkar had brought to Adams, sat at the center of the dais across the room, looking a little bored. Her close-cut brown hair was fluffed around her head. She was slim, with a slightly bulbous nose and small mouth. Her narrow shoulders made her head look a little big. Her mother, a more dynamic and attractive woman, stood next to her with a drink in her hand, talking to some guests with animation. She wore large eyeglasses and appeared to be in her forties.

"The girl doesn't look like she's having such a great time," observed Mary.

"Nothing special, is she?" commented Clara. "But I'll bet that gown is a beautiful fabric when you get up close."

Mary recognized a cheerful voice that rang out nearby. She turned to see the two Wendel sisters approaching them.

"Why, look who's here!" cried Ella Wendel happily, clapping her hands.

"We never expected to see you here, Mary," said her sister Georgiana.

"Lovely," Ella said, looking at them brightly. "And this must be your colleague?"

"Hi, Miss Wendel. This is Clara, my assistant."

Ella Wendel looked beautiful in a luxurious floor-length dark gray chiffon dress of decades before, covered with black lace and trimmed in rich, black velvet ribbons. Her gray hair was upswept in a pompadour style, and she wore a large diamond necklace around her neck. She carried a closed fan.

Georgiana, as usual, looked much younger and very chic in a shimmering black knee-length dress and long strings of pearls.

"Mary, don't turn around," whispered Clara hastily, "but we've got company."

"Is it Detective Sterling again?" Mary demanded, staring straight at Clara. She could see the Wendels react, but they were smiling and waving.

"Yoo-hoo! Over here."

Mary turned around to see Tom Holkar striding toward them with a broad smile on his face. She gasped. "Now we're really in trouble."

"He doesn't look upset to me," answered Clara.

Holkar was suavely dressed in a satin-trimmed tuxedo. His shirt looked both expensive and new, and large gold cufflinks shone at his wrists. He looked subdued but elegant. As he approached the group, he gave them all a slight bow.

"Are you ladies all enjoying yourselves?" he asked solicitously. "Lovely room," he said, glancing around.

"Yes, we've been here many times," replied Georgiana.

"But we can't have you all just standing about," said Holkar, admonishing them gently. "Which one of you ladies would like to dance?" He looked at Ella and then Georgiana pleasantly.

"Oh, no, Mr. Holkar," demurred Ella, obviously flattered, as she fluttered her fan. "We don't know the latest steps. But Miss Adams' envoy here might."

Oh, no! thought Mary, frozen in place. *Please, not me.*

With one quick movement, Clara took Mary's drink out of her hand and pushed her forward with the other. Holkar offered his arm.

"I'm afraid I don't remember your name," he said as he walked her to the dance floor.

"It's Mary."

"Mary. I take it Miss Adams was unable to attend?"

"She—she had a previous engagement," stammered Mary, terrified.

The band began playing a lilting version of Jerome Kern's "Once in a Blue Moon." Holkar led them off, putting his hand lightly on her waist and taking her right hand with the perfect amount of pressure and space between them. Mary was surprised how easily he led her. He danced expertly, his movements relaxed and sweeping, though he gazed past

Mary to the young woman at the table. "The Millers didn't believe in astrology," he commented, "but now that Miss Adams has given me such a good forecast, I think they'll be making an appointment themselves soon." He smiled.

Mary, somewhat stupefied, wasn't sure how to respond.

Holkar continued, "Nancy Ann is a bit under the weather this evening, poor dear. She needs to have her appendix out, I'm afraid. But her mother insisted that she come."

"I'm so sorry," said Mary, genuinely concerned. *Why would this mother insist her daughter come to a stupid party when she was sick?*

"I'm sure she'll be all right," replied Holkar. "I had the doctor look in; it's not an emergency. And Miss Adams also said the operation could wait." They moved together quietly for a bit; then Holkar spoke again. "I haven't consulted Miss Adams very often. Do you find her accurate?"

"She's probably the best you'll find in New York," answered Mary sincerely. "But astrology isn't like a science. She can't always say for sure whether something will happen or not. But when you're aware of what to expect, you can handle things better." Mary thought of how Adams had described her understanding of astrology. "It's kind of like a game of chess. There are several types of pieces all moving and interacting in different ways. Each of us is one of those pieces. We all have our goals, but there are limitations in how we can cross the board. So you can only do so much to control the outcome."

"Ah, a game of chess. I rather like that," said Holkar. "Although in life, when the king falls, the game is not necessarily over," he said a little pensively. "Miss Adams was confident I'd have rather a better year — something to do with Uranus, I believe. Our astrologers in India don't consider that planet."

"I remember. Uranus sextiles your Moon; that shows new conditions, but Saturn will also oppose your Moon this fall, so you need to proceed carefully."

"That's right, I recall now. Mustn't rush into things."

They were quiet once again. Mary softly hummed the melody along with the band. She could almost hear the lyrics, *Once in a blue Moon, you will meet the right one; once in a blue Moon, find your dear, delight one.* She was beginning to enjoy herself and gazed up at the chubby cherubs on the wall. They looked happy. She swayed to the soothing music as she circumspectly studied Holkar. *He's certainly good-looking*, she thought, now that she was near enough to see his long, dark lashes and regular, even features. *And he's a graceful dancer.* The musical number ended, and the guests all came to a stop and applauded.

Mary snapped out of her reverie and returned to reality. "Mr. Holkar," she said, "I hope I'm not being forward, but the detectives have been bothering Miss Adams about that ruby elephant that Mr. Fiske lost."

"Why on earth would they involve *her* in that dreadful business?" he asked, surprised.

"Because she has so many elephants. And she also has clients who are close to Mr. Fiske."

"*What is it about that elephant?*" Holkar asked, bewildered. "I've tried to be rid of the blasted thing for fifteen years," he said candidly. "It's finally gone and I told the police not to bother; it's well insured. But they're rather intent upon returning it to me."

"I think Mr. Fiske told a lot of people about it before he died," said Mary.

"Such an old piece," Holkar said, shaking his head. "Well, not to worry. In the morning, I promise I'll ring up the detectives. They shouldn't be troubling Miss Adams."

The band now began a jaunty arrangement of "I Want to be Happy," complete with saxophone solo. Out of the corner of her eye, Mary caught sight of a sparkling juggernaut heading straight towards them. "Mr. Holkar," she quickly said, nodding toward the lady, "that's Mrs. McLean, and she's desperate to buy that ruby elephant."

"What a bother. Why did Fiske have to expire and leave me with this mess? He promised to handle it for me." He sighed and made to dance Mary toward the center of the floor, but Evalyn Walsh McLean was instantly upon them.

McLean appeared in a flash of white and blue. She wore a sheath-like, shimmering, cream-colored dress with a short, feathered train. An extremely large, teardrop-shaped diamond on a long diamond chain rested on her chest, with the blue diamond, the one her Great Dane, Mike, had recently worn to the office, suspended below it. The jewels were breathtaking and sparkled like the chandeliers. Mrs. McLean was petite and the blue stone looked much larger than it had on Mike.

What would she do with the ruby? wondered Mary. She guessed it would be given to Mike since it would clearly be too large for Mrs. McLean to wear.

"Can I horn in?" she asked assertively, tapping Mary on the shoulder. They stopped. "How nice to see you here, Mary," she said, looking up at the Maharaja expectantly.

"Mr. Holkar, this is Mrs. McLean," Mary dutifully informed him.

"Very nice meeting you," Holkar replied as he bowed lightly and backed away. "Though I must fly — there's Mrs. Miller waving to me from across the room." He nodded and waved. Mary didn't see anyone waving back. "Mary, we'll meet again, I'm sure," he said. "Wish me luck." And he was off.

"Of all the nerve!" McLean complained, standing with her hands on her hips, quite put out.

"You'll have to follow through," returned Mary.

"Yes, indeed I will," said Mrs. McLean as she watched the Maharaja heading toward Nancy Ann Miller and the dais.

Mary was horrified to see Clara standing nearby, amiably chatting with Nancy Ann. She followed in Holkar's wake to intercept her. The Maharaja sat down and the young woman immediately turned all of her attention to him.

Mary drew Clara aside. *"What are you doing here?* I thought we were going to be unobtrusive?"

"I was just complimenting her on her dress. It's a radium silk *crepe de Chine* . . ."

"Forget about the dress!" Mary interrupted her.

"She seems nice enough," said Clara. "Doesn't look suspicious."

"Neither does Holkar. Remember his Sun in Sagittarius rising? He was pretty open. The only thing he seemed to be interested in was Nancy Ann. Everyone is looking for that jewel except maybe its rightful owner," she added. "He really wants to be rid of it. And he was genuinely concerned about the detectives coming to the office, said he'd ask them to leave us alone.

"And as for Mrs. McLean," Mary continued, "I just don't think she has the wherewithal to kill Mr. Fiske. Especially when she's got the means to pay a ransom for that ruby." Mary smiled. "And look around you." She paused dramatically as she scanned the room. "No Jesse. And what about Holkar's secretary? I was too distracted to notice; did *he* look suspicious?"

"Nah, I guess not," admitted Clara.

"So that's it then," concluded Mary. "We're all finished here."

"But the party's just getting started!" cried Clara. "And I didn't even get to dance yet. Luigi'll give us another drink . . ."

"Stay if you like," Mary said. "But it's been a long day. I'm going home." She saw a hesitant young man shyly approaching from one side. She looked up and smiled at him, subtly indicating that he should join them.

"Excuse me, Miss," he asked Clara, a little flustered. "Would you care to dance?"

"You bet!" Clara exclaimed as she took his hand. "Toodeloo, Mary! See you in the morning."

Mary smiled and watched the couple as they shimmied onto the dance floor. She took a long, lingering look around the magnificent ballroom as she made her way toward the door. They had the jewel. And the Maharaja, she admitted, probably didn't kill anyone. In spite of herself, she felt relieved. But she still had an uneasy, lingering feeling that Henderson Fiske's murderer remained free.

Chapter 29

Mary and Clara reviewed their adventures on Friday morning, but it had been an eventful night and they were both a little tired. Miss Adams hadn't opened her office door yet. Mary sat at her desk with a cup of coffee. Clara was reading the morning paper.

"Mary, listen to this. It's about Holkar." She read aloud. "*Seattle Girl Will Not Wed Maharaja, Says Mother. Party to Leave New York on Sunday.*

"*There is no possibility of a romance between Miss Nancy Ann Miller of Seattle and Prince Holkar, formerly Maharaja of Indore, Central India, Mrs. Jennie Miller, the young woman's mother, declared yesterday. Emphatically denying rumors and speculation as to the possibility of a marriage between the American girl and the former Indian ruler, Mrs. Miller said: 'The Maharaja arrived in New York a few weeks after Nancy and I returned from Europe. I have known his highness for many years as I have many friends in Bombay and have visited there often. I saw him several months ago and invited him to come to the U.S. to see the country and be my guest in Seattle. My daughter and I will merely be his guests on our trip across the U.S. The Maharaja is kind, generous and above all else, a gentleman. His views are broad and in the background of his life there is a wealth of culture and liberal education.'*

"*Miss Miller is a tall, slender girl of about twenty-three years. Gracious in manner, she is exceptionally attractive, and while attending a local moving picture theater the other evening with the former Maharaja, attracted considerable attention because of the marked contrast in their complexions.*

"*A student friend of Nancy Ann from the University of Washington, Alpha Phi house, doubted that she could accept a Hindu who already had two wives for a husband. Her mother said Miss Nancy is under the care of physicians for a mark near her right eye and she is taking radium treatments for its removal.*

"Can you believe it?" asked Clara, putting down the paper. "I wouldn't call her 'exceptionally attractive.' And I don't know how they came up with twenty-three! We know for a fact that she's only nineteen."

"Just didn't want to make her seem too young, I guess," commented Mary.

"And the way the mother talks about no romance and all, it just makes it sound more like they *are* involved. They're already going to the pictures together."

"Exactly," said Mary.

"And you think these people have easy lives," Clara added, "but here she has to have a wart or a mole or something removed." Clara looked down at the paper and thought a bit. "I didn't notice it, though . . . couldn't have been *that* bad. Maybe she has nothing better to do but to go in for this plastic surgery." Mary didn't repeat anything about Nancy Ann's medical situation.

Evangeline opened her door and joined them in the inner office. "Good morning, ladies," she said cheerfully. "Do you know, last night I went downstairs to see Will Rogers at the Hall, you remember, the ticket our landlord Mr. Simon gave me? There was a nice crowd, the lights went down, and I was all set for an enjoyable evening when who should materialize in the chair right beside me but Mr. Robert Simon himself!"

"Oh, no!" exclaimed Clara, laughing. Mary smiled and sat back to enjoy the story.

"Oh, yes indeed, my dears. And he proceeded to talk of nothing else but the ruby elephant. I couldn't keep him quiet. Finally, at the intermission, I turned to him and said in the most earnest of tones, 'Mr. Simon, I have it on very good authority — *very good authority, mind you* — that the stone is in the hands of a courier on his way back to India.' He tried to interrupt me and I said, 'Not another word. It's God's honest truth. See if I'm not right. You'll hear no more about it.' Well, he took me at my word and stayed to watch the show. We actually had quite a nice evening. Will Rogers said, 'Good judgment comes from experience. And a lot of that comes from bad judgment.'"

Mary and Clara laughed. Evangeline added, "It's funny because it's true. We learn the most from our mistakes. Now come into my office; I need to discuss things with you both."

Once they were all seated, Evangeline began. "I have a note here from Mrs. Fiske. She's selling the house on West 9th Street. She'll be taking a rest cure up in Saratoga Springs. And then she'll go on to stay with her sister in Newport."

"Good," said Mary. "Now she'll have all of Mr. Fiske's money and won't have to put up with such a horrible husband anymore."

"Did she stay with him just for the money?" asked Clara.

"Oh, no, not at all. Mrs. Fiske always had her own money," Evangeline answered. "That was part of the dynamic of their relationship. Mr. Fiske was extremely wealthy, no doubt about that. But he could never compete with his wife's fortune. She inherited a vast amount of money from her own family."

"Then why stay?" asked Mary. "She didn't sound very happy with him."

"Mrs. Fiske has a Gemini Sun, so she's very adaptable. But she also has Venus in Taurus. It not only attracts wealth, it's also very constant. And her affections, ruled by Venus, are fixed. She'll have quite a time overcoming the loss of her husband, I'm afraid."

Evangeline continued. "I've known Mrs. Fiske for many years. And she does have some challenging patterns in her horoscope. But above all, it's always seemed to me that she lacks a strength of will. And I've often thought that she might be overusing the sleeping draughts.

"Mrs. Fiske is of a certain age, and she's probably been taking laudanum or something like it for decades; it's been a treatment for insomnia for as long as I can remember. The authorities have made it more difficult to obtain in recent years. But Mrs. Fiske, or any person of her class, I can assure you, would have absolutely no trouble whatsoever in getting a doctor to write a prescription for exactly what she wanted to have. And once one is in the grip of a narcotic drug, it eats away at your willpower.

"One of the main ingredients of laudanum is opium. And opiates can cause confusion and even hallucinations. Mrs. McLean once told me that she imagined her home crawling with reptiles while she was attempting to break a morphine habit. Did you notice, Mary, that Mrs. Fiske's story of the jewel included some hallucinatory elements? She felt the elephant was watching her, that her husband was talking to it and so forth? Both sounded somewhat far-fetched to me. And then her recent reaction to the noise from the pipes is also a clue. Sensitivity to noise can be another symptom of narcotic abuse."

"Is she a junkie?" asked Clara, shocked. "You read about them in the papers, shooting up." She made a face thinking about it.

"Oh, no, no," Adams reassured her. "I wouldn't classify her as such. And I don't believe Mrs. Fiske would use a hypodermic needle in any case. Too distasteful. But there is probably an addiction there. These medicines were a necessary evil of our modern times, many thought, to tranquillize a population made anxious by technology. Since I was a girl, they've insisted that we all have great anxiety due to the growth of steam power, the expansion of wireless telegraphy, the spread of the periodical press," she counted each item on her fingers, "and of course, the mental activity of women," she added scathingly. "And in the wake of the Great War, our minds are considerably disordered. A lot of balderdash, if you ask me. But you can't argue with the fact that the pace of life has accelerated and we may be overstimulated, especially with the radio and moving pictures today as well. Perhaps a symptom of the Aquarian Age that's now upon us.

"In any event, opiates were considered miracle drugs for years and probably still are in medical circles. Used properly, they can be helpful. But once a habit, it can be awfully difficult to break.

"Well, now, all of this is by way of introduction to my main point. I believe that Mrs. Fiske killed her husband." She paused. "With the ruby elephant," she added emphatically.

Mary felt a sinking feeling in the pit of her stomach. She instinctively knew that Evangeline Adams was right.

Adams went on. "Mrs. Fiske admitted to being under the influence of a drug. She was hallucinating. Opiates aren't particularly known to make one violent, but Mrs. Fiske had frustrations with her husband for many years, and he appeared to be quite a difficult man. I imagine him asleep in his armchair, with the elephant nearby. She sees it as the evil thing that's destroying their marriage. And in her distress and confusion, she takes it up and knocks him over the head with it. And after hitting him, she returns the jewel to their old hiding place beneath the radiator, goes back to sleep and dismisses it all from her mind.

"I don't like it, but it's the only logical explanation. There were no signs of a break-in, nothing was disturbed, and the authorities are casting a ridiculously wide net for suspects. No one but Mr. and Mrs. Fiske would've known about the jewel's hideaway. And Mrs. Fiske, as I've known for many years, has a strong animal passion indicated in her horoscope."

"Animal passion?" asked Clara. "What does that mean?"

"Judging the temper of the animal passions: an astrological technique for measuring how much we're able to control ourselves in moments of pressure and strain. In this particular case, Mrs. Fiske has Mars in Taurus in the twelfth house squared off against her Moon. We don't see it—it's hidden in her twelfth house. But when activated, by Saturn recently for Mrs. Fiske, it can unleash pent-up violence."

There was a knock at Evangeline's open door. She looked up. "Marco! Just the man I wanted to see."

"Miss Adams," Marco said, glowering, "I'm here only because Mr. Simon is telling me to come and look at your radiator again. I thought we covered everything the other day," he said, aggravated. "There's nothing more I can do."

"Oh, no, Marco, you're quite wrong," Adams said, getting up and coming toward him with much pleasure. "I believe I've actually solved our little problem."

"Oh, you have, have you?" Marco asked bitingly. "And when did you become an engineer?" he asked, putting a hand on his hip and glaring at her.

254 THE PRECIOUS PACHYDERM

Evangeline paid him no mind. "Come right over here and you'll see." She lifted the lightweight grilled cover from the radiator and set it aside. "Mary and I were talking about radiators just the other day and it got me to thinking. See here, where the pipe is leaning against the floor boards?" She pointed. "I watched it last night when the heat came up. As the pipe is heated by the steam, it expands. And when it expands, it pushes against the floor boards and that's where the banging comes from. It's actually more of a snapping noise, but the cover dampens it somewhat, making it sound like a bang."

Marco's attitude instantly changed. He kneeled down to get a better look and examined the pipe closely. "I see what you mean. The pipe is pressing against the board already. When it expands . . ." he looked up at Adams. "You could be right," he said, standing. "I'll send Artie up to take a look at it. He's got a narrow wallboard saw. He'll cut away, just a little, around that pipe. That may just do it." He started walking out. "Leave it open for now; I'll send him up right away."

"Thank you, Marco. But I'd prefer this afternoon, around three o'clock, after my clients have left for the day."

"I'll let him know."

"Thank you, Marco." Adams beamed. "You see, Mary, the housekeeper's story about the hideaway beneath the radiator made me think. Mercury is still retrograde, you know, giving us another little puzzle to solve. And I realized that I had never actually examined this instrument for myself. I needed to do further research. As soon as I looked, it occurred to me right away. However, maybe it's simply our friend the Syamantaka's influence."

"I don't know about that . . ." began Mary.

Evangeline continued. "It's too bad we can't keep it. I've felt very clear and relaxed since it's been in my possession. But under the circumstances, it's simply much too dangerous to consider, linked as it is with the murder. And the ruby is also not a very good stone for a Pisces rising like myself," she said, sitting back down.

Adams then unlocked her drawer, took out the jewel, and placed it before them on the desk. Mary again marveled at how exquisite and luminous it was.

Evangeline announced, "We're in possession of a valuable object and must agree on its disposition. Mr. Fiske is gone for good, and he appears to have been a thoroughly dislikeable figure by all accounts. Mr. Holkar doesn't want it; it's obviously the piece that broke when he was presented to the King and Queen and is probably associated with that most embarrassing incident in his life. And he certainly doesn't need the money. Mrs. Fiske didn't own it—in fact she detests the thing. I almost feel that something in the stone may have compelled her to attack her husband. He was such a materialistic man. It's reminiscent of that character strangled by the necklace of material gain, or the Maharaja falling while trying to exert his status and power. It won't work for that purpose. I like to think it wasn't Mrs. Fiske's fault; that she was only the instrument. But that's just my opinion.

"I see no reason to facilitate anything whatsoever for Detective Brophy or his cock-eyed cohort. They have done nothing but bully me, Mrs. Fiske and countless others, I imagine. And then of course, with a piece like this, there's a spiritual element that comes into play, since this is a large, living stone, Sattva, it's called in India, remember? It's a perfect being; I think we demonstrated that yesterday. And aside from anything else, the detectives are simply not evolved enough to know how to handle it properly."

Evangeline paused, leaned forward on her desk, and looked at them earnestly. "The monks were right. I feel certain that this is the sacred relic that Swami Puri talked about when he came to see me, that he expected to come into my hands—the Syamantaka stone. Treasures like this belong to the incarnation of the god who presides over the temple. But of course the prince of the realm controls that. An unfortunate combination of the religious and secular.

"But first and foremost, this one does have metaphysical properties. It may help the monks reach a higher state of consciousness and attune to the divine. I did a little background reading last night. Krishna let the Syamantaka remain on earth under the condition that it stayed in Dwarka."

She paused to admire the stone, then looked again at her assistants. "I believe it should be returned to the monks. Give to Caesar what is Caesar's; and give to God what is God's. Unfortunately, this jewel falls somewhere in between the two. But since I come down on the side of God, I vote for the monks." She regarded them intently now. "Do we all agree?"

Mary and Clara looked at each other thoughtfully and nodded.

"There's no going back once we decide," Adams added. "You're both sure you won't have second thoughts later on?"

"Miss Adams," said Mary, "we really liked the monks, they should have it. But there was something that happened when they were here . . ."

"It's hard to explain . . ." added Clara.

"We think that they hypnotized us or something," concluded Mary.

"Not *bad* hypnotized . . ." clarified Clara.

Evangeline looked at them, delighted. "No, my dears. Swami Puri only revealed to you your true nature. To do that, you need to detach from the material world. He has one foot on the earth and one in Infinity at all times; that's what makes him so remarkable. You two recognized it—whether you knew what was happening or not. And that makes you remarkable, too." Adams clasped her hands in front of her on the desk and again looked at her assistants attentively. "So we all agree? I can arrange for the stone to return to India with the monks."

Mary said a firm "Yes," and Clara nodded in agreement.

"We're all privy to this secret, but we must try to keep it between ourselves. I won't even be telling Mr. Jordan; no need for anyone else to be involved."

"I won't tell anyone," said Clara.

"Me neither," said Mary. As beautiful as the jewel was, she wanted to get rid of the thing; it had caused enough problems.

Adams picked up the phone and spoke to Dorothy. "Please send Richard in to see me, won't you?"

"Richard?" asked Mary, surprised. "Is he involved, too?"

"He's not involved, not really. Not yet. Richard is a member of the Vedanta Society, the group that sponsored our friend Sri Puri and his colleagues to come to America. They asked me to give Richard an apprenticeship so that he might learn astrology. And he's been a wonderful student, with a natural gift, and has been picking it up admirably."

"Richard's been studying astrology?" Clara asked. "You could've fooled me! When? With Jesse in the evenings?"

"Yes, my dear," Evangeline assured her. "Some people are not the type to advertise their personal affairs to everyone about them," she said graciously. "He'll probably be going to India soon with the monks when they return."

"*With the monks?*" Mary asked, even more surprised.

"Yes, of course. Richard is in training to be a monk. And India is the very best place for him to do it."

There was a soft knock on the door and Richard stepped inside. His eyes shone with a quiet pride that Mary had never noticed before.

"Ah, here's our scholar," Evangeline announced proudly. "Richard has made quite some progress with his astrology."

"I hope so, ma'am," the young man said modestly as he stood calmly in front of them.

"Now Richard," Adams said with authority, "I have another important errand for you. We have an ancient artifact here to be returned to India," she said, indicating the ruby elephant in front of her. "I'm entrusting you to take it over to the Vedanta Society for me, so they may pass it along to Sri Puri to return to Dwarka for us. Do you think you can do that? Today, if possible."

"Yes, ma'am. I go there every day after work, and walk through the park."

"Good. Now I feel I have to warn you that the authorities may be surveilling the office. Can you conceal it on your person somehow, inconspicuously? They may attempt to follow you."

"I shouldn't have a problem. People don't notice me, Miss Adams," Richard said truthfully.

"Well that's fine then. Perhaps you should use the 57th Street exit on the other side of the building, just to be sure. Stop by my office before you leave for the day. You may take the dogs if you like, they'll protect you."

"Yes, ma'am."

"Thank you, Richard. That's all for now." Richard turned to go and closed the door quietly behind him.

Mary was stunned. *Why hadn't she recognized Richard for what he was?* She suddenly saw that he had the same serene composure as Swami Puri and his gang in their saffron colored robes. But she supposed that she didn't know a lot of monks and had nothing to compare him with. Pisces could be mysterious, but it was also the most otherworldly of the zodiac signs.

"That sorted itself out nicely," Evangeline Adams said with vigor. "Now, ladies, let's return to work, shall we? Clara, I'm sure you'll excuse us? I have some letters to dictate to Mary. And our clients for the day will be arriving sooner than we think," she said, glancing at her wristwatch. "Take another look at the ruby before I put it away." She held it up in the palm of her hand. The Syamantaka sparkled brightly; Mary even thought she saw the little elephant wink.

About the Author

Karen Christino was a consulting astrologer for over 20 years. She's written horoscope columns for *Glamour*, *Cosmopolitan* and *Life & Style* magazines, as well as features for *Marie Claire*, *Seventeen* and numerous astrology journals. She was the astrologer for *Modern Bride* for nearly ten years and wrote the "Choose Your Career" column for *American Astrology* throughout the '90s. Karen has a B.A. from Colgate University, also studied at Columbia University, and is professionally certified by the National Council for Geocosmic Research. You can read her blog and more about her work at *KarenChristino.com*. See below for her books.

Astrology Books by Karen Christino

Regal Brides: The Astrology of Five American Women and their Royal Marriages

Consuelo Vanderbilt, Wallis Simpson, Grace Kelly, Hope Cooke and Lisa Halaby, each born in the U.S., became royalty through their marriages. This book analyzes their personal horoscopes and their wedding charts, and looks at the brides' compatibility with their royal husbands and common astrological elements.

Your Wedding Astrologer

Filled with wedding tips for each sign of the zodiac, *Your Wedding Astrologer* helps brides plan the perfect affair and understand a new spouse, in-laws and sexuality. There's even a chapter on choosing wedding dates astrologically.

"It's a great gift for the bride-to-be." — *InStyle Weddings*

What Evangeline Adams Knew:
A Book of Astrological Charts and Techniques

The astrological secrets of America's most famous astrologer: how Adams predicted World War II and the stock market crash of 1929, foresaw death for Enrico Caruso and Rudolph Valentino, and chose presidential winners, travel and wedding dates. Includes chapters on Evangeline's work with the magician Aleister Crowley and for clients like Edgar Cayce, Joseph Campbell, Eugene O'Neill and Tallulah Bankhead, along with court transcripts of her famous New York City fortunetelling trial.

"... brilliantly presented." — *ISAR International Astrologer*

Foreseeing the Future:
Evangeline Adams and Astrology in America

This one-of-a-kind biography tells the colorful story of a woman who defied convention as she single-handedly popularized astrology in the U.S. Adams wrote four best-sellers and had a top-rated national radio show in the early 1930s. She battled legal authorities in New York City for the right to practice astrology, married a man over twenty years her junior, founded a tremendous business enterprise, and made stunning predictions.

"... a major contribution to the history of astrology."

— *American Astrology*

The Best of Al H. Morrison

The collected works of one of the most brilliant and innovative astrologers of the 20th century — Morrison's thoughts on Chiron and the minor planets, the Void of Course Moon, Declination, and a wide array of other topics in astrology and beyond.

"... one of the outstanding astrology books of the year."

— *Geocosmic Journal*

www.ingramcontent.com/pod-product-compliance
Lightning Source LLC
Chambersburg PA
CBHW050024180626
46810CB00002B/570